Sleeping
with the
Entity

Sleeping with the Entity

Cat Devon

St. Martin's Paperbacks

This is a work of fiction. All of the characters, organizations, and events portrayed in this novel are either products of the author's imagination or are used fictitiously.

SLEEPING WITH THE ENTITY

Copyright © 2013 by Cathie L. Baumgardner.
Excerpt from *The Entity Within* copyright © 2013 by Cathie L. Baumgardner.

For information address St. Martin's Press, 175 Fifth Avenue, New York, NY 10010.

ISBN: 978-0-312-59146-5

Printed in the United States of America

St. Martin's Paperbacks edition / June 2013

St. Martin's Paperbacks are published by St. Martin's Press, 175 Fifth Avenue, New York, NY 10010.

10 9 8 7 6 5 4 3 2 1

To my agents Meg Ruley and Annelise Robey and my editor Jennifer Enderlin—without whom these vampires would never have seen daylight. I am deeply grateful to have you all in my life. Special thanks to Neda, the owner of Sugar Monkey Cupcakes in Naperville, Illinois, for her assistance and her delicious cupcakes!

To my agents Meg Ruley and Annelise Robey, and
my editor Jennifer Enderlin-Weston, whom I love
always. I would never have sold a single book. I am
deeply grateful to have you all in my life. Special
thanks to Ruth Thompson of Sugar Grove's
Orchard in Yorkville, Illinois for her assistance
and her beautiful peaches.

Chapter One

"All the good men are taken," Daniella Delaney said. "The rest are vampires."

As soon as she spoke the words into her iPhone, the hairs at the back of her neck prickled and a shiver slid down her spine. They really had the air-conditioning cranked up in this Chicago bar and grill. The place was almost as cold as her pink fridge back home. Sure, it was a warm Indian summer October day outside, but come on.

Tugging her thin black sweater tighter around her, Daniella continued her phone conversation with her good friend Suz Beckman. "I'm telling you, they're vampires. Sucking the energy and enthusiasm right out of you. So don't hook me up with any more blind dates. And you know who else is an energy suck? The head of the local business association. I have no idea what they have against me opening my cupcake shop in this neighborhood, but he's sadly mistaken if he thinks he can get rid of me. I've worked too hard to let anyone stand in my way. I'm meeting him here in a few minutes, and if he thinks he can push me around just because I'm wearing a sweater set, he's in for a big surprise." She'd no sooner said the words than a man appeared at her side seemingly out of nowhere.

"Can I help you?" His deep, smooth voice startled Daniella.

He had a tall rangy build and was dressed all in black. His dark hair was on the long side, and he had the thickest lashes she'd ever seen on a man. His eyes were a surprising shade of wickedly stormy gray. Radiating toughness and sex appeal, he had Mick Jagger–like chiseled cheekbones and fierce yet almost poetic lips.

She'd never been a Rolling Stones fan, however. She preferred her men polished and polite. Dangerous bad boys weren't her cup of tea.

"Gotta go," she quickly told Suz before ending her call and turning her attention to the man standing beside her. "And you are?" she said.

"The manager of this establishment."

"Oh. Well in that case, perhaps you can help me. I did try to order some food when I first arrived but was told that wasn't possible. It's strange having a bar and grill that doesn't serve meals."

"The regulars don't come here for the food. They come for . . . the ambience," he said.

It was all Daniella could do not to laugh as she studied her surroundings—the moose head over the bar, the plastic mackerel beside it, the Chicago Blackhawks hockey jersey lopsidedly stuck to the wall with duct tape. "Right. Because the place has such great ambience." She shook her head in disbelief. "Look, I don't mean to cut our conversation short but I have an important meeting scheduled to take place here with—"

"Me," he interrupted her. "Your meeting is with me. I'm Nick St. George."

Great. The man wasn't just the manager of the place. He was the owner and the head of the neighborhood chamber of commerce. At least she hadn't called him a downer vampire during her phone conversation with Suz as she'd been tempted to. "You couldn't have said that sooner?"

"I could have," he acknowledged, "but I chose not to." He sat in the chair across from her.

"Well, it's nice to meet you at last. I'm Daniella Delaney, but you must already have figured that out. Anyway, I won't take up much of your time. I'm sure you're a busy man. I wanted to meet you face-to-face so that we could go over what exactly your objections are to my opening my business."

"I don't object to you opening your business. Just to opening it around here."

"I'm going to change your mind." Daniella reached into her tote and pulled out a folder with photos of chocolate-frosted cupcakes on it. "My business will be a powerful addition to the neighborhood, improving the local ambience . . . which is clearly needed, I might add. I'm going to spruce things up and offer yummy cupcakes. Come on, what's not to like about that?" She didn't give him a chance to answer—just kept going. "I made hard copies of some of my promotional ideas for my business. Flyers, coupons, that sort of thing. Or I can show you the entire presentation on my laptop if you'd rather do it that way. Which would you prefer?"

"Whatever brings you the most satisfaction." His voice rolled over her like warm honey.

She frowned at him. Why was he staring at her so strangely? Was the man flirting with her? Why? She was hardly a raving beauty. Not even close. She was pretty nondescript. Brown hair, brown eyes, an okay nose and mouth. Nothing special.

She'd chosen to wear a professional outfit of black pants and lightweight sweater set with a string of pearls. Again, nothing special.

Was he deliberately trying to throw her off her stride? "You know what would give me the most satisfaction?" she said. "You stopping your protest about me opening Heavenly Cupcakes."

"You don't really want to open your store in this area." His words had an almost hypnotic rhythm to them.

"Yes, I do."

He frowned and stared directly into her eyes. "No, you don't."

"*Yes,*" she said emphatically. "I do."

His frown deepened, and those stormy gray eyes of his narrowed.

She laughed. "You seem surprised," she said. "Did you really think you could get rid of me that easily?"

"I believe you may turn out to be more challenging than I expected," Nick said slowly.

"I'm sure I will," she said cheerfully. "A *lot* more challenging."

Nick couldn't believe how difficult this was becoming. He might look like a regular bar owner, but deep down he was very different. He was a vampire struggling to stay under the radar. He'd overheard her talking about vampires on her phone. At first his concern had been that he and the rest of his friends had somehow been found out by this cupcake maker.

He no longer thought that was actually the case,

but there was still something strange about her. He supposed it was ironic that he, the vampire, was calling her, the human, strange. But the truth was that he didn't know what to make of her.

His job as a leader was to protect his clan and keep her out. The more that humans hung around the area, the bigger the chance was that their vampire community would be discovered. He had no doubt her business would be a success, but he couldn't allow that to happen. It was much too risky.

When Nick had first set up this meeting, he'd thought it would be an easy fix. His buddy, fellow vamp and body artist Pat Heller from Pat's Tats next door, had even mockingly kidded him that it would be a piece of cake. All Nick had to do was use every vampire's favorite weapon—mind compulsion— and Daniella Delaney would obey him.

It hadn't worked. He'd never had a human resist him before. She was supposed to respond to his vamp thrall by agreeing to do his bidding. All the others had for centuries.

He'd established direct eye contact and done his vamp thing. But instead of surrendering, cheeky Little Miss Cupcake had laughed. She'd actually laughed.

Like all vamps, Nick had a superior sense of smell. He could tell by her scent that she wasn't a vampire herself. But there was something about her . . .

"Do you have a cold?" she suddenly asked him. "Allergies?"

"What?"

"You were sniffing."

Nick glared at her. Daniella eyed him suspiciously. And so she should. He could eat her for breakfast.

Okay, so he didn't actually eat humans. He only

drained them of their blood. And only when they *really* aggravated him.

She finally looked away. "I, uh, brought something that's sure to change your mind about me joining your business community. I brought you . . ." She carefully lifted a sturdy cardboard box from an oversized bag and opened it with obvious pride. "My cupcakes."

Studying her closely, Nick was more impressed by her great breasts even if she was hiding them under that prim sweater. Too bad vamps didn't have X-ray vision like Superman. Still, they did have supernatural hearing, and he could hear her heart beating faster.

Good. He must be having an effect on her after all.

But her focus remained on the box full of elaborately decorated cupcakes with little bats and spiders on them in honor of Halloween in a few weeks.

His focus remained on her. She wasn't the most beautiful woman he'd ever seen. Not even close. But she had a passionate nature and a luscious mouth. And she got to him. Big-time.

"Try one," she said.

"No thanks. I don't like cupcakes."

She gently shoved them a little closer. "They're my specialty. Red velvet."

He eyed them. She'd gotten the red color right but the ingredients wrong. There was no blood in these cupcakes.

"Come on. Just take a bite," she said.

Nick could feel his fangs starting to emerge. Hell, yes he wanted to take a bite. Of her.

Damn. He hadn't been this tempted in ages. Literally ages. Decades certainly. An entire century maybe. He was no raw teenage vampire unable to manage and suppress his desires.

"Just one little tiny bite," she said. "It can't hurt."

He leaned closer. He could see the pulse beating in her throat. He was dying to take a bite. Well, not *dying,* since vamps were immortal. But shit, she was tempting him. Was she doing it on purpose? Daring him?

If so, Little Miss Cupcake was definitely playing with fire. The problem was that vampires could get burned by fire. Garlic and crucifixes didn't bother him. But fire could destroy.

Was she a witch? A demon? All Nick knew for sure was that she was a problem, and he didn't like problems he couldn't solve. He prided himself on being in total control of all situations. In total control of his emotions and his needs.

Exerting his willpower, he was able to overcome his need to feed. For now.

"Come on," she coaxed him. "I can tell you're tempted."

"Lady, you're pushing your luck," he growled.

She sat back and blinked at him in surprise. Good. Maybe now she'd pack up her freaking cupcakes and get the hell away from him.

Instead she said, "If you're a diabetic, I have some sugar-free cupcakes I can offer you."

"I don't want anything you have to offer." His voice was werewolf-rough.

She blushed. Blood rushed to her face. Her heart rate was elevated, her pulse pounding. His undead vampire body responded accordingly. Shit.

Daniella said, "I wasn't trying to seduce you or anything."

It was the "or anything" that worried him. Hell, that wasn't true. *Everything* about Daniella Delaney worried him. He had to get away from her.

"This meeting is over." He stood and quickly turned away.

"Wait," she called after him. "Does that mean you'll drop your protest over my store?"

"No."

"I don't need your approval," she told him. "It would be nice to have, but it's not a requirement."

Nick turned back to her, his scowl forceful enough to send fearless warriors running for their lives. *Run, little cupcake maker. Run*. He sent the mental order with all the considerable power at his disposal.

"I'll just leave these cupcakes here in case you change your mind," she said with her customary cheerfulness. But she did grab the rest of her things and head for the exit. "'Bye now. Have a nice day."

A nice day? Nick didn't have a nice bone in his entire body . . . his painfully aroused vampire body.

He glared at the bumper sticker fastened to the wall above the bar. LIFE'S A BITCH AND THEN YOU DIE. For humans maybe. For vampires, life remained a bitch forever. And no amount of red velvet cupcakes could ever fix that.

The bottom line here was that the cheeky cupcake maker seemed immune to his mind-control powers, which meant that Nick had to figure out some other way to get rid of her.

He could do that. After all, he was a vampire and she was only human.

Or was she? Hell, Nick didn't know for sure. But he'd needed to find out fast whether she was going to be a threat to his existence or merely to his peace of mind.

Getting to know her better might be a tough job, but some vampire had to do it. Might as well be him.

Chapter Two

"That was a waste of time," Daniella told Suz before sinking into one of her friend's comfy armchairs. Daniella loved Suz's office. She specifically loved this particular armchair, which fit her to perfection. "A *total* waste of time."

Suz gave her one of her trademark *Really?* looks over the tops of her colorful designer eyeglass frames. With her short platinum-blond hair and impeccable makeup, she was the epitome of a fashionista and as far away as you could get from the stereotype of an accountant. Suz's office looked like it had been masterfully designed by a top-notch decorator, but she'd actually done it all herself. And that wasn't her only talent. Not only was Suz a whiz with numbers and figures, but she could also throw together an awesome outfit in five minutes flat. Daniella liked Suz despite these talents, none of which she possessed herself, although she did have an eye for decorating and design. But Daniella lacked the fashionista gene.

"You mean you didn't win over the crabby guy with your charm?" Suz said.

"I gave it my best shot. I really did. I even offered him cupcakes."

"And?"

"And he refused."

Suz's eyes widened. "He must not be human. No one refuses your cupcakes."

"That's what I'm saying. *No one* refuses my cupcakes."

Suz leaned forward in her ergonomic office chair. "Does that mean you still have some with you?"

"Well, yeah, but . . ."

"No buts." Suz put out her hand. "Hand them over."

"I thought you were on a diet."

"I am. The cupcake diet. I'm PMSing," Suz warned. "So do not make me get up and come get them."

"Fine." Daniella reached into her bag and removed a small box of cupcakes. "Here." She gave Suz one of her creations.

Her friend was not that easily appeased. "One cupcake? That's all you've got?"

"I left the large box full of a dozen cupcakes at the bar with Nick St. George so I only have a couple as backup. What do you think of the little bats and spiders on top? Cute, huh?"

But Suz was blissfully unaware of the artistic decorations, because she had her eyes closed while chewing her first bite. "Mmmm."

"They're red velvet but I added a new twist. I also am experimenting with dark chocolate cupcakes with root beer buttercream frosting topped with either a root beer barrel hard candy or an A&W Jelly Belly jelly bean. "

"You know I'm your official taster for all your experimental new flavors, right?"

"Of course I know that. I love your philosophy about these things."

"Cupcakes?"

"Life. Some people say the glass is half empty. Some say the glass is half full. You say, are you going to drink that?"

"Right. I'm practical that way."

"I'm working on being more practical myself. I think it would help my business skills."

Suz gave her an appraising look before telling her, "You've already got great skills in that area. You're a pit bull in a twinset and pearls where your business is concerned."

"Only when I have to be," Daniella said.

"Did you 'have to be' with the crabby guy you had that meeting with?"

"He's determined to work against me. Can you believe he actually had the nerve to tell me that I don't really want to open my cupcake shop in this neighborhood? He really thought I'd pack up my bags and go somewhere else just because he said so."

"He doesn't know you very well."

"That's for sure. And he never will with that attitude."

Suz shrugged. "His loss."

"There was something strange about him," Daniella said.

"Aside from his not liking you or your cupcakes?"

Daniella nodded. "Yes, aside from that."

"Describe him to me. How old is he?"

"I don't know. Mid-thirties maybe?"

"That young? I pictured him as a crabby sixty-year-old guy chomping on a cigar. Go on." Suz leaned back in her chair. "Tell me more."

"Dark hair and fierce gray eyes. He seemed

ruthless and arrogantly regal, like he was the king of the world."

"That's Leonardo DiCaprio's job in *Titanic*."

Daniella was not impressed. "For all the good it did poor Leo. His character ended up sinking to the bottom of the ocean."

"Yes, but he did it for love."

Daniella shook her head. "I can't see Nick St. George doing anything for love. I didn't get the impression that he's a people person."

"Yet he's the head of the local business association?"

Daniella nodded. "I think that's more of a power trip than anything else. He seemed very surprised that he couldn't boss me around."

"So the guy is a bully."

Daniella frowned. "That's the thing. I've dealt with bullies before. When I was a pastry chef in New York, my boss was impossible. No, Nick is more than a bully. I suspect he could be charming if he really wanted to and if it would get him something he wants."

"So you think that will be his next step? That he'll try to charm you?"

Daniella grinned. "I sure hope so." She wiggled her fingers in a *come here* gesture. "Let him try. I'll be ready for him."

"That was a waste of time," Nick said. He could feel his jaw clenching as he spoke to fellow vamp Pat Heller at Pat's Tats tattoo parlor. Looking around, Nick remembered Daniella's comments about the ambience at his place. He didn't think she'd like Pat's Tats any better. No doubt the wall covered with various body art designs would offend her dainty sensibilities. He couldn't imagine her as the type of female to get a tramp stamp.

He also couldn't imagine her approving of Pat with his gray hair held back in a ponytail. The vamp was commonly mistaken for George Carlin before he passed away. George had actually been Pat's favorite comedian. Since vampires remain the same as when they were turned, Pat's hair stayed long and prematurely gray as it had when he'd been bitten back in the 1600s.

"What was a waste of time?" Pat asked before he sipped blood from a dainty Wedgwood porcelain teacup.

"My meeting with Little Miss Cupcake Maker."

"What's the problem? You just look her in the eye and use mind compulsion to make her change her mind about opening her store around here."

"I did that. It didn't work."

Pat looked surprised. "It didn't work? I've never heard of that before. She's not a vamp, is she?"

"No, but I have a feeling she's going to be a pain in the ass."

"You have a *feeling,* huh?"

"I meant it as a simple observation. You know I don't do feelings."

"I didn't think so."

"Do not tell anyone about her being immune to my mind compulsion," Nick said.

"Feeling a little inadequate, are you?"

Nick growled.

Pat shook his head with disapproval. "How many times do I have to tell you that vamps don't growl? Werewolves growl."

Nick's silence spoke volumes. So did his glare.

"You've been a vampire long enough to know better," Pat scolded him.

"Is this the part where you go on and on about how many centuries you've been a vampire?"

"I do not go on and on," Pat said.

"I need to figure out more about this cupcake maker," Nick said.

"Her name is Daniella, right?"

Nick nodded.

"It's a lovely name." Pat sat back in his chair. "I knew a Daniella in Paris before the Revolution. Ah, those were the days . . ." He paused, clearly lost in the memories. "Of course his real name was Daniel. I've been gay for a long time. But I've never been happier than I am with my current partner, Bruce. It helps that he's a vamp, too. Not that he's been around as long as I have."

"That longevity of yours and your intelligence are what have saved our clan from the devastating effects of sunlight. You're the reason we can go out in daylight without frying and turning into crispy critters."

"I just wish I could have come up with the answer faster. It took me a few centuries to come up with the right combination of ink and symbols for a tattoo that allows us to tolerate daylight. I knew it involved the fleur-de-lis design, but it was the formula for the ink that had me stumped for so long. I had to get the ratio exactly right to counteract the UV rays that are so deadly to vampires. It was a painful process—I had to sit in a strong beam of sunshine coming through a window to see if I had it right. I can't tell you how many times I'd end up with blistering burns in mere seconds. Once I was back in the shade again, my vamp super-healing abilities restored my skin to normal and I'd try it again. It wasn't until almost thirty years ago that I got it down. With the tattoo it's all about design, ink, and location, location, location."

"Better late than never," Nick said, running his hand over the tattoo on the nape of his neck.

"True. As with all things vampire, each kind finds their own way. Outsider vamps think it has to do with refining the blood. After going through what I have, there is no way I'd give up the secret to our being able to tolerate sunshine here in Vamptown. Do you think I'm going to share that formula with every Tom, Dick, or Harry vamp that walks through my door? No way. Especially not the dicks."

"What about the human dicks? Are you still accepting them as clients?" Nick asked.

"On occasion," Pat said. "It's not like I'm making a meal of them. I don't need to. Doc Boomer has come up with the perfect formula to revitalize the human blood we get from the human-run funeral home. It's better than fresh. He's even added calcium for healthy bones and teeth. After all, dental hygiene is important to our kind. That's why Doc Boomer runs the twenty-four-hour dental clinic here in Vamptown. Doc is currently a dentist but he's also been a physician and a chemist in the past." Pat paused to empty his cup before dabbing at his mouth with a linen napkin. "As for the humans, I only take a small sip from the ones who pass out. That's why I can say with utmost confidence that Doc's blood formula is better than the blood from a still-breathing human. Doc has filtered out all the impurities. No germs, viruses, or cooties. Not that it matters, since we are immortal. But no one goes looking for cooties. Even vamps."

"You know there have been rumblings about us taking over the funeral home," Nick said.

"I'm aware. But that would draw too much attention. No, I believe our current arrangement is the best. Let the humans deal with the boring details at the funeral home; we merely siphon off the blood unbeknownst to them. But getting back to Daniella . . . that is strange that she didn't respond to your mind compulsion."

"It's never happened to me before," Nick said.

"Maybe you should try experimenting with it on another human. Just to make sure you haven't lost your touch or something."

"That's a good idea. I need to talk to Daniella's brother Gordon at the funeral home anyway."

"Make sure your mind compulsion still works before you go into any details with Gordon," Pat said.

Nick glared at him. "I'm not stupid."

"I know that."

Did he? Pat used to trust him completely. His friend had never doubted him before. Yet now Pat was reminding Nick not to make any rookie mistakes. Hell, he might not have as many centuries under his belt as Pat did, but Nick had been around for two hundred years.

This was all the cupcake maker's fault. Nick had only met the female two hours ago and already she was making his life difficult. She'd started complicating things the second she refused to back down from her plans to open the cupcake store down the street. And to make matters worse, she'd been so damn cheerful about it all.

Nick couldn't figure her out, but he would. Because no one ever got the best of him.

"Gordon will be trembling in his boots if you walk into the funeral home with that look on your face," Pat said.

"Good. Humans are easier to deal with when fear keeps them in their place."

"You were human once," Pat said.

Nick didn't welcome the reminder. He didn't want to think about those days so very, *very* long ago.

None of the limited number of humans in Vamptown were aware that they were surrounded by vampires, and Nick was determined to keep it that way. Which is why he began compelling Gordon the instant he walked into his office at the Evergreen Funeral Home. Usually such visits involved some reminder to keep the blood flowing, but this one was different.

"Tell me about your sister Daniella." Nick stared into the funeral director's eyes and watched them go glassy and blank. He was relieved to see that mind compulsion continued to work just fine on Gordon, unlike his sister.

"She was born in Chicago eighteen months after me. Birth date June first. She's twenty-nine. Graduated from college with honors." He quickly stated facts as if by rote. "Went to boot camp at CIA."

"Hold on. The CIA?" Could this explain somehow why Daniella was immune to his vamp mind compulsion? Had spy training taught her to resist any sort of mental coercion?

"CIA—Culinary Institute of America," Gordon said before continuing, "Favorite music groups are Coldplay and The Script. Favorite color is pink. Drives a pink Vespa moped she's named Shirley. Always wears her helmet, which is also pink."

"Tell me more."

"She's very stubborn but usually cheerful. Studied in New York to be a pastry chef. Worked there at some fancy place I can never remember the name of. Her best friend here in Chicago is Suz Beckman, an accountant."

"Are there any men in Daniella's life?"

"Me, my father—"

"No," Nick interrupted him. "I mean romantic relationships."

"She went to senior prom with my best friend Randy Schmidt."

"More recent than that," Nick said impatiently.

"Dave Labelle in New York City. She broke up with him when she moved back to Chicago a couple of months ago. The asshole cheated on her. She nearly whacked him with a cupcake baking tin."

"Anything strange about her?"

"Aside from the baking-tin thing, she always wins at Scrabble. I think she cheats even though she says she doesn't."

"Besides that?"

"She has a kick-ass memory. Almost as good as that actress who used to be on the TV show *Taxi*."

"What else?"

"Sometimes she knows what you're going to say before you say it."

"She has ESP?"

"I guess. She's no good at guessing Lotto ticket numbers or winning horses at the track, though."

Nick knew that Gordon had a gambling problem and had racked up debts, which made him an easy mark for working outside the legalities and regulations involved with running a funeral home. Even if he did sometimes wonder about things, he never asked questions, and that wasn't entirely due to his being compelled. It also was due to the fact that he didn't want to know because money was coming in. He didn't want to rock the boat even if he didn't know exactly what kind of boat it was. It was a lucrative one, and that's all that mattered.

If Daniella really did have telepathic abilities, Nick was willing to bet that she wouldn't help her brother further his gambling addiction. The fact that she didn't accurately predict the numbers or the horse names didn't mean she couldn't do it. It could mean she *wouldn't* do it.

"That's all for now," Nick said. "You will not remember this conversation at all, Gordon. You won't remember me asking about your sister. Do you understand?"

Gordon nodded, blinked, and then said, "We are fully booked for funerals all this week. Business is booming."

"I'm happy for you." A successful mortuary was the lifeblood of the vamps in Vamptown. There were other vampire clusters in the city that had their own ways of obtaining blood. Some had an "in" at the blood bank or a hospital. Others had darker ways of satisfying their hunger.

Mind compulsion kept Gordon and his talented embalmer Phil Phelps in line. Nick didn't need to know all the gory details. He left that to Doc Boomer, who assured everyone that there was no mixing of embalming fluids with the blood drainage. If that meant an adjustment in procedures, so be it. Vamptown had been flourishing lately, having successfully dealt with two of the most challenging aspects of life as a vampire—blood and daylight.

Daniella had the potential to put all that at risk. Nick needed to figure out what made her different, and he needed to do it fast.

Daniella stared at her surroundings with equal parts delight and dismay. The Heavenly Cupcakes grand opening was only ten days away. There was no way she'd be ready in time, was there?

"Stay calm," she ordered herself. Saying the words out loud made her feel better somehow.

Turning on her iPad, she chose "Always Look on the Bright Side of Life" from her music files. As the cheerful *Spamalot* song filled the space, she reminded herself of the things that had gone right. For one thing, her father owned the building, which featured an empty storefront and a one-bedroom apartment upstairs, and was letting her have it rent-free for one year. He also allowed her to remodel the dingy space and even recommended a great contractor.

She'd kept the art deco architectural details, like the decorative moldings, from the 1920s when this building and most on the rest of the block had been built. She'd brightened the walls with subtle blush-pink paint and added black-framed prints of angels she'd collected over the years. The combination of the dramatic black against the pale pink provided a feeling of both class and welcoming warmth. She could have gone for the more traditional look of hot pink and black from the 1950s diner era but had preferred this more restrained ambience.

Daniella had transformed the back into a dream bakery with a huge stainless worktable, an industrial-sized oven, a commercial fridge and freezer, and a pantry with carefully labeled storage bins for the dry goods like flour and sugar. Her pink KitchenAid handheld mixer and huge mixing bowls were stored on wire racks.

The *Spamalot* song repeated. Now that she thought about it, her shop wasn't in dire straits after all. Yes, the pair of cupcake wrought-iron wall sconce light fixtures still had to be installed, but that should be done by tomorrow. And yes, the glass display cases for her trays of cupcakes were the wrong size and had to be sent back, but the vendor assured her the correct ones would be delivered tomorrow. Meanwhile, she really needed to focus on hiring some part-time help. She'd been trying for the past month without much success. Without *any* success, really.

Lost in thought, Daniella sat at one of the marble-topped tables facing the window while she scanned the list on her iPad. It vaguely seeped into her consciousness that the light was diminishing outside as darkness fell. She glanced out the window and saw a lone figure standing on the sidewalk. The hair on the back of her neck stood up. Someone was watching her. She couldn't see their face in the shadows, but she felt their presence.

She raced to the security system panel and punched in a series of numbers, hoping she was hitting the right buttons. Putting her hand on the front doorknob, she felt it turn. Her heart raced. The door opened, and she faced her stalker.

Chapter Three

"I knew you wouldn't be able to resist," Daniella said with a big smile. "Come in!" Daniella pulled Nick into her shop before he could protest. He was looking at her rather strangely. Was that suspicion she saw reflected in his stormy gray eyes, or something else?

"I wouldn't be able to resist? Explain," he said curtly.

"Seeing my store. It was the flyer I left for you, wasn't it? The one with the drawings of what I planned to do with the store. You had to see the finished product yourself. Not that the renovation is completely finished yet, obviously." She waved her hand at the sawhorses reserving the area where the glass display cases would be. "But the space has great bones."

Daniella cheerfully chose to ignore the way Nick was glaring at her as if he wanted to break a few of her bones and continued. "I admit the place doesn't have the gorgeous examples of art deco that other buildings like Chicago's Board of Trade has, but I like to think that it's special in its own charming way."

"No moose heads or plastic mackerels for you, right?"

"Right."

Nick stared deep into her eyes. "You don't want to open your store here." He was using what she'd labeled his hypnotic voice.

She widened her eyes and stared right back at him. "Why do you keep saying that?" she said in exasperation. "Of course I want to open my store here. Duh. That's why I renovated the space."

"Duh?" He appeared somewhat at a loss at her response.

"Yeah, duh. Look at that crown molding. Isn't that cool? The brick buildings all along this block were built in the 1920s. That was an exciting time. The Roaring Twenties with flappers dancing the Charleston and men bootlegging alcohol during Prohibition."

"How do *you* know it was exciting?" His suspicious look was back.

"I can read. And I like reading about history. Do you?"

"Do I what?" he said.

"Like history? Like the 1920s?"

"Sure. It's almost as if I've lived through it," he said drily.

She nodded. "I know."

"You do?"

"Yes. I mean if these walls could only talk. Well, maybe not these *exact* walls, since we had to put in new wallboard and remove what was here before. The space has been empty for a while."

"I know."

"As the head of the local business association, I'd think you'd be happy to see it being utilized." She tilted her head to study him a moment. "Unless you're afraid that I'm going to 'girlie' up the block by adding my classy shop? I mean, you've got a bar next to a tattoo parlor next to a dental clinic."

"My point exactly. Not really the clientele you'd be wanting."

"My father owns this building and he's giving it to me rent-free for a year. I can't afford to go anywhere else."

"You can't afford to stay here, either," he muttered. Or was it a growl?

"My dad tells me this isn't a high crime area," she said.

The corner of Nick's mouth lifted slightly in what was probably his version of a smile. "You could say we've taken a bite out of crime."

"Well, that's a good thing, right? Even so, I have a serious security system installed." She pointed to the panel on the wall.

"No security system is infallible."

"This one is pretty darn close," she said. "Or so the sales rep assured me. Why? Do you know about security systems? Have you heard something bad about this one?"

Daniella didn't even realize she'd reached out to touch Nick's arm until her fingers started humming. Her hand was on his arm where he'd rolled up the sleeves of his black shirt. Her bare skin was on his bare skin, and the result was startling. If she had an internal security system, it would be blaring alarms and flashing lights.

As far as first touches went, this one was incredibly intense and powerful. Her eyes lifted from her hand to his face. Was he feeling it, too?

His eyes darkened as he stared at her as if trying to reach the innermost workings of her mind. She felt drawn to him. He moved closer.

Fearing her heart might jump out of her chest, she stepped back. Okay, she obviously didn't really think her heart would literally do something like that, but her entire body felt strange. She'd never experienced this before. She didn't even know how to label or describe it.

Maybe she was coming down with something? Not that she had time to get sick. Maybe it was just exhaustion and excitement? Yes, she was going to go with that explanation. It beat the chance that she was attracted to Nick.

"What does your ESP tell you about opening your store?" he asked her.

"My what?"

"Your ESP. Your brother mentioned something about you having a talent in that area."

"When did you speak to my brother?"

Nick shrugged.

She wasn't about to let him off the hook. He couldn't bring up a subject like that without her following up. "That's not an answer."

"Naturally, as fellow business owners, Gordon and I talk from time to time."

"About me?"

"Your name may have come up briefly in one of our conversations," he said.

"I don't have ESP," she said.

"You don't get feelings about certain things?"

"I definitely have the feeling that you didn't come here to look at the things I'm planning for this space. You came here to try to talk me out of opening my shop again."

The corner of his mouth lifted. "So you do have ESP."

"Oh please. A two-year-old could figure it out."

"Figure what out?"

"That you don't approve of me," she said. "No big deal. I'm not sure I approve of you, either."

"Why not?"

"Oh, I don't know," she said sarcastically. "Maybe the fact that you've been so outspoken in your disapproval of me."

"Not you."

"Right. Not me. Just my store's location," she said.

"It's not personal. It's business."

"Yeah, for you and Donald Trump maybe. But for me, my shop is *very* personal. I've thought through every little detail. For example, I looked through dozens and dozens of cherub designs before picking this one for my logo for Heavenly Cupcakes." She held up one of the flyers for her grand opening.

Nick was not impressed. "It looks like a fat baby who has eaten too many cupcakes."

She was as upset as if he'd insulted her own child. "It does not!"

"It does to me."

"Which just goes to show what you know," she muttered. "You're clearly no expert regarding angels."

"You've got that right."

She doubted Nick had an angelic bone in his body. "Well, I'm happy with the way my logo looks. I spent weeks selecting the font. I love the way I've decorated my shop with some art deco touches. Chicago is one of the most art-deco-influenced cities in the world. I can't believe you're not interested in highlighting those aspects in your own building."

"Believe it," he said curtly.

"Has anyone ever told you that you're a real Debbie Downer?"

"No."

"Well, maybe the correct term would be Donnie Downer since you're not a female."

"I'm having a hard time keeping up with your scatterbrained conversation."

"Scatterbrained?" She put her hands on her hips. "Who are you calling a scatterbrain?"

"You. Obviously." He frowned at her as if she were a few cupcakes short of a dozen before adding, "Duh."

She cracked up.

His frown deepened. "What's so funny?"

"You are." She grinned at him. "There was just something about the way you said duh."

"I don't appreciate being laughed at," he said coldly.

"And I don't appreciate being called a scatterbrain, so I guess we're even."

"We'll never be even," he said.

"Why not? Because you're a man and I'm a woman?"

Because I'm a vamp and you're not. The words were on the tip of Nick's tongue, but he held them back. This was another first for him. He'd never been the least bit tempted to reveal his secret before. Yet here he was with her, on the verge of doing something stupid.

Was she some sort of witch whose touch melted his brain and sent his undead body into overdrive? She'd put her hand on his arm and gotten to him with a simple touch. He refused to acknowledge that she might have rattled him. He refused to give her that power. But he knew he'd hidden his reaction well.

She appeared rattled by the physical contact as well. Good. That meant he could get to her. Nick took that discovery with him as he abruptly made his departure. He'd sensed her rapid heartbeat in a way that made him hunger for her. Next time he approached her, he'd be better prepared . . . and fed.

Daniella began the next morning with her plan to win over the neighboring businesses. She wasn't going to waste her time trying to convince Nick any longer. Instead she'd go directly to the other entrepreneurs on her block. Nick's abrupt exit last night was a clear indication that the man had no intention of siding with her. He also had no manners.

He hadn't even bothered coming up with an excuse or one of those white lies like *I've got somewhere else I need to be.* No, last night he'd simply turned on his heel and walked out, leaving her standing there wondering what had just occurred.

That was all in the past. She'd moved on to Plan B. Her first stop was Pat's Tats. She'd grown up in this neighborhood and Pat's Tats had been there for as long as she could remember. Even so, she'd never actually gone into the tattoo parlor before. There was no need. It wasn't as if she'd ever want a tattoo. That was so *not* on her bucket list.

The first thing she noticed was the buzz of needles inking skin. Her stomach turned and her squeamish self wanted to abandon Plan B and run back to the safety of her own shop.

But her Inner Cupcake Diva insisted she stay. The noise soon stopped as her presence was noted.

"Don't let me interrupt," she said with forced cheerfulness.

She recognized the owner, Pat Heller, who set

down his tools and came toward her. "Are you here for a tattoo?" he asked.

"No way." She quickly realized that her emphatic refusal might be rude so she added, "I mean, no thank you."

The tattoo victim checked out the addition to his arm, which was already covered in blue ink. He reminded her of the creatures in *Avatar*. Pat didn't have many tattoos on his arms, but those he did have were nicely done. Not that she was any expert on such things. He also had some strange kind of symbol tattooed below the knuckle on each of his fingers, a different one on each digit.

"I thought you and your customers might want to try some of my cupcakes," she said. "And I wanted to introduce myself as a new fellow entrepreneur. I realize I'm the new kid on the block in a manner of speaking and that you've been successful in business for a long time."

"Are you saying I'm old?"

"That wasn't my intention, no. Not at all."

"And you're hardly the new kid on the block. You were born here."

"Well, not right here in this tattoo parlor. I was actually born in a hospital, but I know what you mean. I am a local. Like you."

"Not really like me," Pat said.

"Well, of course not since you're a man and I'm a woman and you're doing tattoos and I'm baking cupcakes. But there is a creative element in both our lines of work. In fact, the Chicago Department of Cultural Affairs includes both our professions in their latest online survey." Realizing she was getting off the beaten path conversation-wise, she paused to take a deep breath before continuing. "Are these your tattoo offerings displayed on the wall?"

Pat nodded. "Are you interested in getting a tattoo?" he asked her.

"No way. I mean, it's not my thing. But I can still admire your artwork without having it embedded in my skin." She studied them closer. "Many of these designs are really unique. I mean, I'm no expert obviously, but you've gone beyond the standard motifs of hearts and butterflies and barbed wire. Were you trained as an artist?"

Pat said, "I consider what I do to be art."

"You're clearly very talented. Would you be interested in branching out?"

"In what way?"

"Doing some drawings for my business."

"Do you mean cupcake tattoos?" he asked.

"I was thinking more along the lines of flyers and that sort of thing."

"You've already got your logo," he said. "I saw your sign in the window advertising your grand opening. The cloud background with the angel perched on top is clever."

"Thank you," she said. "I really appreciate that. Especially coming from someone like you."

"Someone like me?" He sounded insulted.

"Someone with such an artistic gift," she hurriedly explained.

"Well, I do tend to see what others don't."

She nodded. "Creative people are like that. We notice the little things in life."

"That's true."

She smiled at him. Finally she felt like she was on the same page with someone on this block. "I'm really glad I stopped by today and we had this talk."

"I'm glad, too," Pat said. He leaned forward to kiss her hand. "It's been a pleasure."

His gesture could have been sappy or icky but was courtly instead. She'd never had anyone kiss her hand before.

Feeling confident, Daniella left a box of cupcakes next to the cash register as Pat suggested and then moved on to the Happy Times Emergency Dental Clinic next door.

Once again she was greeted by the sound of drilling.

"May I help you?" the receptionist asked her.

Daniella checked the older woman's name tag before replying. She was helped by the fact that the receptionist looked like Mrs. Cunningham on the classic TV sitcom *Happy Days*. The other woman radiated maternal vibes. "Hi, Lois. My name is Daniella Delaney and I'm the owner of Heavenly Cupcakes. Our grand opening is a little over a week away so I'm stopping by the other businesses on the block to introduce myself."

"Your family owns the Evergreen Funeral Home, right?" Lois said.

"That's right," Daniella said. "But I'm here about my own business venture."

"I saw you had a HELP WANTED sign in your window along with the sign for your grand opening. Adorable angel by the way," Lois said.

"Thanks. Yes, I still am looking for some part-time help. Why? Do you know someone who might be interested?"

"Me," Lois said. "People who come here have problems or they wouldn't come to an emergency dental clinic. It might be nice working someplace where people are happy."

"Have you worked in retail before?" Daniella asked.

Lois nodded.

"I wouldn't want to steal you away from the dental clinic or anything . . . ," Daniella said.

"Not a problem," Lois said. "I'm not the only receptionist working here. Tell me more about your shop."

Nick was not having a good day. You'd think that being a vamp would make life easier, but the opposite was true. He was only now appreciating how much he'd depended on using mind compulsion to deal with humans who gave him a hard time. He'd just made that comment to Pat as the two of them met to discuss Daniella.

"She was here a short while ago and I have to admit that it was hard saying no to her," Pat said.

Nick frowned. He didn't know whether he should be pleased or aggravated by the fact that he wasn't the only vamp having trouble dealing with the cupcake maker. "Saying no to what?"

"She liked my designs and asked if I'd be willing to do some for her."

"For her? You mean as a tattoo?" Nick asked. He tried to imagine tats on her alabaster-pale skin, but couldn't. It would be a violation somehow.

"No, not tats. For flyers and ads. She said I was a very talented artist."

"She probably knew that complimenting your work was the way to your heart. Not that you have one," Nick said.

"Are you saying I'm *not* a talented artist?" Pat said.

"I'm saying that Little Miss Cupcake Maker is smart. Very smart. Which could make her very dangerous."

"She doesn't look dangerous. By the way, I tried mind compulsion on her and I wasn't successful, either. So it definitely isn't just you who isn't able to compel her." Pat paused before adding, "There's something about her . . ."

"Any idea what that something is?"

"Not yet. But I have complete confidence that you'll figure it out. One suggestion, however. I think you'd be more successful if you pretended to be her friend rather than her enemy."

Nick nodded slowly. "I've already come to the same conclusion myself. I can learn more about her by pretending to help her instead of fighting with her. She'll come to trust me."

"If you're lucky."

"Luck has nothing to do with it," Nick said with total certainty. "It's all about skill."

"If you want to practice your *skill* on Daniella, she's gone over to Doc Boomer's dental clinic."

"Why?"

"To be neighborly and introduce herself," Pat said.

Nick swore under his breath.

"Remember, you're going to charm her, not curse her," Pat said. "And since your vamp skills don't seem to work on her, you'll have to depend on your human skills, which are no doubt rusty from lack of use."

"I'm not human."

"True. But you were once."

That had been so long ago, Nick barely remembered what it was like. Sometimes things hit him strongly, like the memory of a great meal. Being charming had never been his strong suit, however.

Even so, how hard could it be?

Nick soon found out when he walked into the dental clinic and found Daniella talking to Lois, the middle-aged receptionist there. "What are you doing?" He directed the question to them both, but Daniella was the one who answered.

"Being neighborly. What are you doing?" she countered. "Do you have a toothache? Is that why you're so crabby?"

Lois giggled. It wasn't a pretty sound. Nick sure wasn't amused.

"He's always like that," Lois said.

"You mean he's always brooding, morose, and negative?" Daniella said before adding, "Oh, and bossy, too."

"Yes, I have to say that's a fairly accurate description," Lois said. She and Daniella exchanged a grin.

"I knew there was a reason I liked you," Daniella said. "Here, have a cupcake."

"Sorry, hon, but I can't," Lois said with real regret. "I have a ton of food allergies."

Now Nick was the one who snorted. Lois had food allergies all right. The same ones he had. Because Lois was a vampire.

Chapter Four

Daniella didn't like the way Nick was smirking at her. He managed to act all arrogant and superior without saying a word. There was also something about his eyes that she had yet to figure out. Was it the strange stormy gray color or the fierce intensity of his gaze? Whatever it was, she didn't like it or his smirk.

"It doesn't sound as if Lois would be one of your customers," Nick said.

"She might be something even better," Daniella said. "A part-time employee."

That wiped the smirk right off his face. "You're kidding, right?"

"Not at all."

"She already has a job," Nick said.

"Yes," Daniella said. "But she's expressed interest in coming to work for me."

He turned his disapproving glare toward Lois. "Why?"

"Don't answer that," Daniella told Lois. "It's none of his business."

"Everything in this neighborhood is my business," he said.

"Despotic much?" Daniella said.

"A lot," he said, undaunted. "Get used to it."

"It seems to me that you have a thing against women entrepreneurs. Is it just me, or do you also have a thing against Tanya's Tanning Salon on this block?" Daniella demanded.

"I do not have a thing against businesswomen."

"So it's just me. That's nice to know."

He had no response for that, which was fine by her. She'd prefer he keep his mouth shut. She'd prefer he disappear entirely.

Daniella reminded herself that Nick's disapproval didn't matter. She was in charge of her own destiny. She had a smart business plan and a delicious product. Everyone said so. Except for Negative Nick.

She smiled at her nickname for him. She liked it. Yeah, Negative Nick. That worked.

"Lois and I are having a private conversation," she informed him in her haughtiest voice. "Your opinions are neither requested, required, nor desired."

His gaze traveled over her in a way she should have found insulting but instead made her heart beat a little faster. It was as if he was visually telling her that he knew she desired *him,* which was ridiculous. She narrowed her own eyes and gave him a *you must be kidding me* look. Turning her back on him, she asked Lois, "How do you put up with him?"

"He's not usually this bad," the older woman said.

"So I bring out the worst in him," Daniella said. "Good to know."

"I didn't mean it that way."

Daniella shrugged. "Sometimes people just don't get along. It happens."

"I was actually trying to be nice to you," Nick had the nerve to say.

She turned back to him. "Really?"

He nodded.

"Well, you stink at it. You're no good at all at being nice to me. But that's okay. You may not have the communication skills needed to get along with people. They offer classes for that, you know," she added.

"I don't need classes," he growled.

Daniella shrugged. She realized she did that a lot around him, but there was nothing she could do about it. The motion made her feel better. It was as if she were shaking off any influence he might have on her. "I'm just saying."

"I communicate just fine."

"You communicate your disapproval just fine," she agreed. "It's the *nice* part that you definitely need help with. You seem to be lacking in that area."

"I am not lacking in anything," he said.

"You don't have to get all insulted."

"I'm not insulted."

"Then why are you growling?" Daniella said.

"You would drive a saint crazy."

"I sincerely doubt that," she said. "You, on the other hand, would definitely be a challenge to a saint. Not that I'm a saint by any stretch of the imagination. Look, all this anger probably isn't good for your blood pressure. Perhaps you should look into some anger-management classes while checking out those communication classes."

"I told you, I don't need classes."

"Because you're already perfect. I know you obviously think that but it's not really true." Daniella turned back to Lois. "We'll talk later. I'm going to stop at Tanya's Tanning next."

She moved toward the exit, stepping around Nick. She could feel his heated glare on her back as she exited the dental clinic and headed down the sidewalk to the tanning salon.

She could also feel him following her. Damn, the man moved fast. He was standing in front of her a second later.

She refused to be impressed or intimidated. Instead, she tapped her foot impatiently. "What now?"

"I want to apologize if I've offended you," Nick said.

Her eyes widened in surprise. That was the last thing she expected him to say. "You don't seem like the kind of man who apologizes much."

"I don't," he readily admitted. "But I came off strong and—"

"Bossy?" she inserted.

"I've never met anyone like you before," he said quietly.

It was the first time she'd heard him use that tone of voice, and she had to admit it got to her. For the first time since meeting him, she was speechless. She studied him carefully, trying to read his thoughts by his facial expression or his eyes. She didn't detect any mockery there. He seemed genuinely baffled by her.

"I've never met anyone exactly like you, either," she said.

"Finally, something we have in common," he said.

"So why don't you like me?"

"I never said I didn't like you."

"Right," she scoffed.

"Maybe if I knew you better . . . ," he said.

"You'd like me more?" she finished for him. "I suppose that's possible."

"And maybe you'd like me more."

She volleyed his words back at him. "I never said I didn't like you."

"Touché."

She'd never had a guy say *touché* to her before. Surprisingly, she liked it. His smile was pretty stunning as well. It consisted of a slight lifting of those fierce lips of his.

"Do you want me to introduce you to Tanya?" he offered.

"I'm sure you must have other things to do . . ."

"I insist." He ushered her into the tanning salon.

No drills here but Daniella couldn't help noticing that all three of the establishments she'd visited so far had displayed a definite lack of clients. Business was not brisk—and that didn't bode well for her shop.

Maybe it was just a slow time of the day. She didn't feel comfortable asking why each place was so empty. That would be rude.

Being rude didn't seem to bother Tanya, however, as she glared at Daniella. "What do you want?"

Okay, maybe that was the reason for the lack of business in the tanning salon. Tanya had a definite attitude problem. Or maybe she just had low blood sugar. The young woman didn't look like she'd eaten recently. She had that super-skinny look that the fashion magazines made so popular these days. It wasn't a look that Daniella would ever achieve in this lifetime.

Daniella was the first to admit her own body had curves. She had thighs. She had breasts. Thighs, breasts . . . okay, now she was getting a mental photo of the drive-thru menu at KFC. Her stomach growled.

Tanya turned her attention to Nick, moving forward to curl her fingers possessively around his arm. "I'm glad to see *you*."

"This is Daniella Delaney," Nick said. "She's opening a cupcake shop down the street."

"Cupcakes?" Tanya shuddered in horror. "They're poison!"

"I never use poison in my recipes," Daniella said drily.

"Do you use sugar and butter?" Tanya demanded.

Daniella nodded.

"Poison." Tanya shuddered.

Daniella was getting ticked off. It was one thing to insult her; it was another thing entirely to insult her cupcakes. Still, she tried to be professional about it all and stay calm. "I have some sugar-free cupcakes as well."

"You're killing people!" Tanya shouted.

"Tanning beds harm more people than cupcakes do," Daniella retorted.

Things went downhill from there and ended with Tanya kicking Daniella out of her salon. Not literally, of course, although she did look tough enough to do some damage with those spiky heels of hers. Tanya's tanned body was slim, but there was some muscle there as well. And she looked angry enough to be dangerous.

Daniella was angry, too. She was angry that Nick just stood there like a dummy while Tanya unloaded her vitriol on Daniella, yelling something about the salon focusing on spray tans instead of tanning beds.

At this point, Daniella really didn't care. She only knew that Tanya was not worthy of her cupcakes, although eating one might make her disposition a little sweeter.

In Daniella's world, cupcakes represented comfort. In Tanya's world, cupcakes clearly represented dangerous calories.

As for Nick, who knew what his world was? Daniella didn't care. She left him to deal with Tanya's tantrum and made her departure, turning at the last minute to add, "Have a nice day."

Daniella raced out before Tanya could throw a bottle of self-tanning solution at her.

"To the Vamp Cave," Nick said. The voice-recognition-activated security system immediately opened a hidden entrance in Nick's small office in the back of the All Nighter Bar and Grill. The building and many others on the block were connected by underground tunnels dating back to Prohibition in the 1920s, when bootleggers used them to bring in illegal alcohol. The maze-like layout was hard to follow if you didn't know where you were going.

Nick always knew where he was going. Being nice to Daniella today hadn't gone as well as he'd planned, so he decided to try another tack. He entered an underground room filled with the latest cutting-edge computer equipment and flat screens displaying, among other things, neighborhood surveillance camera footage.

Chicago had more surveillance cameras than any other American city. The city's security was top-notch but no match for vamp super-nerd Neville Rickerbacher, who could hack any firewall without breaking a sweat. Now that Neville was a vampire, he could do it all at super speeds mere humans couldn't hope to rival.

"I need you to do a background check," Nick told him.

"I'm one step ahead of you," Neville told him,

pointing to the large screen in front of him. "Daniella Delaney, right?"

Nick nodded.

"Here's the factual stuff. Date of birth, education, that sort of thing."

Nick quickly looked it over. "I already know that info."

Neville changed screens. "Here's her financial stuff. Her business plan looks good to me."

That meant a lot coming from Neville, who played the stock market and had for decades. He'd been turned in the 1980s when his own stockbroker, Howard Hanes, had bitten him after referring to Howard as a greedy bloodsucker. Since then, Neville and his elite team made the money that kept Vamptown going.

"She's never had any run-ins with the police or with the IRS," Neville said. "Drives a—"

"—pink Vespa she called Shirley," Nick said. "Yeah, I already know that."

"I didn't know she named her scooter." He rapidly typed in this info. Neville pointed to one of the surveillance screens before calling it up on his own display. "She wears a pink helmet while driving."

"It's her favorite color," Nick said. Seeing Neville's curious look, he added, "I talked to her brother."

"I have to tell you there's a lot of chatter about the fact that Daniella appears to be immune to vamp mind compulsion."

Nick swore under his breath.

"There's no way to keep something like that quiet," Neville said. "You weren't the only vamp to try mind compulsion on her. Nobody was successful."

"Put the word out to keep that on the down-low," Nick said.

"Okay, but it may already be too late. With social

networking and tweets, news gets out really fast. And not just in Vamptown."

"Meaning what?"

"Meaning other vamps are taking notice and are curious," Neville said. "It's only a matter of time before some of them coming sniffing around. I may be able to buy us some time by spinning it—saying the story is an urban legend."

"Do it."

Neville's fingers flew over the keys. "Done. But I don't think the vamp community is going to buy it."

"Did you find anything in her background to indicate why she's immune?"

"Not yet."

"She may have some ESP talent."

"Duly noted."

"Keep digging," Nick said.

"Sure."

"I tried being nice to her today. It didn't go well," Nick admitted.

Neville blinked at him. "I'm not good with dissecting relationship dynamics."

Nick knew that. The fact that he'd confided in Neville showed how badly Daniella had thrown him. But he couldn't seem to stop himself. "I've never had trouble being nice to a female before."

"So I've heard."

"She isn't that special," Nick said. "I mean, aside from the mind compulsion immunity. She's not that pretty."

"Agreed. She's no supermodel."

"But there's something about her," Nick said.

"She's smart." Neville called up her educational records. "Great SAT scores. Graduated with honors."

"I've dealt with smart women before and never

had any trouble with them." Nick's irritation came through in his voice.

"So it's not her education. I don't see any indication that she's been involved with anything metaphysical. By the way, I hacked her laptop when she was using the Wi-Fi at Starbucks this morning and checked her recent online orders. She bought a popular book."

"About what?"

"It's a baker's memoir. She also ordered a cupcake bracelet from Amazon. Then she emailed her website person about tweaks to the site, saying she wasn't happy with it yet."

"Keep monitoring her."

"She's had no contact with any other vamps outside of Vamptown. No computer contact with any in Vamptown, either. She seems to like face-to-face meetings."

"She asked Lois to work for her," Nick said.

Neville's face reflected his surprise. "Lois from Doc Boomer's office?"

Nick nodded.

"What did Lois say?"

"She's considering doing it," Nick said.

"That might be a good idea," Neville said. "To have one of us working there, I mean."

"You're right."

"Lois is pretty discreet. No one would guess she's a vamp."

"Maybe I'm going about this backward," Nick said. "Maybe I should just use mind compulsion on her father. He supplied the building for her."

"He did. But he also drew up an airtight contract. I looked it over when I was pulling her information.

And you know that he's gone on a monthlong cruise in the South Pacific, right?"

"I forgot about that," Nick muttered.

"Forgetting isn't something you usually do," Neville noted.

Nick glared at him. "I'm aware of that."

Neville leaned back in his chair as if trying to put as much distance as possible between himself and Nick.

"How did you find out about the contract between Daniella and her dad?" Nick said. "I didn't know it was a matter of public record."

"That doesn't stop me. I have my ways."

"Right." Nick had his ways as well, some of which were clearly rusty. Charming Daniella had proved to be more challenging than he'd expected, but he wasn't about to give up now. The clock was running. As Neville pointed out, it was only a matter of time now before other vampires came sniffing around.

Daniella refused to be discouraged that no one in the neighborhood was willing to sample the cupcakes she'd brought along as she went door-to-door and introduced herself to the business owners today. Some, like Pat from Pat's Tats, she'd known since she was a kid.

And yes, there were some new faces like Tanya from Tanya's Tanning Salon, who obviously never ate sweets to keep her super-skinny figure going. Clearly, Daniella's meeting with Tanya hadn't gone well. Daniella was willing to consider the possibility that perhaps it was partly her fault. Gorgeous women tended to intimidate her a little. Especially gorgeous stuck-up bitchy women. *Nice* gorgeous women were just fine.

Remembering the condescending *you're nobody* look Tanya gave her made Daniella feel irritated all over again.

But come on. The woman ran a tanning salon. She was hardly America's Next Top Model.

Okay, so she *did* look like a supermodel.

Nick liked Tanya. Daniella had been stunned by the smile he'd flashed at the other woman. He'd never smiled that way at her.

Maybe he reserved those for women with perfect features and sun-kissed blond hair.

Daniella really shouldn't be wasting her time even thinking about either Tanya or Nick. She needed to focus on the cinnamon frosting she was trying to perfect. To add crimson fondant leaves or not? That was the question.

She was totally focused on achieving culinary excellence when she heard a noise coming from the alleyway outside. No doubt it was Nick, coming to give her a hard time again.

Wiping the frosting from her hands with a nearby kitchen towel, she quickly untied her baker's apron and headed for the back door.

Chapter Five

Nick was holed up in his tiny office when the feeling hit him. *Daniella is in danger.* The realization crashed into him with the force of a cannon. All his vamp senses were immediately on high alert.

Neville's call came an instant later. "The cameras outside the bakery have gone black."

"I'm already on my way."

Nick used his vamp super speed to get to Heavenly Cupcakes in less time than it took a human to blink an eye. His sense of smell led him to the back alley, where he found Daniella surrounded by a motley trio of vampires. They weren't locals.

He could tell that they'd each tried their mind compulsion on Daniella and that it hadn't worked.

"If you need help, there's a homeless shelter three blocks away," Daniella was telling them.

"We came for you," the tallest one said.

"You can't have her," Nick said. "Step away from the cupcake maker."

Instead of obeying his order, the tall one made a grab for Daniella.

"Big mistake," Nick growled. He had to rein in his fury or he'd go full vamp in front of Daniella. He could sense the others were on the verge of doing so as well. He had to get her away from the scene.

"Let me go!" Daniella shouted before removing a small can from her cargo pants pocket and spraying the tall one with pepper spray. While the deterrent didn't have the same powerful effect that it did on humans, it was enough to make the tall one release her.

"Get inside," Nick ordered her. "And lock the door." The outsider vamps wouldn't be able to follow her in without an invitation.

"I'm calling the cops," she warned them before racing indoors.

Nick waited until she was inside before turning his back to the shop so she couldn't see his transformation. He could already feel his fangs emerging. The alley was dark enough that the three others stood in the shadows. The darkness increased as Nick knocked out the nearest streetlight with the force of one look.

"You boys don't belong here," Nick said. "Leave now."

"We've heard about you," the tall one said. "The tough Nick St. George. But the odds are against you tonight."

Nick had been in enough fights in his lifetime and certainly in his afterlife that he didn't look forward to them. But he'd never been one to walk away from a battle, and he wasn't about to start now. He might be outnumbered but he wasn't going to be outsmarted.

Neither he nor the trio of vamps was afraid to die. Being immortal did that to you. But there was nothing pleasant about getting your face bashed in or your arms and legs broken. Sure, they all had the power to heal quickly. But the process was not fun.

Some vamps got an adrenaline rush out of fighting their own kind. Humans didn't provide enough of a challenge for them so they sought out other vampires for a sort of World Wrestling smackdown. But these guys seemed to have a more deliberate agenda.

"Who sent you?" Nick growled.

The tall one responded by attacking, fangs in full force. Nick launched him into the air with one hand before whipping around to kick the shorter vamp in his solar plexus. The third one didn't even attempt to enter the battle.

Nick was relieved to see that this trio talked the talk but weren't skilled enough to walk the walk. They weren't as battle-tested as he was. It was all over in less than a minute. The outsiders wisely took off.

It took a few more minutes for Nick's anger to abate and his fangs to retreat so that he could face Daniella. He knew that his eyes had darkened to a feral glow, and he could feel them returning to their normal state. But still he waited. He couldn't risk the chance that Daniella would see him for what he was. Finally he felt normal. Which was a lie. Nothing about him was normal.

"It's Nick. Let me in," he told Daniella through the locked back door.

She quickly obeyed. "The police are on their way. What happened out there? The light went out and I couldn't tell what was going on."

Instead of answering, Nick asked his own question. "What were you thinking going out there by yourself?"

"I heard a noise and I thought it was you."

"Your ESP couldn't warn you that it wasn't me?"

"I told you before, I don't have ESP."

"Obviously," he said. He wished he knew who had sent the trio to check her out. This latest development was not a good one.

"So are you going to tell me what happened?" she said. "Who were they? What did they want?"

"They were just a bunch of thugs lurking about and looking for trouble," he said.

"Were they gang bangers?"

He shrugged. Vampires felt a loyalty to their clans that gangs shared. He knew there were some gang members who were also vamps. "They're gone now," he said.

"What if they come back?" She sounded nervous.

"They won't." But others might. He was glad that she wasn't acting as cocky as she had before. Going outside had been damn stupid and could have ended her life. That realization hit Nick in the gut. Humans had never been at risk in Vamptown before. The two species had always lived in relative peace. But things were changing. Rapidly.

"Why did the one guy say they came for me?" Daniella asked.

"Who knows?" Nick said, but it was a lie. He knew why they'd come. It was because they'd heard she was immune to mind compulsion and they wondered why. Such immunity was extremely rare. "He was probably high on drugs."

"His eyes were very red, and he did seem strange," she said.

"Drugs," he said curtly.

"So they were drugged gang bangers lurking about? You don't hear that much these days. Lurking about. It sounds very BBC America. Unless you've spent time in England?"

Nick had. Centuries ago. Not that he planned on sharing that information with her. Instead he asked, "Did they say anything to you before I arrived?"

"They just stood around looking menacing and trash talking a bit. I was trying to be nice by telling them about the nearest homeless shelter. They looked like they needed help. I didn't realize they were gang members. What if they'd pulled a gun or something?"

It was the "or something" that worried Nick.

"If they come back, do not invite them inside," he said.

"Do I look stupid?" she countered.

"You look like someone who's too nice."

She didn't appear pleased by his observation. "What gave you that impression?"

"The fact that you told them where the nearest shelter was located."

"I won't make that mistake again."

"Good."

"And I'm not always nice," she said. "I haven't been nice to you. I didn't bend when you tried to order me around. In fact, I've been described as a pit bull in pearls and a twinset where my business is concerned."

Nick had no idea what a twinset was and he didn't get why she seemed pleased with the analogy to a pit bull. They were hardly the cutest canines. And the cupcake maker was definitely cute . . . and hot and sexy. The more time he spent with her, the more he felt the attraction. She wasn't obvious the way Tanya was. Daniella wasn't into displaying yards of cleavage. She didn't have to.

"I wonder where the cops are," she said.

Nick didn't have to wonder. He knew that Pat would have waylaid them and compelled them into believing everything was fine and the call was a false alarm.

No, the police weren't the problem. Daniella was. Clearly he needed to watch out for her from now on, and the best way to protect her was to keep her close. "I've changed my mind," he said. "I think you opening your store in this neighborhood is a good idea after all."

She narrowed her eyes at him. "Why the sudden change of heart?"

He couldn't blame her for being suspicious. "As you said, you're going to open your shop whether I approve or not."

"Right," she said. "So there's no logical reason why you should suddenly decide that my being here is a good idea. Were you behind the trouble here tonight?"

"No. Why would I do that?"

"To scare me away."

"Then why did I save you?" he said.

"You didn't save me. You happened to arrive at an auspicious moment. And perhaps you did that in order to be a hero," she said.

"Trust me, I'm nobody's hero."

"People in the neighborhood seem to think highly of you."

"That should tell you something," he said.

"It tells me you've got them bamboozled." She sighed. "Okay, now I'm sounding like BBC America, too."

"You should be glad that I'm on your side."

"Really?" She didn't look as impressed as he felt she should be. "Why's that?"

His words were deliberately curt. "Because you don't want me as your enemy."

He saw her shiver. Good. Maybe the seriousness of the situation was finally getting through to her. The incident tonight meant that word about Daniella's immunity to vamp compulsion had gotten out. Nick couldn't be sure which of the rival clans of vamps had sent the troublemakers tonight.

Drawing herself up to her full height—all of five feet, seven inches—Daniella loftily informed him, "You don't want me to be *your* enemy, either."

"Agreed." Nick could tell his response surprised her. "So aren't you glad we can get along so much better now?"

"Are we getting along well enough that you'll try one of my cupcakes?"

"No, but I did eat a few of the samples you left."

"You did?"

He nodded. He was lying, of course, since vamps couldn't eat. He hadn't had food in ages and he missed it badly. Some of his kind considered humans to be nothing more than a source of sustenance. They looked at them and thought—*lunch*.

They drained them of life and blood and in doing so destroyed the last bits of humanity within themselves. Nick knew how that felt, and he'd fought it hard. That's why he'd been so glad that Doc had discovered a way to recycle blood and keep it fresh and full of life even though it came from corpses.

Frankly, Nick didn't like thinking about the source of his meals. Did that make him that different from meat-eating humans who didn't want to know about animal cruelty? Yeah, it probably did, he admitted to himself. He *was* different from humans and always would be. He couldn't afford to forget that.

Daniella seemed different, too. Which meant what? He had to figure that out because time was clearly running out.

"So what did you think?" Daniella asked eagerly.

"About what?"

"About my cupcakes? You said you tried some of the samples I left."

"Uh, they were good."

"Good?" She appeared insulted.

"*Very* good?"

"Talk about damning with faint praise," she huffed.

He briefly considered telling her she looked cute when she was irritated but decided she'd probably brain him with a mixing bowl if he did. "They were the best cupcakes I've ever had."

"Do you have a lot of them?"

"Not many."

"Did your mom ever make them for you when you were a kid?" she asked.

"No."

"My mom did. She used to bake cookies and cupcakes for the families of the deceased. She'd tell me, 'I can't bring their loved one back, but I can try to bring them some comfort.' So from an early age, cupcakes meant comfort to me."

It was the first time Daniella had talked about her past, and it made Nick feel as if he was finally making some progress with her.

"Your mom sounds like someone special."

"She was. She died when I was sixteen. I still miss her. I think she'd be very proud of what I'm doing here with Heavenly Cupcakes."

"I'm sure she would," Nick said.

"What about your parents?" she asked. "Are they from Chicago? Are they proud of you opening your bar and grill?"

"My parents are both dead."

"Any siblings?"

He shook his head. "I don't have any family."

"That must be rough."

"I manage," he said.

"I'm sure you do. You seem like the kind of man who can deal with anything."

"I have to." As a vampire he couldn't afford to show weakness.

"You also don't seem the kind of man to suffer fools easily."

"I never thought you were a fool."

"Good," she said. "Some people think I'm a push-over because of my appearance."

"What's wrong with your appearance?"

"Asks the man with the plastic fish and the moose head on his bar's wall," she said wryly.

"I'm merely saying that you look fine to me."

"Gee, thanks." Once again she was irritated.

What had he said wrong now? You'd think he'd know how to deal with females after two centuries. But the truth was that without mind compulsion, he was finding it much more challenging . . . to put it mildly.

He studied her lush mouth with the intensity of a scholar.

He detected the change in her heart rate instantly. So he did get to her. Good. That meant he had some power over her, and he intended to use it to get what he wanted. Self-preservation and the preservation of his clan demanded that he break the spell she seemed to cast over him. He needed to be the one with the upper hand. And that hand of his couldn't be caressing her breast the way he wanted.

Nick wanted to make Daniella his, but a vampire mating with a human never worked out well. So he had to fight this attraction he had for her and instead increase *her* attraction for him. He could do it. He had to do it. He just needed to figure out how. And in order to that, he needed to get away from her before he tossed her onto the stainless-steel worktable and had sex with her. "Later," he growled at her before abruptly leaving.

"The outsiders were responsible for the cameras going out, so I've changed the interface and passwords," Neville told Nick as he entered the Vamp Cave. "I assume you were responsible for the streetlight going out?"

Nick nodded. "Who were they?"

"You tell me."

"Did you get them on any of the other cameras?"

"Nothing on the city's cameras that we've hacked into. But our own vamp cams did pick up something."

Neville had developed a camera fast enough to capture the image of a vampire on the move and slow it down so that it was more easily visible.

Pat and his companion Bruce joined them. "I heard there was an altercation," Pat said. "I took care of the police presence. Do you know who the vamps were?"

"We're trying to get a look at them now," Nick said.

"Got it," Neville said. A moment later an image came up on the multiple large screens in the Vamp Cave.

"What are they wearing?" Bruce shuddered. "I

hate the pants-on-the-floor look. I thought we were past that fashion faux pas. And look at the hair on that short one. It's like steel wool. A good conditioner and an eyebrow wax would make a world of difference."

"Recognize them?" Nick asked Pat.

Bruce answered first. "They are fashion don'ts, that's for sure."

"I don't think they were worried about their looks," Nick said.

"Clearly," Bruce said. He might look like a linebacker for the Chicago Bears with his stout and sturdy build, but he was a self-proclaimed fashionista. Pat liked to describe his partner as a combination of toughness and tailored tenderness—part Hulk and part Armani.

"The tall one looks familiar," Pat said. "But I can't quite place him."

"He seemed to be the leader of the trio," Nick said.

"That's the problem with living four hundred years," Pat said. "You meet so many people and vamps it's hard to keep them all straight. Don't worry. It will come to me eventually. Any idea what they wanted?"

"They wanted Daniella."

Pat's expression was worried. "That's not good."

"No, it's not," Nick agreed.

"Did they say why they wanted her?" Pat asked.

"We didn't stop to have a lengthy conversation about it," Nick said. "But I got the impression that they'd heard about her immunity to vamp mind compulsion and were curious."

Pat raised an eyebrow. "Just curious?"

Nick nodded. "For now."

"It must have been a pretty strong curiosity for them to stray into our territory," Pat said. "They know the rules. Each vamp tribe keeps to its own areas unless invited to do otherwise."

"I want to know who sent them," Nick said.

"It could be the Gold Coast vamps," Pat said. "They don't want to get their fangs dirty, so they send enforcers to do their dirty work."

"The Gold Coast vamps are very natty dressers," Bruce said. "I can't see them hiring help wearing that attire. Tim Gunn would have a hissy fit."

"This isn't *Project Runway*," Pat told Bruce. "This is serious business."

"*Project Runway is* serious," Bruce retorted. "I still haven't recovered from Gretchen beating Mondo in season eight."

"Any face recognitions yet?" Nick asked Neville.

"Not yet."

"I suspect they're recent," Nick said. "They had that edginess that comes from new converts to vampirism."

"I'll keep checking," Neville promised.

"Do that," Nick said. "Because the clock is clearly ticking at a faster speed now."

Daniella was in her shop before daylight the next morning. She kept to her usual schedule despite what had happened the previous night. She did keep her pepper spray in hand as she sprinted the few steps in the front of the building housing both her business and her apartment. She planned on avoiding the alley in the dark for the next few days.

After a successful morning creating culinary mini masterpieces, she decided to include a small and elite collection of them on her cupcake menu. The cookies 'n' cream and the amaretto were two of her favorite concoctions in this new smaller version.

Around noon, Daniella moved to the front of the shop. She was surprised to find a young woman knocking on the door. Her dark blond hair had streaks of statement-making neon red throughout.

"We're not open yet," Daniella said.

The woman held up her smartphone. "I saw on Craigslist that you're looking for help."

Daniella unlocked the door and temporarily disabled the security system to let her in. Daniella had a good feeling about this applicant for some reason. Maybe it was the wild Technicolor dreamcoat she was wearing, which should have clashed with her hair but didn't. Daniella had loved the play *Joseph and the Amazing Technicolor Dreamcoat* when she'd seen it.

Once inside, the woman started reading the ad aloud. "In need of a permanent part-time worker. Must be able to frost, work with fondant, take accurate orders, be flexible, willing to get dirty, willing to put up with my entertaining singing, able to take criticism, able to handle customers, and—this is important, remember, so I'm repeating it—able to take accurate orders!" She paused before adding, "My name is Xandra Stevens and I can do all that. I worked in a cupcake shop in Vail and another in Lake Tahoe. I'm the best person for the job. I'm totally stoked about cupcakes and it looks like you are, too."

Xandra's energetic enthusiasm was contagious. Daniella handed her an application to fill out and watched the young woman as she sat at one of the tables by the window. She was definitely a free spirit, from the tips of her paisley boots to her dangly bottlecap earrings.

Daniella opened her laptop and checked out the names of the cupcake stores that Xandra had listed. They were valid. She then Googled Xandra's name and found her photo on the blogs of both stores with high praise for her.

"Why did you leave Vail and Lake Tahoe?" Daniella asked.

"It was too expensive," Xandra said. "I had to come back home and move in with my parents."

"How do I know you won't take off for the slopes as soon as you have enough money?"

"I'm not a skier or snowboarder myself. I just liked to watch. I actually do have a plan. I plan on returning out west when I'm twenty-five."

"How would you deal with an unhappy customer?" Daniella asked.

"It depends on what made them unhappy, but I'd try to help them in any way I could. Maybe they are just having a bad day—but that doesn't mean that I can just dismiss their complaint. I'd do whatever I could to make them chill out."

Daniella was impressed. The only other applicant had answered by saying "What do you expect me to do about it?" in a defensively crabby way.

"We close early when we run out of cupcakes for the day," Daniella said. "We bake them fresh every day."

"By 'we' you mean you and who else? Do you need help in the kitchen?"

"Sometimes."

"I can do that," Xandra said. "I've done it before. Just consider me to be one of the Keebler Elves, only better."

When something sounds too good to be true, it usually is. Suz told Daniella that all the time.

But it wasn't as if tons of people were lining up at her door for the minimum-wage job. Daniella wasn't sure why not. Times were tough, and people needed work. She wondered if Nick was somehow behind the lack of applicants.

"I'm also great at using social networking tools to bring in business," Xandra said.

That did it. Daniella trusted her gut and hired her. "Providing your references check out."

"They will."

Daniella held out her hand and one of the custom-designed navy-blue T-shirts with the hot-pink shop logo. "Welcome to Heavenly Cupcakes."

"It's gonna be sick," Xandra said with a grin.

"*Sick* isn't really a term you want to use in the culinary arts," Daniella said.

"Right. I know that. Sorry. I'm just really stoked."

Daniella grinned back at her. "Me too. I think we're going to get along just fine."

Chapter Six

Daniella loved Shirley, her pink Vespa, for many reasons. First was the freedom she provided. Parking was never an issue, which in a big city like Chicago was a huge plus. Second was the sheer exhilaration of riding the scooter, zipping from one place to another. Third was the incredible gas mileage, especially given the price of gasoline these days.

Yes, she loved Shirley, which was why she took special care of her when not using the scooter. She didn't leave her parked at the curb overnight. Instead she carefully sheltered her in the funeral home's large garage. Sure, the perky pink Vespa did look out of place next to the solemn black hearse. After all, they did represent opposing ends of the vehicle spectrum. The Vespa was full of life and the hearse . . . well, it wasn't.

The 2010 Cadillac Medalist, with its shiny yet somber black exterior and blue interior, was her brother Gordon's pride and joy. He'd handpicked the hearse from the Internet, bragging about the great deal he'd gotten on it. The last time her brother had bragged about a hearse was back in high school when he'd taken their old discontinued hearse and had it custom-painted with red flames on an orange background. He'd been a big hit with his buddies, since Gordon had transformed the back of the vehicle into a plush bed for makeout sessions.

Their father had not been equally enthusiastic about the old hearse's transformation, saying it looked like Hell on Wheels.

Now that their dad was almost sixty, he'd shifted a lot more responsibility onto Gordon's shoulders. The cruise their dad was currently taking had been a surprise he'd sprung on them at the last minute.

"My friend Franny was going to go with someone else," her dad had told Daniella, "but they canceled so she suggested I go instead. Franny and I knew each other in college but we lost touch after that. We reconnected on Facebook about a year ago and we've met a few times since then."

She wondered if Franny was his girlfriend. Since Daniella's mother's death thirteen years ago, her dad had been 110 percent focused on the business. Independent funeral homes like theirs were finding it harder and harder to stay afloat. The death care industry was big business ruled by large corporations, as was much of the country these days.

But here on her block, the Evergreen Funeral Home lived on. Her dad said business was booming since Gordon stepped in. She found that a little hard to believe given her brother's gambling habits. But she'd never had any interest in the family business per se. Embalming wasn't her thing. She and her mom had focused on comforting grieving people, while her father and brother were more interested in completing procedures. Daniella and her mom were into people. Her dad and brother were into the process.

Daniella was so deep in her thoughts that she shrieked when Nick suddenly materialized beside her. The large garage door leading to the alley was still open, which was clearly how he got in.

"You need to be more aware of your surroundings," he chastised her. "You haven't forgotten that incident in the alley a few nights ago, have you?"

"No."

"Good. Here, let me help you with that." He took one of the canvas bags filled with food from her. "So this is Shirley, huh?" He eyed her pink scooter.

Daniella returned the favor by eyeing him suspiciously. "How did you know I named my Vespa Shirley?"

"I must have heard it in the neighborhood," he said smoothly. "Where are you going with all this stuff? To the shop?"

"No, to my apartment above the shop."

She hung her pink helmet on the scooter's handlebars, set the garage security system, and closed the door before heading down the alley to the narrow walkway between her building and the neighboring one.

"This is a danger zone," Nick said.

"If the bag is too heavy for you—"

He interrupted her. "I meant you're in an enclosed area."

"There's a security camera mounted on the front corner of the building," she said. "It covers this area as well as my shop."

"Does it cover the alley?"

"No, but I'm looking into adding one there."

She passed the shop's door and headed for the

one next door. Nick followed her, watching her as she jingled her key in the lock.

"Do you need my help?" he asked.

"I'm okay." Her nerves were caused by his proximity. She could feel the heat emanating from his body. He was wearing his customary black, and he looked better than she remembered. He smelled better, too. Not that he'd smelled bad before.

Right. She was definitely losing it here. She needed to focus . . . and not on how sexy Nick was. No, she needed to focus on practical things like opening this darn lock. There. She finally got it and yanked the door open.

A steep flight of stairs led up to her one-bedroom apartment.

After unlocking her apartment door without any trouble and punching her code into the security system, she turned to see Nick still standing in the hallway. "Come on in," she said. "Would you like something to drink or anything?"

"No, thank you." He closed the door behind him and set the tote bag of food on the kitchen counter to the right of the entrance.

Daniella had kept the vintage feel of the kitchen with white subway tile on the kitchen walls and the pink refrigerator. Granted, pink wasn't the usual color for the appliance, but it added a nice dash of color. The original wood flooring had been sanded and varnished throughout the apartment. While the kitchen might look Old World, her cooking equipment was top-of-the-line.

Danielle noted the way he was surveying his surroundings. "I'll bet you were expecting lots of pink and ruffles, right?" she said

"You do drive a pink scooter and you have a pink refrigerator."

"I like pink," she readily admitted. "A lot. But I also like other things." She gestured toward her living room with its bright palette of raspberry red and ivory. Stationary floral curtain panels subtly defined a cozy reading corner with a window seat beneath large tall windows.

Instead of commenting on her decorating, Nick said, "I wanted to talk to you about security measures. Your windows are locked, right?"

"I have a security system here and as you already know, I also have one in the shop."

"You shouldn't be down there alone in the dark," he said.

"At this time of year there aren't enough daylight hours," she said. "I go make the cupcakes in the dark and I come home in the dark."

"Then I'll come with you."

"Don't be silly. You saw it's only a few steps from the entranceway downstairs to my shop's front door."

"Even so, I'll escort you."

"Why?" she asked him suspiciously. "What do you think is going to happen?"

"I don't want a repeat of that incident in the alley the other night."

"Neither do I."

"Good. Then it's settled."

She paused in the process of putting the last of her groceries away to look at him. "No, it's not settled. You're being bossy again."

"I'm trying to be nice."

"I'm not a kindergartner who needs her parent to hold her hand as she walks to school."

"I'm not your parent," he said before asking, "Did they really do that? Hold your hand and walk you to school?"

"When I was a little kid, yes. My mom did that. The school is only a couple of blocks away. When I got a bit older, my brother had to walk me home. He hated it," she said.

"Why?"

"He wanted to hang out with his friends, not take care of his sister."

"Are the two of you close now?" Nick asked.

"We get along okay," she said. "Why?"

"No reason. I was just making polite conversation." He abruptly changed the subject. "I saw there was a buzzer outside by the front door. What do you do if someone buzzes? You don't automatically just let them in, do you?"

"I use the intercom to ask who it is. Why the interrogation?"

"I told you. I'm concerned for your safety," he said.

"You're sure you're not trying to scare me?" she countered. "Gaslight me?"

He frowned. "I don't understand."

"*Gaslight* was a classic movie from the 1940s about a husband who was trying to manipulate his wife into thinking she was crazy."

"And you think I'm trying to manipulate you?" he said.

"You've tried to do it in the past. The first time we met, you thought you could merely tell me not to open my shop and I'd blindly obey."

"I admit we got off on the wrong foot," he said. "And I've said that I have no objections any longer to your shop. I looked at your business plan. It's good."

"I had help with that from my friend Suz, who is an accountant, and my baking mentor Cookie."

"Cookie?"

"It's her nickname. I met her when I was working in New York City. She owns a very successful cupcake shop there and was generous enough to share her knowledge with me."

"I don't recall you mentioning her before."

Daniella paused to fold her reusable grocery bag and put it away before saying, "I don't tell you all my secrets."

"Why is she a secret?" he immediately asked.

"She's not. It's just an expression."

Nick looked deep into her eyes. "You can tell me your secrets."

"Really?" she retorted. "Will you tell me yours?"

A small part of Nick wanted to. Luckily it was a *very* small part of him. The huge majority of his vampire brain cells declared war on that stupid and dangerous impulse.

"No?" she said. "I didn't think so. No worries. So we each have secrets. No big deal, right?"

"Right." He nodded. "So does this mentor of yours have a last name?"

"Marelli. Why?"

"No reason." He made a mental note to have Neville check her out.

"Cookie could give you some tips on improving your business," Daniella said. "She managed several restaurants and bistros before opening her own shop."

"I don't need any help."

"Says the man with the plastic fish on his bar's wall," she teased him.

"You seem to have an obsession about that fish,"

he said. "Do you have a thing against talking mackerels?"

"As examples of the lunacy of some consumers, no. As a decoration, yes."

"So you're saying I shouldn't get you one as a present for your grand opening?"

"You're kidding, right?" She eyed him uncertainly.

"Am I?" His lips lifted slightly.

"I can't tell," she admitted. "I haven't experienced you kidding me before."

"A milestone in our relationship," he said drily.

"Are you saying we have a relationship?"

"A business relationship."

"Sure. A business relationship." She narrowed her eyes at him. "You're being much too nice to me all of a sudden. Is there something you're not telling me?"

There was a lot that Nick wasn't telling her, that he *couldn't* tell her. Staring into her eyes, it was so tempting to just lean a little closer so his lips touched hers. She was wearing a jean jacket over a white T-shirt and jeans. Nothing fancy. Nothing to make him want her so intensely. Every time he saw her, his desire for her grew.

"There *is* something. I knew it. Tell me," she said.

"I want to kiss you."

"Wha . . . at?" Clearly stunned by his reply, she stumbled over the word.

"You asked me a question. I answered it."

"You're kidding, right?"

He swooped in and answered her question with action instead of words. His mouth brushed against her soft lips, coaxing them to part for him. When they did, he rewarded her response by intensifying the kiss.

He could feel her heartbeat, feel the throb of her pulse drawing him in.

"What are you doing?" she whispered as he nuzzled her earlobe.

"Kissing you."

"But why?"

"Because I want to," he murmured against her mouth.

"Is this your way of trying to convince me not to open my shop?"

"Forget about your shop."

"I can't." She pushed him away. "Don't try to make me."

"I'd never make a woman kiss me against her will."

"I meant don't try to distract me with kisses. It won't work. Any more than my kissing you would distract you."

Nick wasn't about to admit that her mouth was capable of making him lose track of everything. Every thought. Every good intention.

"You don't believe me? I know this doesn't distract you." She moved swiftly, placing her mouth over his.

He fed on her. Not her blood but her essence— the essence of her soft lips, the texture of her tongue. Because there was plenty of tongue going on. He doubted she'd intended that to happen when she'd kissed him to make a point. But the fact that it had happened proved how volatile the two of them were together.

At their very first meeting, he'd thought she was playing with fire. Now he was doing that, too. Fire had the power to destroy vampires. But damn, she tasted so fine.

He'd fed earlier so it wasn't her blood he craved.

It was her body. He wanted to take her then and there, up against the wall, with her jeans around her knees and him embedded deep within her.

But the need to protect his secret took priority above all other needs. Pushing her away, he regained control. "Lock your door," he growled before storming out.

"Are you ready for your grand opening in four days?" Suz asked Daniella as the two of them sat in the back work area of the shop where Daniella was still tweaking some of her specialty frosting recipes.

"Sure," Daniella replied. "I can't wait!"

"You're lying," Suz said.

Daniella made a face. "What gave me away?"

"The way your right eyelid is twitching."

Daniella put a hand up to her face.

"Now you've got frosting on your forehead," Suz said.

"Great," Daniella muttered.

"How nervous are you on a scale of one to ten?"

"I don't think in terms of numbers," Daniella said. "That's your thing, not mine."

Suz nibbled on the remnants of what once was a naked chocolate cupcake. "You're avoiding the question."

"Because I want to focus on the positive. The shop looks wonderful. The specialty Halloween cupcake flavors are ready to go."

Suz said, "I love the names. Devil's Feud. Whipped Scream Delight. Ghostess Twinkies."

Daniella grinned. "Phil the embalmer at the funeral home is incredible with stuff like that."

"With embalming?"

"Yes. But also with coming up with brilliant puns.

As for the cupcakes themselves, our test runs in the kitchen have gone smoothly for the most part."

"You know they say that in the theater it's bad luck to have a smooth dress rehearsal."

"This isn't the theater." Daniella piped frosting in a swirl design on top of a spice cupcake.

"You've had enough drama to make it theatrical."

"Not really." Daniella added little fondant fangs to her evil masterpiece.

"What do you call that harassment?"

"By Nick?"

"I thought he rescued you from those guys hassling you?"

"Right. He did. It was no big deal."

"Yeah, it was," Suz said. "A very big deal. I would be totally freaking out if I found a group of gang bangers hanging around outside my workplace."

"I refuse to let them win by scaring me. Plus I have a kick-ass security alarm system."

"And a kick-ass protector in Nick, right?"

"He's been supportive of me opening my business."

"Right. Anything else?"

"Like what?"

"Like anything seductive going on?" Suz asked.

Daniella recalled that kiss they'd shared upstairs in her apartment. Nick had initiated the first kiss, but when she'd kissed him, he'd taken off as if his feet were on fire. She hadn't seen him alone since then. Was he afraid she was going to jump him or something? He didn't seem like the kind of man who feared anything.

Besides, she'd only kissed him to prove a point. She no longer could recall exactly what that point was but she'd had a reason, a logical reason, at the time.

Something about distracting him the way he had distracted her.

Suz pounced on her silence. "Aha, so there *is* something. I knew it! Wait. Where are you going with that bowl?"

"To wash it." She nodded her head toward the three-bin stainless-steel sink.

"No way. Hand it over."

"Why?"

"There's still some frosting in there." She eagerly grabbed the bowl from Daniella. "Waste not, want not."

"This is why you could never work here. You'd eat everything."

Suz swiped the edge of the bowl with her index finger. "You said you did find two people to work with you."

Daniella nodded, relieved that she'd distracted Suz from asking her more about Nick. "Lois and Xandra."

"Which one did the awesome job on the website and social network stuff?"

"That's Xandra. She worked in cupcake shops in Vail and Lake Tahoe."

"Then what is she doing in this neighborhood? I know you grew up here, but after you've seen Vail and Lake Tahoe I can't imagine coming back to Chicago."

"Why not?" Daniella said.

"It's so flat, for one thing."

"Yeah, Xandra does say that. But she didn't come here for the scenery. She had to come back for economic reasons. She's living at home with her parents."

"Times are tough," Suz said.

"I know. And to belatedly answer your question, I

am nervous about the grand opening for that reason. But cupcakes aren't expensive and they are comfort food. In tough times, people need comfort. My brother placed a standing order for several dozen for every funeral package he has scheduled. I made sure they are for the more somber cupcakes."

"Somber cupcakes?" Suz said. "Is there such a thing?"

"I for sure don't want to send over the funfetti-decorated ones. So I'm going with the more traditional vanilla or chocolate."

"See, stuff like that would never occur to me," Suz said.

"I'm sure you wouldn't send over happy-face cupcakes to a funeral. Unless they were a special order. Some funerals are stranger than others. I'll never forget one widow requesting the song 'Up, Up and Away' by the 5th Dimension be played over and over again."

"Did they request smiley-faced cupcakes, too?"

"No."

Suz took the empty bowl to the sink and started cleaning it herself. "Speaking of cupcakes, I'm surprised you use a handheld mixer instead of one of those stand models."

"The bowls are too small in the stand models."

"These are mega-sized."

Daniella nodded. "I call them 'arms-around size' because if I make a circle with my arms and have my fingertips touch, it matches the size of the stainless mixing bowls for the batter. It's true that I'll need a new handheld mixer every couple of months, but for now it's worth it."

"These frosting bowls are a little smaller but not much."

Daniella cleaned her sticky fingers in the separate hand sink. "Tell me again that there's no reason for panic."

"There's no reason for panic," Suz obediently said before adding a hug. "Everything will be fine. You'll see."

But Daniella did panic when strange noises woke her in the middle of the night. They were coming from the street below. She got out of bed and tiptoed to the living room. Pushing aside the curtain covering the window, she snuck a peek outside. The streetlight on the corner illuminated two people throwing something at her front window.

Chapter Seven

Nick was not amused. "Egging? Come on," he said in disgust. "That's pitiful. What has the world come to that vampires are egging a cupcake shop? That kind of juvenile behavior is for wimps, not vamps."

"They were trying to get Daniella to come outside," Neville said.

"She didn't fall for that, did she?"

"No. She called the police, but egging is a minor issue on a busy Chicago police schedule."

"Was it the same group of vamps that came before?" Nick asked.

Neville shook his head. "No, this is a different bunch."

"Great. So now we've got two groups of outsiders trying to get Daniella. A trio of gangsta vamps and a pair of vampire wimps."

"I heard that Tanya wasn't real pleased with Daniella's visit to her tanning salon. Tanya thinks her human clients will get fat on the cupcakes and not want to wear swimsuits or get tanned."

"That sounds like a lame excuse to me," Nick said.

Neville shrugged. "You know Tanya. She likes being the only female business owner in Vamptown."

"She's still the only female vampire business owner in Vamptown."

"You don't think she has anything to do with these incidents, do you?"

"I'll check it out," Nick said.

He left the Vamp Cave and headed for Tanya's Tanning Salon. She was clearly pleased to see him. "Nick!" She came closer to kiss his cheeks in the European fashion, even though she'd never stepped foot on the Continent. She then planted her mouth directly on his.

She was trying to stake a claim.

Nick didn't like anything to do with stakes. It was a vamp thing.

Firmly setting her aside, he gave her a hard stare. He wasn't going to be distracted by sex. "Why the warm welcome?"

"Why not?" Her smile was sultry. "I'm always glad to see you, Nick. You know that."

"You seem unusually pleased today. Not suffering from a guilty conscience, are you?"

"I'd have to have a conscience in the first place and I don't."

Nick could tell the salon was empty at the moment. He sensed no human or vampire presence. So he was direct.

"Egging, Tanya? Really? Come on," he mocked.

"I have no idea what you're talking about."

"I'm talking about those lame minions you had egg the cupcake shop last night."

"Why would I do that?"

"Jealousy."

"Oh, please." Tanya drew herself to her full height,

which was even higher thanks to the stiletto sandals she wore. "Why would I be jealous of her?"

"Then why egg her place?"

"She doesn't belong here. You said so yourself."

"I changed my mind," Nick said.

"You mean *she* changed your mind. She may be immune to vamp mind compulsion, but are you immune to her?"

"She isn't a vampire," he said. "She can't do mind compulsion."

"Can't she? Are you sure about that?" Tanya said.

"Yes, I am sure. And I want you to promise you won't pull another stupid stunt like this."

"I swear. Cross my heart and hope to die. Oh wait. That doesn't work for us since we don't die."

"You can die. Fire. Decapitation. Ring a bell?" he said.

"Are you threatening me?"

"I'm just reminding you of the facts. Daniella is no threat to you. But you causing an incident that required the police to be called in and that heightened the attention of the other vamp communities creates a threat for all of us."

"Why is she so special?"

"She's not."

"Come on," Tanya said. "She's the only human I know who is immune to mind compulsion."

"You never said how you knew she's immune?"

"I tried it on her myself when I told her that her cupcakes were poison," Tanya readily admitted. "You saw her response."

"She is protective about her cupcakes," he said.

"Just be sure you keep your hands off her cupcakes."

Nick just stared at Tanya. It was enough to make

her take several steps back. "You've been warned."
He left without saying another word.

There was no place like home. Especially when home
was a funeral home.

Daniella gently rearranged the fresh floral arrangement on the marble table in the front foyer of
the Evergreen Funeral Home. Along with the comfort of cupcakes, her mom had also been proud of
the lovely flower arrangements that the neighborhood florist Saul Alexander did for them. But her
mom had always stopped to do a tweak or two each
time she passed the vase on this table. So Daniella
did the same, as a sort of nod to her mom.

Two smaller tables stood on either side of the front
entrance with a Boston fern on each of them. The
lower part of the walls was finished in a dark wood
while above was soothing neutral wallpaper in a
muted leaf design. Daniella had helped her father
pick it out a few years ago. Otherwise, not a lot had
changed.

The funeral director's office was straight ahead,
and that's where she found her brother Gordon. He
looked a lot like their dad. The two men shared the
same lanky build as well as similar blue eyes and
dark brown hair.

Gordon looked up from the laptop computer on
the desk. "Hey, sis, I hear you had an egg incident
last night."

"Hey, yourself." She sat in one of the brown leather
wing chairs facing her brother. Sitting there reminded her of the many times when, as a little girl,
she'd brought a specially decorated cupcake to her
dad. He'd always ignored the lopsided frosting and
the overabundance of sprinkles and would praise

her for creating such a beautiful masterpiece. "Dad seems to be having a great time on the cruise judging by his emails."

"He'll be back soon. Do you know who egged your place?"

"The last time I remember getting egged was when Rodney Livermore did it to the funeral home's front windows back when we were in high school. Hey, you don't think it was Rodney again, do you?" she said, sort of kidding and sort of not.

"No. He moved to Sacramento and opened a Subway franchise there."

"What about your gambling friends? Is this something they would do?" she asked,

Gordon shook his head. "They're more into using baseball bats to break legs and kneecaps. Not that they'd do that to me," he hurriedly added.

His words concerned her. "Are you in debt again?"

"No." His voice turned totally defensive as it always did when this subject came up.

"Are you going to any Gamblers Anonymous meetings?"

"I don't have a problem," Gordon said. "Besides, I'm not the one who got egged. You were. Or your shop's windows were."

"I spent two hours this morning cleaning the slime from the glass. It wasn't time I could spare."

Her brother was not empathetic about her plight. "No one has time to spare these days. I've got two viewings scheduled for tonight so I really can't chat."

"Have you been talking to Nick St. George about me?" she asked.

Gordon frowned at her abrupt change of subject. "No."

"Then why did he ask me if I had ESP?"

"How should I know?" her brother said. "I'm not the one with ESP. Go read his mind." He shooed her out of the office and closed the door on her.

Yes, there was no place like home. But she had a new home now and she had to get back to preparing for one of the biggest days of her life—her grand opening.

An hour later, Daniella was in heaven. Cupcake baking heaven. True, she was covered in flour and powdered sugar, but that didn't matter. She had the place to herself. The only sound was her mixer and Muse singing "Supermassive Black Hole." Perhaps not the first song that might come to mind for a woman who wore pearls and twinsets, but this was her inner diva side.

She danced her way from the oven back to the stainless-steel worktable with a cupcake tin filled with freshly baked cupcakes. She'd been experimenting with new autumn flavors this afternoon, like pumpkin cinnamon and apple cider spice.

The music moved on to the next song on the playlist she'd selected for today. They were all songs guaranteed to keep you awake and dancing. "Letters from the Sky" by Civil Twilight certainly qualified. She stood back to eye the spice-cake-based apple cider cupcake she was working on. It needed something more . . . a touch of lemon juice in the frosting maybe? She added some.

Daniella loved playing with recipes and combining different ingredients, flavors, and texture. One of her recent faves was a Baileys Irish Cream cupcake with espresso buttercream frosting dunked in chocolate sprinkles and topped with a chocolate-covered espresso bean candy.

But her favorite part was decorating the cupcakes. She frosted a batch of Halloween cupcakes to the sound of Róisín Murphy's "Ramalama." She used cookie cutters on the fondant she'd made to create various designs. A leaf could be turned into an evil eye when turned sideways.

The hairs suddenly rose on the back of her neck and she pivoted to find Nick standing there. It was as if he'd materialized out of nowhere. She put her hand on her pounding heart, thereby placing a powdered sugar-laden handprint on her black I LOVE NY T-shirt. Her apron didn't cover that part of her anatomy, falling just below that point. "You scared me!"

He seemed consumed with staring at that fresh handprint on her chest.

"How did you get in?" she demanded.

"Through the back door."

"It was locked. And the security system was set." When he kept his gaze focused on her breasts, she added, "Hey! Eyes up here." She used two fingers to point to his dark gray eyes and then back to her own.

"I apologize," he said but she wasn't sure he really meant it.

"What are you doing here?"

"I came to talk to you about what happened last night," he said.

"The egging? Do you know who did it?"

"I have my suspicions."

She reached for a pad of paper. "I want names."

"I can't give them to you," he said.

"Why not?" She angrily clicked the ballpoint pen in her hand. "Because you side with them against me?"

"Because I don't have any proof," he said. "But I did issue them a warning."

"Big deal," she scoffed.

"It was a big deal. I don't issue many warnings."

"Tell me the name of the person you suspect and I'll issue my own warning," she said.

"That's not necessary. I took care of it."

She hated to admit it, but part of her was relieved. She really didn't need more things to add to her to-do list before the opening. But another part wanted to make sure that he knew she was perfectly capable of sticking up for herself. Especially where her cupcakes were concerned. "You don't think I can issue warnings, too?"

"I think you look adorable covered in flour and sugar."

She rolled her eyes. "Adorable?"

"Sexy?"

She laughed. "Okay, now that's just a lie."

"It is not."

"Come on. There is no way I look sexy in these clothes. I'm not wearing any makeup. My hair is scraped back in a ponytail to get it out of the way."

"You don't need makeup. You look good enough to eat."

She laughed again, despite the fact that he was actually eyeing her with an expression of hunger. "You'd have to be starving."

"Maybe I am."

"Then have a cupcake."

He turned his head just as she held an apple spice one to his mouth. She ended up smearing the frosting on the corner of his mouth and his cheek. "Ooops." She automatically wiped her finger across his lips. "Sorry about that."

She might as well just have placed her hand in the oven. Her skin was hot. His was hotter. She wouldn't have been surprised to see sparks flying between them, so powerful was the attraction. You'd think that would make her move away, but instead she stood there transfixed.

She lifted her gaze to his eyes and tried to decipher the look she saw there. Hunger and heat. Power and passion. Sex and secrets.

She belatedly snatched her hand away.

"What was that about?" She didn't realize she'd said the words aloud until he answered them.

"You know the answer to that," he said.

"I do?"

He nodded and returned her hand to his lips. "You feel it, too."

"I do?" Right, that sounded brilliant. But her brain wasn't functioning normally at the moment; really, it was miraculous that she was able to form full words at all and not just moan with sensual yearning.

"You know you do." His voice was roughly husky as his tongue skimmed against her skin.

"But I don't want to."

"Are you sure about that?" he said.

Daniella shook her head. She wasn't sure about anything aside from the powerful rush of need pulling her under. His smoky gray eyes reflected a similar need. Her lips parted as she tried to draw in enough breath to calm the hormones raging within her. His gaze instantly shifted to her mouth. A second later his mouth covered hers in a kiss that was all-consuming.

If their first kiss was exploratory, this one was raw and no-holds-barred. His tongue tangled with hers. She responded with a wild abandon she'd never experienced before. The oral skirmish was sexy and liberating.

The taste of spices blended with the taste of Nick. There were no words to describe the combination. Sweet and salty. Dangerous and addictive.

She couldn't stop with just one kiss. She needed more. So did he.

Nick lifted her to the only clear space on the edge of the table. She hooked her legs around his thighs. The music played on with the primal beat of Muse's "Undisclosed Desires." The lyrics from the song were a description of his embrace.

Undoing the ties on her apron, he slid his hands beneath her T-shirt to fondle her breast. The brush of his thumb against her satin-covered nipple was enough to make her melt like butter. Yet she could feel every pulse in her body beating in a primitive rhythm that dated back to the beginning of time.

She was so hot for him in that moment that she was actually burning up. Burning . . . no, wait. That was the smell of her latest batch of cupcakes turning into cinders.

His spell on her was broken as she rushed to the stove to save her baked goods.

Grabbing a pot holder, she wailed, "Look what you made me do!"

"I'm looking." But he wasn't staring at the cupcakes. His eyes were glued on her derriere. She turned to look over her shoulder. Sure enough, she now had flour on the backside of her jeans.

She smacked the cupcake tin on a cooling rack and turned to confront him. "What was that about?" She was asking herself the same question she'd asked earlier.

This time his answer was much more blunt. "Sex. It was about sex."

"I do not have sex while I'm baking cupcakes," she informed him. "It would be sacrilegious or something."

"It was definitely something." His voice went all hungry husky.

"If you think you can control me with sex, you are sadly mistaken."

"Some things are very hard to control."

She couldn't help herself. Her eyes slid down to the zipper of his black jeans. The blatant bulge there attested to his arousal.

"Do you like what you see?" he murmured.

The confidence in his voice made her want to smack him while simultaneously making her want to kiss that slight grin off his lips. Talk about a conflict.

Which was weird because normally Daniella wasn't about conflict. She was all about comfort.

Yes, she could be tough. But not where sex and men were concerned. In those areas, she tended to be more cream puff than hot peppers.

Wait, maybe cream puff was the wrong analogy. That made her sound totally wimpy. Maybe she was more chocolate chip cookie than hot peppers.

"Hello?" Nick waved his hand in front of her face.

"Sorry. I was just thinking about cream puffs and hot peppers."

"How did we go from talking about sex to talking about food?" he demanded.

"Both are meant to satisfy a physical hunger," she said.

She took a few steps away from him before she was tempted to do something foolish, like kiss him again. He had kissed her in her apartment and then walked out only to mysteriously appear in her work area while she was baking and kiss her again.

Yes, sex was definitely in the mix here. But so was stupidity on her part. What was she thinking? That he was an awesome kisser?

Okay, while that was true, she couldn't ignore the fact that he'd been ignoring her for several days. Not that she craved his attention or his kisses or his body or anything.

Right. Who was she kidding? She craved all that from him and more.

"I don't have time for this," she told him and reminded herself. "Not when my grand opening is only three days away."

"I just want you to be vigilant."

"For what? You coming to kiss me?"

"I didn't come to kiss you," he said. "I came to tell you that I had the egging incident under control."

She eyed him suspiciously.

"Why the look?" he demanded.

"I can't help thinking that there is a possibility that you are behind these incidents that keep happening. First those guys in the alley and then the egging last night."

"Stupid pranks are not in my DNA."

"What about making out with me to distract me? Is that in your DNA?" she demanded. "You say you're happy about me opening my shop here, but is that the truth? Or is this all some devious way of intimidating me?"

"If I wanted to intimidate you, you'd know it." His voice was harsh.

She wanted to believe him. She really did. Well, she actually *did* believe that he could be a powerful intimidator. What she *wanted* to believe was that he supported her move into the business community. She also wanted to believe that when he kissed her, he did so because he wanted to without having any ulterior motives.

She closed her eyes for a moment, trying to get her thoughts together. When she opened them, Nick was gone.

Chapter Eight

"I called this meeting of the Vamptown business community for several reasons," Nick said as he addressed the group gathered in the Vamp Cave's conference room.

"I still want to know why you changed your mind about the wisdom of having a human open a cupcake business here," Tanya said. "Her grand opening is only two days away. The *Chicago Trib* ran a feature about her shop today, and you know what that means. A crowd of humans flooding into our neighborhood. It's only a matter of time before some vamp looks at one of them and thinks, *Lunch*."

"You all have human clients who come into your businesses, and you don't feel the need to feed on them," Nick said.

"Who says we don't feel the need?" Tanya said. "We just don't act on it."

"Need I remind you all that we have a great thing going here with our arrangement with the funeral home? A lot of vamps aren't as lucky," Nick reminded them.

"You're into her. That's why you abruptly changed your mind about her shop," Tanya said.

"We already had this discussion," Nick said. "Daniella is the daughter of the funeral home owner, so we owe her some level of appreciation."

"She was the funeral home owner's daughter two weeks ago when you were throwing a hissy fit about her opening her business," Tanya pointed out. "And it's not as if the funeral home owner or his son has any idea that the drained blood of their deceased is being recycled and rejuvenated to feed vampires. We've used mind compulsion on them without any problems. Yet it doesn't work on her. Something is very wrong with that."

"We're looking into it. In the meantime, I don't want to see any repeats of that juvenile egging incident. We're not in high school anymore."

"You never went to high school," Tanya retorted. "I'm no history buff seeing as how I was turned in 1954, but I don't believe they had high schools in England in 1812. So you have no idea what American high school is really like."

"But I do," Neville inserted. "You've been a vamp decades longer than I have, Tanya. As a member of the graduating class of 1972, I confirm Nick's observation."

"You're just a geek," Tanya retorted. "What do you know?"

"A lot, actually," Neville said. "Mega gigabytes more than you do."

"We all need to get along in times like these," Bruce, ever the pacifist, said.

"If we could get back to the reason I called this meeting," Nick said. "As you know, we've had several incidents involving outside vamps. I want you all to be on heightened alert for a possible repeat. Just because things have been quiet for the past thirty-six hours doesn't mean we're safe. This could just be the calm before the storm."

"And I want to remind you all that revealing our agreement with the funeral home to any vamp outside our clan is cause for permanent banishment," Pat said. "Ditto for sharing any information about our tats."

"We don't have much information about our tats or how they work," Tanya pointed out.

"And I plan on keeping it that way," Pat said.

"I'm not going to betray any of you," Tanya said. "You're family but not in a yucky way. In a loyalty kind of way. I mean, it's not like I think of Nick as a brother or relative or anything. And he certainly doesn't think of me like a sister, right?"

"I don't think of you as a sister," Neville piped up to say.

"If you're such a genius, why haven't you figured out what Daniella's secret is?" Tanya's narrow-eyed look was meant to squash him, but Neville was tougher than that.

"Don't mock me. I know how to hack into your Facebook page, and you have no idea the havoc I could create there," Neville warned.

"Enough!" Pat shouted. "You're acting like a bunch of brainless zombies."

"He is." Tanya pointed to Neville. "I'm not." She fluffed her hair. "Vampires rule. Zombies and humans drool."

"You're not in high school anymore." Nick's voice was taut with pent-up anger and aggravation. "This behavior stops now."

Tanya's eyes widened as she realized he meant business. "Okay, okay."

"Just so we all understand. Vamptown is on Code Orange alert from now until the cupcake shop's grand opening," Nick said.

"I do love that little angel on the Heavenly Cupcake sign," Bruce said. "It's so adorable. Reminds me of Raphael's work."

"Was he someone you knew in the circus?" Tanya asked.

Bruce had been a clown in his other life. His pre-dead life.

"I was referring to the Italian Renaissance painter Raphael," Bruce said. "He was known for his paintings of angels."

"Was he a vampire?" Tanya asked.

Bruce frowned. "I don't believe so."

"I'm sure he's not as good a painter as Pat." Tanya sent Pat a brilliant smile.

Lois, who'd been silent all this time, raised her hand. "Now that we have that out of the way, I just wanted to say that Doc Boomer is sorry he couldn't attend today's meeting but he had an emergency vamp dental procedure he had to perform. I said I'd give him the highlights. And lowlights. Anyway, a reminder that I'm actually going to be working at Heavenly Cupcake's grand opening this Saturday. I'll keep you posted regarding any unusual activities."

"I don't know how you can stand working there," Tanya said.

"Believe me, after hearing the constant sound of a dental drill, this is a piece of cake. Or a piece of cupcake," Lois said.

"How do you deal with all those smells? Those baking smells?" Tanya shuddered.

"It is pretty intense from a vamp's point of view," Lois admitted. "Or maybe I should say point of scent.

But you get used to it. Nick has adapted and so have I. Not that I've started working there yet, but I've stopped by the shop a few times since I was hired. Thanks again for creating a résumé for me," Lois told Neville.

"No problem," he said.

"Great. We're done here then," Nick said impatiently. "Meeting adjourned."

Nick was fed up with all this talking. He was not a chatty kind of guy under the best of circumstances. It didn't matter whether they were vamps or humans.

He was more into action than Italian Renaissance angel painters or American high school antics. As for baking smells . . . when he was around Daniella, he was consumed by her unique scent.

He felt a connection with her that went beyond the physical and that made him uneasy. The physical chemistry was powerful enough. He didn't need to admire her toughness or the way nothing got her down. Or the way she laughed at him. No one did that. Ever. But she did. And the crazy thing was that he kind of liked it.

Shit. That couldn't be a good sign. Instead of admiring her toughness, he needed to focus on his own.

"Let the countdown begin," Suz said. "Less than twenty-four hours to go until your grand opening."

Daniella nervously nibbled on her bottom lip before nibbling on a chocolate cupcake. She and Suz were perched on stools around the worktable in the back work area of Heavenly Cupcakes. "Maybe I should have gone with a soft opening instead of making a big deal out of things."

"This is a big deal. Your to-die-for cupcakes are a

big deal." Suz waved a delightfully decorated spice cupcake in the air. "I'm sure the food blogger coming to the opening will think so, too."

"What food blogger?"

"The Cupcake Q-tea. I contacted her,"

"Oh, no." Daniella felt the blood drain from her face.

"Why oh, no?"

"Because she's mean."

"How mean?"

"*Very* mean. She described one cupcake as 'a gross mushy mess.' Another one was listed as being 'a greasy and tasteless waste of time with a bitter aftertaste.' "

"Uh, I guess I should have checked with you first, huh?"

"Yes."

"Sorry about that," Suz said.

"What if she writes a terrible review? What if I have a grand opening and no one comes? What if the egg throwers come back and ruin the opening?"

Suz addressed her hysterical laments one at a time. "If she writes a terrible review she would be lying. And if she lies about your cupcakes, she probably lies about her taxes so I'll anonymously report her to the IRS. A number of my clients promised they'd be coming to your opening, so you will have customers. As for the egg throwers . . . you told me Nick had set up a neighborhood watch at night."

"Right. That doesn't help me if no one shows up," Daniella said. "Your clients may just have been polite in telling you they'd show up."

"You're offering BOGO."

"Buy one get one half off for the first twenty-five customers. Yes, that might help."

"What happened to thinking positively?" Suz asked.

"Panic got the best of me."

"Never." Suz squeezed Daniella's shoulders. "I refuse to let that happen. Remember, you won't be alone. Xandra is coming to help bake the cupcakes at five tomorrow morning. And I'll be here, too. At six or so. You open at eight."

Daniella resumed her nervous lip nibbling. "Maybe I should have opened on a Monday instead of a Saturday. At least then we'd have the commuter foot traffic heading for the CTA bus stop on the corner. I don't know if you've noticed, but there isn't a lot of foot traffic otherwise, and the parking around here isn't great."

"We discussed both of those issues when you first came up with the idea of opening your shop," Suz said. "Besides, Monday is the one day you are closed. And the location is what it is."

"It's not like I had a lot of choice. I couldn't afford the rent anywhere else. Not and get the equipment I needed."

"Bake it and they will come," Suz said.

"The floor is uneven."

"You told me that was charming."

"I lied," Daniella said.

"Well, the place was built almost a hundred years ago. What do you expect?"

Daniella took a deep breath. "I expect a great grand opening. I have to believe that. I have to visualize that." Instead she visualized Nick lifting her onto the stainless-steel worktable and sliding his hands under her T-shirt.

She hadn't seen much of him since that eventful night. She wondered if he was avoiding her. The possibility stung. Which was ridiculous. She had enough to worry about as it was. She certainly didn't need to add a brooding sexy man to the mix.

"Why do I not believe you're thinking about cupcakes?" Suz said.

"I was wondering why I couldn't get the dark chocolate and orange frosting combo to work out right," Daniella lied.

"I'm sure you'll figure it out eventually. You have enough varieties as it is. Three standards."

Daniella nodded. "Vanilla cupcakes, chocolate cupcakes, and red velvet. Of course for this week I'm calling them Blood Red Velvet."

"And then you've got the specials that change each day. Like the spice cupcake with the cinnamon frosting and the little fondant leaves."

"I wasn't sure about the leaves at first, but I think they add a nice touch."

"You already know I love the s'mores cupcakes. That combo of a chocolate cupcake, chocolate frosting, marshmallow cream piped in the center, and then crumbled graham crackers on top." Suz made a smacking noise with her lips. "Yumm."

"We can even torch the marshmallow if the customer wants."

"As long as you don't torch the shop. I'm kidding," Suz quickly added.

"The fire department already checked us out." Daniella pointed to the fire extinguisher on the wall near the oven. "We passed their inspection and the health department's."

"So there's nothing to worry about. You're going to do great."

Daniella kept telling herself that even as she kept doing stuff in the kitchen. She couldn't seem to stop herself. Baking was therapeutic for her. But she knew she was risking burning out if she didn't get some sleep. She'd considered sleeping on a fold-up cot down here but decided that would be silly since her bed upstairs was so nearby.

She was bone-weary by the time she slid between her sheets. She wore her cupcake cotton pajamas for good luck. Suz had given them to her last Christmas.

The next five hours involved lots of tossing and turning but little sleep. Daniella was simply too excited. She leapt out of bed before the alarm went off.

A quick shower was followed by multiple gulps of coffee. She got dressed in her jeans and Heavenly Cupcakes T-shirt in record time. Ditto for brushing her hair into a ponytail and firmly clipping it in place.

She was downstairs unlocking the door to her shop at four fifty AM. A hand on her arm made her shriek like a girl before turning à la tough chic Nikita with pepper spray in hand. No one was messing with *her* grand opening.

"Whoa, it's me," Nick said.

"Way to scare a person," she said. "What are you doing out here?"

"I told you we planned a neighborhood watch."

"You were out here all night?"

"Part of it," he said.

She didn't know what to say to that. "Uh, thanks."

"You're welcome." He reached out to gently smooth a loose strand of her hair behind her ear.

She reached up to secure her wayward hair. Some rebellious strands were too short to stay in her ponytail. Her fingers awkwardly bumped into his. "This can't continue," she whispered.

"Why not?"

"Because you can't have people standing guard

all night to protect my business. This is just for the grand opening, right?"

He shrugged.

It was still dark outside and the corner streetlight highlighted his chiseled cheekbones, casting his face in sharp angles and shadows.

As soon as she unlocked the shop door, Nick reached around her to hold it open for her. This wasn't the first time he'd done something . . . well, almost chivalrous. Not that she wanted to fall into a simpering-miss mode where she needed someone to protect her. She didn't. She'd been looking after herself just fine, thank you very much.

Okay, it was true that her dad had helped her out big-time by letting her use this building rent-free. But she planned on paying him back when her business took off. Not if her business took off, but *when*. Of course, that could take a while . . .

She raced to the back to disarm the security system before its alarm went off, then raced back to the front to relock the front door. "I guess I should use the back door," she said.

"This way is safer," he said.

"Well, um, I've got to get started. Oh, here's Xandra. She's one of my employees." Daniella let her in.

Nick abruptly got all dark and broody. "Later, ladies," he said curtly before leaving.

"Who's he?" Xandra asked as she trailed Daniella into the back work area.

"His name is Nick St. George. He's in charge of the local business association."

"St. George. He's the one who killed a dragon to rescue a beautiful lady."

"I don't think Nick has killed any dragons lately,"

Daniella said as she reached for one of the oversized stainless bowls she used to mix the cupcake batter.

"I didn't mean him personally, although he does look a little . . ."

"Like a hero from a Brontë novel?" Daniella inserted. "Or maybe Austen?"

"More a combo of Brontë and edgy rock and roll."

"Hmm, an interesting observation. You know, when I first met him, I thought he had a bit of a Mick Jagger thing going on. I mean, with the fierce lips and those cheekbones."

"Are you a Stones fan?"

"Not at all," Daniella said.

"Yet you like Nick," Xandra said.

"I didn't say that."

"You didn't have to."

"Let's focus on getting this batter done. Then you can use the ice cream scoop to fill the cupcake liners," Daniella said.

"Okay."

She and Xandra worked well together. The baking tins held twenty-four cupcakes and the oven held four tins at a time. Twenty minutes later, she switched out the vanilla cupcakes for red velvet ones.

Daniella was a bundle of nerves until the room filled with the aroma she loved so much. The warm and sweet scents of freshly baked goodies never failed to take her back to her childhood days, when her mom would open the oven door and retrieve the cupcakes. "Don't they smell just heavenly?" her mom would say. "Like a vanilla cloud of happiness or a joyful breath of divine chocolate."

Those memories made Daniella feel all warm and safe inside, as if her mother were looking down on her now with approval. Her mom's frequent use of the word *heavenly* resulted in the name Daniella had chosen for her cupcake shop.

Xandra interrupted Daniella's sentimental flash-back to ask, "Do you mind if we play some music? Would Coldplay be okay?"

"Sure."

Seconds later, the sound of the unique piano opening of "Clocks" boomed out of the iPod dock-ing station. "Too loud?" Xandra asked.

"No." Daniella tilted her head to the beat of the music while using the hand mixer on the bowl of pow-dered sugar, melted butter, and warmed milk. Seeing Xandra's quizzical look, Daniella said, "Warming the butter and milk prevents lumps in the buttercream frosting. That's why I use the microwave to do that."

Xandra appeared to be impressed. "You've got such a great bag of tricks. Neither one of the other shops I worked in did that. They used lard for the frosting."

"Everybody has their own thing," Daniella said.

Time flew by after that as they both focused on getting the cupcakes baked, cooled, frosted, and decorated.

The night before Daniella had used special neon-colored chalk to write the cupcake descriptions on the front of the glass case. An hour before opening time, she took the first tray of completed Blood Red Velvet cupcakes out. The sun was just coming up. And a line was just beginning outside her door.

She blinked. A line? Really? She had a line? For her cupcakes? That BOGO special offer must be working.

The first woman in line actually had a stool she was sitting on. She looked up from the *People* magazine she was reading and waved at Daniella, who waved back.

A second later Suz appeared at the door. Daniella quickly let her in.

"It's wild out there," Suz said. Despite the early hour, she was looking fashionista-fabulous in a leopard-print fuzzy vest, black sweater, and pants. Even her glasses sported an animal print. "The people in line are saying that Xandra is tweeting updates from the kitchen. Look." Suz showed her the screen of her smartphone. " 'Just frosted the cookies 'n' cream.' She even includes a link to a photo she calls a cupcake cam close-up."

"Good job, Xandra," Daniella said as she returned to the back to frost and decorate more cupcakes. It was bedlam after that with Suz carrying completed trays out to the display case as fast as Daniella and Xandra finished them.

The three of them took a brief moment to share a three-way high five before Daniella opened the door. "Welcome to Heavenly Cupcakes!"

"I've got good news," Neville told Nick the moment he entered the Vamp Cave that morning. "I finally got that vampire facial recognition software to work. It's running right now. Ah." Neville pointed to one of the large flat screens. "Bingo. Those three outsider vamps have worked for the Gold Coast clan before." He hit several keys and more info popped up. "You're right. They were recent recruits."

"And the ones who egged Daniella's shop?"

"I don't know yet. But I did discover something interesting about Daniella a few minutes ago."

"What?"

"She's adopted."

Chapter Nine

"Adopted?" Nick repeated. "Why didn't her brother tell me that?"

"Maybe he doesn't know."

"Does *she* know?"

"You'd have to ask her that question," Neville said.

"Right. Like that would be a wise move."

"Like what would be a wise move?" Pat asked as he and his partner Bruce entered the Vamp Cave. He glanced at the surveillance screens before adding, "All quiet on the cupcake front this morning?"

"What a colorful crowd," Bruce noted. "Look how politely they've all lined up." He moved closer. "Oh, I want that person's scarf!"

"Daniella is adopted," Nick said.

Bruce turned to face him. "So? I'm adopted. Do you have something against adopted people?"

"No, of course not. It just means that we now have a new line of investigation to follow in the attempt to find out why she's resistant to mind compulsion."

"She's not just resistant, she's completely immune," Pat said.

"I suggested Nick ask her about being adopted," Neville said.

"Ah." Pat nodded. "I see where *not the wise move* comment comes from."

"Her brother never said anything about her being adopted," Nick pointed out. "There is a good chance she doesn't know."

"What do you know about her birth mother?" Pat asked.

Neville answered, "Nothing yet."

"Keep digging," Nick said.

"Okay. I will say this much. The fact that Daniella was adopted was buried very, *very* deep. Someone clearly didn't want that information easily accessible— and believe me, it wasn't. It was barely accessible at all. It's one of the strangest things I've run into on the Internet, and there's plenty of weird stuff out there," Neville said.

"Strange in what way?" Nick demanded.

"I'm not sure. I haven't figured it out yet but I will." Neville pointed to the surveillance camera display. "I thought maybe Tanya would try to use mind compulsion on some of them to get them to leave."

"She knows better than that," Nick said.

"Does she?"

Neville pointed to the screen and turned up the volume. Nick watched and listened as Tanya handed out coupons for her business to those standing in line for Heavenly Cupcakes and told them, "You don't want a cupcake. You want a tan."

Pat put a hand on Nick's arm to prevent him from going outside and doing Tanya bodily harm. "She's not using compulsion on the humans," Pat pointed out. "She's using marketing skills but no vamp powers."

"Let me handle this," Bruce said. "It could be the perfect opportunity for me to use my clown skills."

Pat rolled his eyes but stopped the instant his partner looked to him for support. "What did you have in mind?" Pat asked cautiously.

"Everyone loves a clown," Bruce said.

"Actually some people are afraid of them," Neville said, ending in a gasp as Pat elbowed him behind Bruce's back.

"I thought I'd get in costume and makeup and work the crowd on Daniella's behalf." Bruce's face lit up.

"I'm not sure that's a good idea," Nick said.

Bruce's face fell. "Why not?"

"We don't want this turning into a circus," Nick said.

Pat glared at him.

Nick frowned and gave him a *what now?* look. "Not that a circus is a bad thing," he grudgingly added.

"Of course it isn't." Pat put his arm around his partner's broad shoulders and hugged him. "Circuses are good things."

"Providing they don't abuse their animals," Neville said. His comment resulted in him getting another subtle elbow from Pat.

"I totally agree," Bruce said. "No animals would be harmed in the idea I'm proposing today. No humans or vampires would be injured, either. I'd better go get ready. My public awaits."

He was gone an instant later. Nick wondered if Bruce could apply makeup with vamp super speed. "I don't believe this," he muttered. "We have a quiet existence in Vamptown for years and now we've got a PR-crazed vamp pushing tans and a clown handing out balloons."

Since Bruce was already out on the sidewalk, Nick got his answer. Apparently vamp super speed *did* work on clown makeup and costumes.

"I want a balloon in the shape of a cupcake," one kid told Bruce.

Nick stood there watching, as Bruce patiently said, "How about a cat or a dog instead?"

"No! I want a balloon cupcake!"

Nick winced. "Turn down the volume," he ordered Neville. Super hearing was another vamp ability, and this kid's voice had a sharpness to it that was worse than fingernails on a blackboard.

"Hey, this is my turf," Tanya said. "Who invited you?"

"Who invited you?" Bruce countered.

Tanya made a grand gesture to those in line. "The people did."

"They invited me, too." Bruce turned to the crowd. "This is America, so let's have a vote. How many of you want a tan?" A few hands were raised. "How many of you want a clown?" A few hands went up.

"How many of you want a mini cupcake?" Daniella demanded from behind them. The crowd cheered their approval.

"It's me, Bruce," he told her. "I was just trying to help."

"If you want to help, hand these out," Daniella gave him the tray of samples before fixing Tanya with a glare. "What are you doing here?"

Nick was outside in a millisecond. "Tanya, we need to have a talk."

"This is a public sidewalk. I have as much right to stand here as she does." Tanya pointed to Daniella.

"I don't have time for this," Daniella growled. To the crowd, she added, "Thanks for your patience, folks. The line will be moving faster now because we've added another cashier."

Nick clamped his hand around Tanya's arm and dragged her back to the Vamp Cave. "Watch her," he told Pat.

"I'm going to file an official complaint about your behavior," Tanya said. "The council will not be pleased."

"No, they won't," Nick agreed. "Because once again you were making trouble and drawing attention to yourself."

"I didn't use mind compulsion on anyone," Tanya protested. "I was merely doing what any good businesswoman would do, vamp or human."

"The line is really moving now," Neville said. "I think we're over the worst."

Nick sure hoped so. He watched Bruce wave goodbye and hand out his last balloon. Humans were more trouble than they were worth. One female human in particular was making him gnash his teeth, which for a vampire was not a good thing.

"Let's talk, Gordon," Nick told Daniella's brother a few moments later. "In your office."

Gordon's eyes got that slightly glazed look that indicated the mind compulsion was working. He obediently went and sat behind his desk while Nick closed the door. "Did you know Daniella was adopted?"

"Yes."

"Do you know anything about her birth mother?"

"No."

Nick swore under his breath. He'd been hoping

that Gordon would know something, but it was obvious he didn't. "When does your father return?"

"Halloween morning."

Nick would have to wait until then to question Jay Delaney.

"Why do you keep asking about my sister?" Gordon's question startled Nick.

"I haven't asked you anything about your sister," he told him. "You won't remember this conversation at all."

"My dad always treated her like she was special," Gordon rambled on. "I think he likes her better than me."

"Did your dad ever tell you why he thinks Daniella is special?" Nick leaned forward, hopeful that perhaps he'd finally gotten a clue.

"She has ESP."

"Yes, so you said."

"But she won't help me with the cards."

"What about your dad?"

"He doesn't play cards," Gordon said.

Nick found himself grinding his teeth again. "Why does he think Daniella is special?"

"How should I know?" Gordon sounded as irritated as Nick felt.

"Did he ever tell you she was special?"

"All the time."

Nick leaned forward again. "What else did he say about her?"

"That she's his little princess."

"Don't a lot of fathers tell their daughters that?"

"I guess. He always gives her compliments but always acts like I'm going to screw up."

"Yet he selected you to run the business."

"Only because she didn't want to do it. She wanted to open her own business instead."

"Are you unhappy that she's opening a business?"

"Not really," Gordon said. "It keeps her out of my hair."

"Don't you like your sister?"

"Of course I like her," he said indignantly. "She's my sister."

Nick sensed something odd about Gordon, but he couldn't put his finger on exactly what. Had another vamp come to compel Gordon? Was that why he brought up the fact that Nick was asking about Daniella? That had never happened before. He tried to read the other man's mind.

Two viewings this afternoon. Should I bet on the Bears winning tomorrow's home game? I want a deep-dish pizza. I need to get laid. No one wants to hook up for party sex with a funeral director. Did I pay my Visa bill? Maybe I should download some porn. Or play online poker with a naked porn star. Scratch two urges at once. Did the flowers arrive yet for the Grabowski viewing?

Gordon's thoughts were in such a jumble that Nick couldn't make out any consistent train of thought—aside from sex and gambling. The experience was more like mental buckshot. Mind reading had never been Nick's forte.

He'd check with Neville about any surveillance footage that might indicate another vamp had visited Gordon. But Nick didn't sense or smell any recent vamp trespassers.

This was all making him realize how precarious their situation was. They'd spent a great deal of time and money to get things going here in Vamptown.

Now more than ever they needed to secure their investments.

Somehow Daniella was the key. Identifying her birth mother would bring them much closer to finding an answer to this puzzle. Or so he hoped.

"We did it!" Daniella high-fived Suz, Xandra, and Lois.

"And you did it without getting into a fight with Tanya," Lois said. "Well done!"

"I didn't have time to stay out there and yell at her," Daniella said.

"I volunteered to do it for you," Lois said.

"You have such a kind face, I can't imagine you yelling at anyone," Xandra said.

"I believe in standing up for what's right," Lois said. "Sometimes it gets me into trouble." A strange look crossed her face before her customary smile chased it away. "But not today."

"Because I needed you more working the counter and acting as cashier rather than going out to confront Tanya. Your being here got the line moving much faster, so thank you for coming in early when I called you."

"No problem," Lois said.

"I just want to thank you all for making today's grand opening such a huge success," Daniella said. "I couldn't have done it without you."

"Knowing you, you probably could have," Suz said with a grin. "But it would have been a lot harder."

"And special thanks to Xandra for all her online marketing and tweets," Daniella added. "And for constantly reminding people that we close when we run out of cupcakes. You even created a sign for the window that is great."

"Reminding customers about the possibility of running out of cupcakes adds a sense of urgency," Xandra said.

"Speaking of urgency, I think it's time we all call it a day. I'll see most of you tomorrow." She paused to give each a hug. "Lois, are you okay? You feel chilled." Daniella rubbed the older woman's arms a little.

"Poor circulation," Lois said, stepping away.

Suz stayed with Daniella while she secured the shop, set the alarm, and locked the doors. "Thanks again for everything. Are you sure you don't want to come up?"

Suz shook her head. "I've got a date tonight."

Upstairs in her apartment, Daniella kicked off her shoes and wiggled her toes. She'd learned early in her days working in the culinary arts that comfortable shoes were a must so she invested in the same shoes that nurses wore. Being on her feet for twelve hours or more a day was something she and the medical profession shared.

Checking her watch, Daniella realized that she had to hurry or she'd miss her Skype setup with Cookie in New York City. A few minutes later her mentor's face filled Daniella's laptop screen. From her corkscrew silver gray hair to her slightly crooked nose, everything about Cookie screamed *Individual*.

"Judging by the exhausted smile on your face, I'm guessing that your grand opening went well," Cookie said.

"Yes, it did."

"It was a busy day here at my store, too, but then weekends are always high-volume."

"Thanks for telling me to bake more for the event," Daniella said. "We ran out a few minutes before closing time."

"It's a tough balance. You don't want to run out so early that you aggravate customers."

"We sold out of absolutely everything. The Blood Red Velvets were a particular fave. Some customers sat at the tables we have so I got a chance to watch their faces as they bit into my cupcakes."

"That's a great feeling, isn't it?"

Daniella nodded. "There was this little girl who put her entire fist in the frosting, grabbed a handful and shoved it straight into her mouth."

"As you know, that's my favorite part of what we do. Watching people enjoy what I create. I'm not a sweets person myself, which some people think is a little weird for a baker. But I like feeding people. That's better than eating the goodies myself."

"I like seeing people enjoy my cupcakes," Daniella said. "But I have to test them myself, too. *I* have to think it tastes good before I can give it to someone else. Oh, I forgot to tell you that we got almost a dozen special orders today! Everything from a request for a caterpillar-themed kid's birthday to Boston cream cupcakes for a bar mitzvah."

"I love the special orders," Cookie said. "This time of year we've got bat, black cat, and witch's hat decorations coming out of our ears."

"Don't forget the vampire fangs," Daniella said.

Cookie nodded. "Vampires are big business. Aside from the Halloween stuff, another trend I'm seeing here in the city is savory cupcakes with flavors like grilled onion."

Daniella shook her head. "I can't imagine that."

"Or fig and goat cheese. Those cupcakes are more like scones."

"Still having a hard time," Daniella admitted.

"How about chocolate-covered potato chip, rimmed with crushed potato chips?" Cookie said.

"Now, that's something I can relate to," Daniella said. "Sweet and salty. I'm going to have to add that one to my must-try list."

They talked awhile longer before signing off.

Knowing she'd be too beat to cook dinner, Daniella had stashed some homemade soups in the freezer for this opening week. She pulled out a container of potato leek soup and set it in the microwave before cutting a slice of tomato basil Parmesan artisan bread a baker friend had made for her. She watched an episode of *Cupcake Wars* she'd recorded on her DVR before deciding she was ready to call it a day.

She was heading for bed when the buzzer from her front door downstairs sounded.

"Who is it?" she demanded in a deliberately crabby voice.

"It's me," Nick said.

"Me, who?"

"Very funny," he said. "I need to talk to you."

"It's late and I'm going to bed."

"This won't take long."

She supposed she owed him for handling Tanya for her. Instead of replying, she buzzed him up. He was at her door a second later.

"That was fast," she said.

He wore his customary black attire—only tonight he had a sweater under his black leather jacket.

"Have you ever thought about adding some color to your wardrobe?" she asked.

"No. I like black."

"Yeah, I can tell," she said.

"You wear a lot of black."

"But I mix it up with other colors," she said.

"I didn't come here to talk to you about clothing issues."

"What did you want to talk about?"

"Your brother," he said.

"What about him?"

"Has he been acting strange?"

She eyed Nick suspiciously. "Why?"

"Just answer the question."

"Not until you answer mine first," she said.

"Why do you always have to be so stubborn?"

"Why do you always have to be so impossible?" she countered.

Instead of answering, Nick kissed her.

Chapter Ten

Instead of protesting, Daniella kissed him back. Seriously. Intensely. As if she meant it, which she did. She really, *really* did.

Her entire focus was on him, centering on his mouth as his tongue erotically tangled with hers. So many textures and tastes. So much hunger. Her appetite grew, as did her need for him.

He cupped her face with his lean hands and angled her head to intensify their oral lovemaking. Because that's what it felt like. Like he was making love to her.

He'd kissed her before but each time his lips met hers, things got more out of control. *She* got more out of control.

Her body was pressed tightly against his. The black cotton of his sweater was soft beneath her fingers as she shoved his leather jacket aside to slide her arms around him. She could feel his arousal through the placket of his jeans. When he rubbed against her, she almost went over the deep end.

He shouldn't be able to bring her to the brink of an

orgasm with one kiss. Or even this series of sizzling-hot kisses. But that's what was happening to her. Fireworks and shooting stars were soon to come.

Until Nick abruptly broke off their embrace to glare at her. "This is all your fault."

She blinked at him, her mind and especially her body still swirling with need. Unable to form words yet, she gaped at him like a fish out of water.

"You mess up my mind," he finally growled.

"So?" she growled back. "You mess up my mind, too, but you don't see me blaming you."

"I mess up your mind?" he said. "Because I kissed you?"

"Because you're *you*."

"What does that mean?"

"I can't figure you out," she said.

"Same here."

She rolled her eyes. "Don't be ridiculous. I'm not hard to figure out. I don't have any hidden agendas."

"And I do?"

Daniella nodded. "I think you might."

"What are these hidden agendas?"

"I'm still trying to figure that out. And I will," she warned him. "I have total confidence that I *will* work it out in the end." She may have been bluffing a bit. The truth was, she was *hopeful* she'd work it out but when dealing with Nick, she knew that it was better to be overconfident. "And until I do, I don't think we should be kissing or making out." Especially when he left her aching for more. Why had he broken things off? She should be grateful he had instead of irritated.

Daniella rapidly came up with several possible reasons for his behavior—but the one she liked best was that he kissed her to distract her and got more than he bargained for. Maybe she got to him as much as he got to her. She preferred that to the possibility that he just wasn't that into her. His body had certainly communicated the fact that he wanted to have sex with her, but maybe he was like that with every woman he kissed.

"You kiss me instead of answering my questions," she accused him. "And then you chicken out when I kiss you back." She knew those were fighting words, which is why she said them. She could tell by the stormy anger in his gray eyes that she'd scored a direct hit. As he took a step closer to her, it belatedly occurred to her that he could also perceive her words to be a challenge. "No more kissing," she reminded him, backing up.

"I never chicken out." He reached out to trail his index finger from her temple to the edge of her mouth. "Never."

She wanted to ask him why he'd broken off their embrace but was smart enough to keep her mouth shut. He brushed the ball of his thumb over her lower lip, which still throbbed from the intensity of their kiss. He used his other hand to cup the side of her neck where her pulse was pounding.

Looking into his eyes was like looking into a swirling eddy pulling her into its dangerous undertow. His eyes got even darker before he once again abruptly stepped away.

"This isn't over," he warned her before walking out.

When Nick returned to the Vamp Cave, he found Bruce viewing the video from earlier in the day. "Why didn't you tell me the camera adds ten pounds? And my face looks so pasty," Bruce lamented. "Maybe

I should get a spray tan like Tanya keeps telling me."

"You were wearing clown makeup," Pat reminded him. "And you're a vampire. That's a double whammy."

"Clown vampires do have more than our fair share of issues," Bruce agreed. "They make those horror movies about clowns and then about vampires. I boycott them all. Except for the *Twilight* saga. Those are romantic. But I have to close my eyes for some of the fight scenes."

"Yet you watch and love the *Fast and Furious* movies," Pat said.

Bruce nodded. "I do love great car crashes."

"Which is why he's also a NASCAR fan," Pat told Nick.

"What movies do you like, Nick?" Bruce asked.

"I don't have time for movies."

"Nick, you're growling again," Pat said. "You must have just seen Daniella."

"You probably watched me on the surveillance screens going to her apartment," Nick said, only now belatedly realizing that possibility. He hadn't been thinking clearly when he'd kissed Daniella. Which is why he'd stopped kissing her.

Vampires hooking up sexually with humans never ended well. Mostly for the human. The thought of Daniella getting hurt due to something he did was like a claw through his heart. Not that he was supposed to have a heart. Or feelings. They were a weakness that clouded both thinking and actions.

"We don't actually have cameras placed inside Daniella's apartment. Although I could arrange that if you think it's necessary," Neville said.

"No." Nick focused his attention on the surrounding screens instead of the memory of her melting in his arms. "What about her brother?"

Neville frowned in confusion. "You want me to put cameras inside his place?"

"No," Nick said impatiently. "I want you to check the video and see if he's had any vamp visitors lately aside from me. Including Vamptown vamps."

"Okay, but why?" Neville asked before seeing the menacing look on Nick's face. "Never mind. Forget I asked that."

Nick nodded his approval before saying, "Later." He headed for the peace and quiet of his small office upstairs. He wasn't alone for long, however, as Pat came to join him.

"Anything you care to talk about?" Pat asked, taking a seat across from Nick's desk.

"No." Nick's voice was curt.

"You know, the fact that you're investigating Daniella's background made me realize I don't know that much about *your* background. You never talk about it."

"That's right."

"Why?"

"I'm not a chatty guy," Nick said.

"Understood. But you've been here in Vamptown, what . . . five years now?"

"Six."

"And before that you were in . . . ?"

"Seattle and Boston. You know this already. You know the history of everyone in Vamptown. Human and vamp."

Pat shrugged. "That doesn't mean I remember it all. The other vamps have talked about how they were turned, but you never refer to it. I know about Neville's boss and about Bruce's circus owner. I even know more than I really want to about Tanya's biker boyfriend who turned her so she'd stay forever young. But you . . ."

"It wasn't exactly the highlight of my life," Nick said.

"Yet it forever changed your life," Pat noted quietly.

"It forever changed my afterlife." Nick leaned back in his chair and fiddled with a gold letter opener showcasing a large bloodstone. "You know that wars are a big recruitment time for vamps. The Civil War here, the War of 1812 in Europe, the two world wars, Korea, Vietnam. The vamp population grew with each one." He paused, keeping his eyes on the letter opener. "I was a British officer in the Battle of Waterloo under Wellington. It marked the end of Napoleon's reign in France, and it was the end of me. I was hit in the back. The cannonball went clear through me. I don't remember much after that beyond the stench of blood and the moans of the mortally wounded as we all lay dying on the battlefield. I heard a woman's voice asking if I wanted to live and I said yes." Nick could still remember that moment as if it were yesterday. He hadn't realized the ramifications of his reply. "She was a vampire named Magdalene and she turned me."

Pat gave him a thoughtful look. "Do you regret that?"

"I don't do regrets," Nick said curtly, dropping the letter opener onto his desk. "They are a waste of time. End of discussion."

Daniella's dreams that night were filled with sex and rejection. One was so real and detailed, it felt as if she was living it. She was offering herself to a man she cared deeply for. Removing her clothing as he sat before her, she was filled with nervous anticipation. Every movement shifted to slow motion. Each button of her shirt was undone with her trembling fingers while he watched.

The process seemed to take forever. She kept her bra on but removed her black skirt and stepped out of it. She was left wearing a matching lace set of tiny panties and bra.

Moving closer, she parted her legs and straddled him. She was so damn nervous as she reached out to unbutton the top button of his white shirt.

"Not now," he said.

She sat there frozen for a moment, suddenly realizing they were alone in a classroom and the door wasn't locked. Was he a fellow student or a teacher? She wasn't sure. She only knew that she had to get out of there ASAP.

"You're right." She scrambled off his lap and grabbed her clothes. She didn't even bother putting them on before heading for the door. She pushed it open and peered out to see if the coast was clear. She couldn't let him see how much his rejection had hurt her. She'd burst into tears if she stayed a second longer.

"See ya," she tossed over her shoulder before scurrying out into the hallway, terrified someone would see her in her underwear.

Daniella woke with tears streaming down her face. She had to get up and make a cup of hot chamomile tea to settle her nerves. While she was awake, she Googled the meaning of underwear dreams. *Underclothes may represent your hidden attitudes and fears. If you dream of feeling ashamed at being seen in your underwear, this may indicate an unwillingness to reveal your feelings.*

Reading on, she saw that the color of her underwear in the dream could also have meaning. She was sure it wasn't white. She thought it was black, which could represent dark thoughts. No kidding. It didn't take a rocket scientist to figure that out.

Since it was one in the morning, she went back to bed but didn't get much sleep after that. It seemed like she'd barely closed her eyes when the alarm went off for her to go bake more cupcakes. She went on autopilot—shower, coffee, downstairs. In the shop she almost forgot to turn off the security system. By the time Xandra joined her, Daniella had the music cranked up. They were all edgy songs intended to keep her awake. "Radioactive" by Kings of Leon qualified.

"You okay?" Xandra asked.

Daniella just nodded and kept mixing the batter. She was too busy to think for several hours after that, which was fine by her. When she did have a moment, she brooded over the cupcake blogger instead of brooding about Nick.

What if Cupcake Q-tea hated Daniella's cupcakes? She wasn't even sure who she was or what she looked like. She only knew that the blogger had come to the opening yesterday and would be posting her review soon.

When Suz stopped by later in the afternoon, Daniella said, "I have a feeling something is up. I've just got all this pent-up anxious anticipation that I just can't seem to get rid of." She shook her arms like a sheepdog shaking off water.

Xandra was in the front of the shop, taking care

of customers, so it was just Suz and Daniella in the work area.

"It's just nerves from the opening," Suz said. "And about the blog. I should have checked with you about that first."

"No, it's more than that. This feels personal."

"Like your store isn't personal? It's your baby."

"I know," Daniella said. "I can't explain. It's just this weird premonition I've got."

"Does it have anything to do with Nick St. George?" Suz asked.

"There could be a connection, but it's bigger than he is."

"Really?" Suz's perfectly arched eyebrows lifted over the edge of her multicolored glass frames. "So you already know how big he is?"

"I didn't mean that literally," Daniella said.

"So you two haven't done the deed?"

"No! I haven't even known him that long."

"You've known him long enough to make out with him."

"I am not discussing this here."

"Fine. I'll bring a bottle of wine and pizza to your apartment tonight and we'll talk then."

As promised, Suz showed up at Daniella's apartment. Not only did she bring wine and pizza but she also brought a surprise. "Special delivery," she called out the minute Daniella opened her apartment door. "Keep that open," she told Daniella before calling over her shoulder. "You're almost there, guys."

Two buffed and burly Vin Diesel look-alikes came into her place. But it was what they were carrying that really got Daniella's attention. "Your chair! The one I love from your office."

"It's yours now," Suz said. "They don't make it

anymore or I would have gotten you a new one. Where do you want it?"

Daniella pointed to the reading alcove near the window. "There." She jumped into the chair the moment the men set it down. "It's like it was meant to be here all along." She snuggled into it. "Mmm, perfect."

"The chair or the men?" Suz murmured so only Daniella could hear.

Daniella just grinned and kept quiet.

"Anything else you need, ladies?" Vin number one asked.

"We aim to please," Vin number two said.

"No, we're good," Daniella said.

"Thanks for the tax help," Vin number one told Suz.

"No problem," she said. "You guys take care and I'll see you soon. Thanks again for the help with the chair."

"Was it rude not to invite them to stay for dinner?" Daniella said.

"I can call them back up if you want."

"No, I'm really beat. I'm not up for company tonight."

"What am I?" Suz said.

Daniella hugged her. "You're my BF, not company."

"True."

"I can't believe you're giving me your chair."

"Consider it a congratulations gift for your successful grand opening. Besides, I'm redecorating my office."

"Again?"

"It's been over a year."

"That long, huh?" Daniella teased her.

"Shut up and eat your pizza. It's extra-thin crust with mushrooms and black olives just the way you like it."

Just the way she liked it . . . sort of like kissing Nick. His mouth blended with hers just the way she liked it. More like the way she loved it. Or the way she craved it. The way she could easily become addicted to it if she wasn't very, very careful.

So that's what she'd be from now on. Totally careful. Which was why she refused to answer Suz's questions about Nick and instead changed the subject. After several attempts, Suz got the hint and let it go.

Daniella wished she could let the memory of Nick kissing her go as easily.

"You. Me. Flash mob. Brilliant," Xandra said, just about bursting with excitement as she bopped into the back room of Heavenly Cupcakes a week later. Xandra didn't glide or meander. She bopped. Daniella wasn't sure how else to describe her employee's energetic movements. She radiated energy like those extreme-sport people she'd followed in the Rockies. "For our first week we sort of worked the kinks out. Since then we've stayed mentally strong and just sort of chilled out."

"*You* have, maybe. I wouldn't say I've totally chilled out."

"Which throws a bit of a variable in," Xandra acknowledged. "But now we've got a flash mob. And not just any flash mob. A 'Thriller' flash mob. At noon."

"That's in an hour."

"I know. I am totally stoked."

"You'll be working here from noon to five," Daniella reminded her.

"And for a few minutes I'll be working the flash mob. There will be a big crowd, and they're going to be hungry after dancing to 'Thriller.' That's why we give them coupons for cupcakes. I printed these earlier." She waved them at Daniella. "I take video at the flash mob with my phone and put it up on You-Tube where it goes viral. News crews come to the store. You change your Killer Chocolate cupcake to Thriller Killer Chocolate. If they buy three cupcakes, they get a fourth one free. Only for a few hours."

"Do I have to dance in the flash mob?"

"No. I've seen you dance, and no offense but . . ."

Daniella grinned. "I like dancing when few people are watching instead of a crowd. And I don't have time to learn the steps to the dance in 'Thriller.'"

"I know them by heart," Xandra said.

"You weren't even born when the song came out, were you?"

"My mom loved that CD, and she taught me the steps," Xandra said. "So do we have a plan?"

"It appears we do," Daniella said.

"It appears we do what?" Lois asked as she entered the shop.

"Xandra is participating in a 'Thriller' flash mob."

"It's at the city park two blocks away," Xandra said. "Today at noon. The word is continuing to go out on Twitter as we speak."

"How many people are coming?" Lois asked.

Xandra shrugged. "Who knows? The more the merrier."

Noticing the frown on Lois's face, Daniella said, "Is there a problem?"

"Parking is already hard to find in this neighborhood. I'm just worried about crowd control," Lois said.

"It's only for a few hours. It will be good to get some new blood in the neighborhood."

Lois's face went blank, making Daniella wonder what her employee could be thinking.

" 'New blood in the neighborhood'?" Nick repeated in amazement.

He and Neville were in the Vamp Cave watching surveillance video live from Heavenly Cupcakes.

"I'm just verifying that Daniella doesn't know we put hidden cameras in her bakery last night," Neville said.

"It's a cupcake shop," Nick corrected him.

"Right. So that makes it okay to spy on her without her knowledge?"

"It's not like we've got cameras in her shower or bathroom. In fact, we don't have any cameras in her apartment. Yet."

"What do you think Daniella is going to say when she finds out you're spying on her?" Neville asked.

"I'm doing it for her own good. And ours."

"What are you going to do about the flash mob 'Thriller' thing?"

Nick pointed to another surveillance display. "They're already gathering in the park."

"You can't compel an entire crowd."

"I know that." Nick sounded as irritated as he looked.

"I bet they're in costume under all those trench coats."

"Halloween is only a few days away."

"Wait a minute," Nick said. "Can you zoom in on

that tall one there? We're not the only group of vamps to figure out how to deal with sunshine."

"Especially when it's a gray and cloudy day like today."

"That's one of the vamps that tried to accost Daniella in the alley behind her shop." At Neville's amused look, Nick said, "What?"

"*Accost.* It's not a word you hear that often."

"So Daniella has already informed me."

"Where are you going?" Neville asked.

"To tell that vamp that he's not welcome at this flash mob."

Neville pulled up the vamp recognition app. "His name is Andy and you can't fight him with that many witnesses."

Nick gritted his teeth, which was painful for a vamp. Especially one who was already angry. He could feel his fangs emerging. But Neville was right. Nick couldn't make a scene. Which no doubt was what the outsider vamp was counting on.

"You could join them if you know how to dance to 'Thriller,' " Neville said.

Nick glared at him.

Neville shrugged. "Okay then. Not a big Michael Jackson fan. You probably only know how to do some dance from the early nineteenth century, right? Mozart, maybe?"

Instead of answering, Nick frowned at the sight of the crowd of people who had dumped their overcoats and started gyrating. "Where do they learn to do this stuff?"

"Online."

"They look like a bunch of zombies," Nick said in disgust.

"With an overabundance of eye shadow," Bruce

said as he entered the Vamp Cave. "Oh, a 'Thriller' flash mob! I wish I'd known about it sooner."

"Why?" Nick said. "What would you have done about it?"

"I would have joined it, of course. Not dressed as a zombie, though." He pointed to the screen. "Xandra is doing a great job. I don't mean to be critical but the guy in the back row doesn't seem to know the steps very well."

"That's because he's a vampire," Nick said.

"Vampires can dance," Bruce said as he started moving to the music, matching the beat perfectly.

Neville was impressed. "You're good,"

"There's no dancing allowed in the Vamp Cave," Nick growled.

"Party pooper," Bruce said.

"Has it occurred to you two that we have an intruder?" Nick said.

"Who can't dance," Bruce said.

"This is the second time he's invaded our territory," Nick said. "I intend to make sure there is no third time."

"What are you going to do?"

"Send him to his doom," Nick said.

"Hey, that sounds like a line from the song 'Thriller,' " Bruce said. But Nick had already left the room.

Chapter Eleven

The tall vamp named Andy eyed Nick cautiously as the humans around them chattered among themselves and took the coupons Xandra was handing out. The dance was over, but the crowd lingered. Andy wore a long-sleeved hoodie that covered much of his face. "I'm not here to make any trouble," he said.

"I am," Nick said. "You're not welcome here."

"That's not very hospitable of you."

"Tell your boss that just because he's a Gold Coast vamp, that doesn't mean he can break the rules."

"My boss?"

"Miles Payne. We know you work for him."

A burst of sunshine broke through the clouds, making the intruder wince and step into the shade provided by a large pine tree.

Nick slid on his sunglasses. "Time for you to leave."

"Miles suggested that our clans work together to try to figure out the deal with the cupcake maker."

"The deal?"

"Why she can't be compelled."

"You tell Miles that the cupcake maker is mine," Nick said. "All mine. I'm not good at sharing. Ask anyone."

The other vamp gulped.

"Message received?" Nick said.

Andy nodded before adding with a touch of bravado, "We'll be back."

"Would you two like a coupon?" Xandra asked them. "Buy three cupcakes and get a fourth one free."

"You work for the cupcake maker?" Andy asked.

"We're not interested," Nick said.

Xandra grinned. "That's not what I heard."

Leaning closer, he growled, "Go away."

"There's no need to be rude about it," she said before hurrying off.

"So you want the cupcake maker for yourself," Andy said.

"I already told you that," Nick said. "She's mine."

"Miles is my sire. He gets whatever he wants."

"He gets you to do his dirty work. You're just his minion."

Nick saw the anger flash across the other vamp's face. Minions were below vamps and just above zombies on the supernatural hierarchy scale.

"You don't scare me, St. George."

"Which proves you aren't very smart," Nick said.

"Strength is more important than brains."

"Strength and brains are the most powerful of all."

"Miles has both strength and brains," Andy bragged.

"If he did, then he wouldn't send a minion like you," Nick retorted.

Nick saw the hatred in the other vamp's eyes, eyes that had gone dark with feral fury. "You will regret insulting my sire."

"And you will regret ever coming here if you don't leave right now."

Andy gave him the finger before turning and walking away.

"How was the flash mob?" Daniella asked as Xandra bopped through the door with her customary enthusiasm.

"Everyone is totally stoked about your cupcakes." She pointed to the crowd that followed her in as if she were the Pied Piper.

The next hour was bedlam as a steady stream of customers lined up for Daniella's cupcakes. The Blood Red Velvet was a big favorite, as were the Thriller Killer Chocolate and the Ghostess Twinkies.

Daniella was glad she'd scheduled both Lois and Xandra to work today as that allowed her to focus on taking special orders from customers. And there were tons of special orders. She had to be careful not to overextend and take more jobs than she could complete, but Xandra had assured her that she could work as many hours as Daniella needed

They sold the last cupcake ten minutes before closing time. "Another sellout," Xandra said before turning the sign on the door to CLOSED and flipping the lock.

"Your feet must be killing you," Daniella said to Lois, who was wearing stiletto boots for some reason. It was a strange footwear choice for someone as maternal as Lois.

"No, I'm fine. I don't get aches and pains like other people my age. That is to say, these boots are comfortable," she quickly added.

"My mom swears she wore four-inch heels the entire time she was pregnant with me," Xandra said,

"She claimed it prevented her from getting back-aches."

Since Daniella was adopted, she didn't have any tales about her birth mom's pregnancy with her. Her mom did use to laugh about how she'd used her tummy as a shelf to temporarily set trays of cookies and cupcakes on when she was eight months' pregnant with Gordon. How she'd craved White Castle slider hamburgers with a dollop of whipped cream from a can on top. How Gordon had kicked whenever a Foreigner song played on the radio.

Daniella didn't have any of those stories. But she had others. Of how thrilled her mom had been the first time she saw her when Daniella was only a day old. Of how Daniella loved being hugged and cuddled so much more than Gordon had as a baby.

Daniella rarely thought about being adopted because it wasn't a big deal to her. Her parents had made sure of that. The fact that she was adopted was a part of her the same way that her fear of the dark and her being double-jointed was a part of her.

"Your flash dance was very successful," Lois was telling Xandra.

"It was a flash mob dancing, and yes it did work out. It helped that Halloween is just around the corner. Are you dressing up, Lois?"

"I have some fangs," Lois noted.

"Righteous," Xandra said, giving her a high five. "Perfect for working in a dental clinic and a cupcake shop. I might pick up a pair myself. I saw some on the Internet that claimed to be the most realistic around."

"I doubt they could be more realistic than mine," Lois said drily.

Xandra bounced up and down, reminding Daniella of Tigger from Winnie-the-Pooh fame. "A challenge! I love it. You're on. We'll compare fangs. The shop is closed on Halloween because it's a Monday so we could do it the day before. What do you say? Daniella, you should wear fangs, too."

"I was going to be Glinda the Good Witch from *The Wizard of Oz*," Daniella said.

"Because of the dress, right?" Xandra guessed.

Daniella nodded. "And the glitter and the magic wand. Who doesn't like magic wands?"

"I saw *Wicked*," Xandra said. "It was pure awesomeness. I have the music on my iPod. We should play 'Defying Gravity' while we're baking."

"Are you into magic?" Lois asked Daniella.

Daniella laughed. "Only when it involves cupcakes."

Lois appeared surprised. "You put something magical in your cupcakes?"

"A lot of love. And all-natural ingredients like butter and sugar and flour and eggs." Daniella's voice reflected her pride.

"Tomorrow is your day off," Lois said. "Do you have any plans?"

"There's a chocolate and potato chip cupcake recipe I'd like to experiment with," Daniella said. "Plus I have tons of errands to run."

"Chocolate and potato chip. Sweet and salty." Xandra gave her a fist bump in approval. "Awesome."

"Thank you." Daniella grinned modestly. "I got the idea from my mentor, a fellow cupcake maker in New York City."

"That reminds me . . ." Xandra paused to check her smartphone. "Yes!" She punched her fist into the air with the triumph of a Shaun White, snowboarder extraordinaire. "Blogger Cupcake Q-tea has her new review up about Heavenly Cupcakes."

Daniella immediately crossed her fingers. "Is it okay?"

"No."

Daniella's heart dropped with dread.

"You stomped it."

"That's bad, right?"

"No way. You tell a snowboarder they've stomped it when they solidly land a snowboarding trick with joyful confidence. It means they did a fiercely awesome job."

Daniella looked over Xandra's shoulder to try to read the review on her smartphone. "Cupcake Q-tea says I stomped it?"

"No. She's unaware of that term. Here's what she did say." Xandra cleared her throat before beginning. " 'Heavenly Cupcakes is a welcome new addition to the Chicago cupcake scene. The Blood Red Velvet, so named for Halloween, is a staple at most cupcake shops, but this was one of the best I've had. All-natural ingredients is a motto of theirs, and that comes across in the perfect blend of moist cake and cream cheese frosting. Other favorites included the cookies 'n' cream with just the right amount of cookie crumbs in the buttery icing. The cleverly named Ghostess Twinkie had real whipped cream piped inside. They close when they run out of cupcakes so go early!' "

Daniella did her own version of a moonwalk, shuffling backward.

"That looked more like a Snoopy happy dance than Michael Jackson," Xandra said with a laugh.

Daniella laughed with her. "Which is why you went to the flash mob dance and not me."

"There's never been a dance as good as the Charleston that the flappers danced in the Roaring Twenties," Lois said. She proceeded to show them how it was done, kicking up her heels before bending forward to put her hands on her knees and shifting them back and forth.

Neither Daniella nor Xandra was able to keep up with her. "You're good," Daniella gasped, breathless from the energetic dance.

"Those were the days," Lois said wistfully. "Chicago had hundreds of jazz clubs. We bobbed our hair and wore short skirts. Not short by today's standards but certainly by that time period's. We were brash and bawdy. When Prohibition arrived, we kept the party going in back-alley speakeasies." There was an excited light in her eyes.

"You sound like you were around at that time, which isn't possible," Daniella said.

"Right." Lois's expression returned to her customary sedate state. "My grandmother used to tell me about it. Or maybe it was my great-grandmother."

"There was a popular documentary on PBS about Prohibition done by Ken Burns," Daniella said. "I watched it."

"Yes, it was good but not the same as actually living through it." The wistful note was back in her voice.

"Chicago was at the center of bootlegging and speakeasies," Daniella said. "The buildings on this block were all built in the early 1920s. I wonder if any of them was turned into a speakeasy. It would be fun to check that out someday. When I have the time. In a few years or so." She shook her head at the thought of her already pages-long to-do list.

"Time is something I have a lot of," Lois said.

"That must be nice." Now Daniella was the one who sounded a bit wistful.

"It sure beats the alternative," Lois said.

"Which is?"

"Having your time run out."

Daniella felt a chill run up her spine. "Well, on that happy note, let's call it a day."

"How did the flash mob go?" Neville asked Nick as he entered the Vamp Cave.

"You saw it on the surveillance cameras."

"You looked like you wanted to decapitate Andy."

"I did want to decapitate him, but I restrained myself."

"Restrained yourself from what?" Pat asked as he joined them.

"From decapitation of one of Miles's latest recruits," Nick said.

"Probably a good thing," Pat said. "Not in broad daylight in front of a crowd. That would not be a good idea."

"Yeah, that's what I figured." Nick started impatiently pacing.

Pat frowned. "This is the second time Andy has shown up on our doorstep, so to speak. On our territory."

"Nick told him the cupcake maker is his," Neville said.

"I can speak for myself," Nick growled.

"Right." Neville lowered his head and focused on his laptop.

"So this is all about the cupcake maker?" Pat asked.

"So it would appear," Nick said.

"I still want to know how word got out about her. We've had a truce with the Gold Coast vamps for years now. An uneasy truce, granted. But a truce, nonetheless," Pat said.

"Miles has always been jealous of our ability to tolerate sunlight better than they can," Nick said.

"But he's never acted on that jealousy," Pat pointed out.

"He's tried to hack into our computer system to find out how we managed that," Neville said.

"But we're always a few steps ahead of him in that regard. This is a much more direct challenge. Sending a minion sired by him . . ." Nick shook his head.

"He's not really a minion. Andy really is a vampire. A recently turned vamp, but . . . . Oh, you were just using the term as an insult." Neville nodded and pushed his glasses farther up the bridge of his nose. The frame had bits of duct tape holding the earpiece together. "Right. I get it now."

"What happened to the pair of designer glasses Bruce got for you?" Pat asked. "They were done by that *American Idol* guy. What's his name again?"

"Randy Jackson," Neville said. "I wear them when I go out but not when I'm in the Vamp Cave."

Pat gave him a puzzled look. "Why not? Bruce said they made you look smart."

"I *am* smart," Neville said. "But I feel even smarter when I wear my real glasses."

Pat laughed. "This is the kind of small talk that drives Nick nuts."

"Yet knowing that, you do it anyway," Nick said.

"We just like yanking your chain." Pat grinned.

"Consider it yanked," Nick said. "Can we move on now?"

"Sure."

"What if they try to compel Gordon to talk about the blood recycling at the funeral home?" Neville abruptly asked.

"We already implanted a default in Gordon's mind and his dad's to avoid that issue. And they can't compel any of us because vamps can't compel other vamps," Nick said.

Neville nodded. "They can only decapitate them or burn them."

"Humans can do that to us, too," Nick pointed out. "We can't forget that. We do not want our existence known to humans."

Neville nodded even more emphatically. "I know. I saw the Dracula movies of the townspeople at the gate with their torches."

"I saw the real thing," Pat said quietly. "I don't want to experience that again."

"Right," Nick said. "Which is why we have to exercise extreme caution."

"I thought that's what we have been doing," Neville said.

"We need to do it even more," Nick said.

"How do we do that?"

"By reassessing the threat and responding accordingly."

"It seems a lot of trouble for one cupcake maker," Neville said.

"She's not just a cupcake maker," Nick said. "She's much more than that." And that was part of his problem. She had the power to get to him, and that was as rare as finding a human immune to vamp compulsion.

Daniella started her Monday morning half an hour late, having missed her alarm wake up. It felt strange sleeping until sunrise when she'd spent the previous week getting up in the dark to make cupcakes. Not that she was complaining. She wasn't.

But sleeping those extra thirty minutes meant she was already late in her quest to get two pages of errands done. Daniella hated being late.

Her favorite weather forecaster on WGN-TV had predicted the weekend would be a little chilly. He'd been right. He'd also predicted that today would be mostly cloudy and mild. A peek out her window confirmed that this was true as well. Commuters had their trench coats open as they hurried to the bus stop on the corner.

Daniella knew the commuters liked stopping at her shop in the mornings, which was why she included coffee as part of her offerings. Xandra was as good a barista as she was a baker.

Knowing Chicago weather as she did, Daniella knew that all too soon the snow would be flying, making it difficult to use her Vespa to get around. So she had to enjoy this time. Maybe it wouldn't be really bad until January. Some years were like that. She hoped this would be one of them.

As a little girl she'd longed for the first snowfall when the flakes had been as big as hamsters and she'd caught them on her tongue. Gordon had teased her about never eating yellow snow and licking frozen flagpoles or street signs. Her mother had warned her never to lick *anything* outdoors, frozen or not, while her dad had laughed at them all.

After a shower and a quick breakfast of fresh fruit and Greek yogurt, Daniella checked her appearance in the mirror by her apartment's front door. She was wearing her customary errand attire of jeans, a plain white T-shirt, and a jean jacket.

She hadn't talked to Nick all week and assumed that since things had been quiet following her grand opening, that increased community policing was no longer required. Which was a big relief as far as she was concerned.

She was pleased not only at a renewed sense of security but also at the lack of temptation resulting in Nick's absence. Of course, that same absence meant that there were times she missed him. She hated to admit it, but it was true.

She didn't regret telling him that they couldn't make out again. She was proud of herself for drawing her line in the sand and sticking to it. Nick was a huge distraction that she did not need right now.

But at night, when her defenses were down, she dreamed about him. Raw sexy dreams. Explicit and erotic dreams that sometimes woke her on the verge of an orgasm and left her gasping for breath. One time she'd actually gone over the edge, waking to the powerful pulse gripping her entire pelvic rim.

Her face went bright red just remembering that moment. She was taking that secret to her grave. No way she was letting Nick know the incredible power he had over her, without him even being in the room or the building. It was more than a little disconcerting; it was downright spooky.

Daniella tried to transfer her focus to her *War and Peace*–length to-do list as she locked up and headed for the funeral home garage and her Vespa.

There weren't many trees on the block, but there was one at the side of the funeral home that sent several dried-up leaves tumbling down to the alley. She'd been so wrapped up with opening her shop that she hadn't really paid attention to the fact that not only was autumn here but it was already past its prime. Unlike Shirley. Daniella smiled as she ran her hand over the curve of the front of her pink Vespa.

"Good morning," she greeted her scooter. Feeling a little guilty at ignoring the hearse, she muttered, "You too." She returned her attention to Shirley. "We've got a lot to do today, so let's get going." She walked the Vespa out to the alley, closed the garage door, and reactivated the security system before reaching for her pink helmet hanging from the handlebars.

Something made her look up to see a huge yellow Hummer that was as wide as the alleyway barreling down on her, racing at such a fast speed that there was no way she'd have time to move out of the way.

She saw a blur out of the corner of her eye as Nick moved with freaky fast speed like a character in some superhero movie, grabbing her in his arms and rolling to the safety of a small patch of grass to the side of the funeral home.

He'd cushioned her fall with his body so she rested atop him. She stared down at him in disbelief. There was no way any human being could move that fast. "What just happened?" she croaked.

"You were almost in an accident."

Her eyes remained saucer-sized as she looked at him with confusion and fear. "What . . . are . . . you?"

Chapter Twelve

"I'm Nick," he said. "Did you hit your head? How many fingers am I holding up?" He waggled them in front of her nose.

"I know *who* you are. That's not what I asked." Daniella looked at him and then the distance he'd covered to save her before stuttering, "No one can run that fast. That was . . . freaky fast."

"I was on the track team in school," he said with false humility.

"Stop it. I'm not stupid. You're not normal."

"I never claimed to be normal," Nick said quietly.

"Then what *are* you?" she whispered.

"What I am is glad you're not hurt."

His calmness did not reassure her. This was beyond weird. Beyond strange. This was . . . well, she didn't know what it was. That was the problem. "Did you drug me? Is that why it looked like you moved so fast?"

She saw him pause but noticed as a squirrel scampered across the grass that nothing else seemed to move at hyperspeed. Just him. So she wasn't drugged.

"Forget it," she said. "Don't try using that as an excuse. It would be a lie."

"You're in shock."

"Yes, but that isn't it . . . I saw something like this in a movie once." She frowned, trying to gather her foggy thoughts.

"Did you see the vehicle that sideswiped you?"

"It was a yellow Hummer. I noticed that much." She looked around before trying to get up. "My Vespa!"

"Your Vespa is fine. Don't try to move yet." He ran his hands over her body. "Does anything hurt?"

"I can't believe the way you just grabbed me in your arms so fast."

"I can't believe some idiot was racing down the alley so fast," he growled.

"It's almost as if they were trying to hit me." She saw the truth on Nick's face. "Oh my God! They *were* trying to hit me. And you saved me. Like Clark Kent without the glasses or the cape."

"If he was wearing the cape then he'd be Superman, which I am not."

"What are you doing?" she demanded when he turned and shifted before sliding his arms beneath her and scooping her up.

"Taking you to your apartment."

"I can walk."

"I think not." She didn't protest because the truth was her head was incredibly swimmy and he was incredibly dreamy. Pressed close against his body this way was shockingly fine. It had been days since he'd kissed her. Days and days. She didn't remember exactly how many because she couldn't think clearly at the moment. But she could definitely feel . . . feel the movement of his muscles as he easily carried her inside and up the stairs. She'd never actually been cradled and carried in a man's arms before. It felt better than she expected. *He* felt better than she remembered. Had his shoulders always been this broad?

Her thoughts distracted her until he entered her apartment and carefully set her in her chair, the one Suz had given her. "Something new?" he asked with a tilt of his head.

Then it hit her. "The movie. It was *Twilight*."

"Never saw it," he said.

"But surely you've heard of it?"

He shrugged.

"You always do that when you don't want to talk about something," she noted.

He reached out to gently run his finger across the wrinkle in her forehead. "And you always frown when you get suspicious."

"Don't try to change the subject. I was not hallucinating or imagining things. You moved with superhuman speed. So did Edward."

"A friend of yours?"

"The hero in the movie. *Twilight*. He's a vampire. Don't tell me you're a vampire, too," she mocked.

"Okay, I won't tell you that."

"Because it wouldn't be true, right?"

He shrugged.

She socked him. "Don't keep doing that."

"What do you want me to say?"

"The truth."

"You can't handle the truth."

"What, now you're quoting movies at me? Jack Nicholson talking to Tom Cruise in *A Few Good Men*." She paused to study him carefully. "Did that Hummer hit you?" She grabbed a handful of his long jacket and saw that indeed it was ripped along his left flank. So was the shirt he wore under it. "It did hit you! You're hurt." Pushing the material aside, she saw the large bleeding wound. She also saw the skin miraculously rejuvenating itself until all signs of his injury were gone. She stared at it before raising her eyes to meet his. "Okay, that is definitely not normal. Even for an abnormal person, that is just not normal. Not even in the cheap seats of the ballpark of normal."

He yanked his clothing back into place. "Forget you saw that."

She wished she could, she really did. Because panic was streaking through her. She was shaking so hard inside, she was surprised that there was no outward sign of her fear. She hadn't really been serious before when she'd talked about him moving with superhuman speed like a vampire. Well, yes, she had been serious, but she'd been hoping for some sort of logical explanation.

Vampires weren't real. No way. So there had to be some other reason for all this.

Maybe she hit her head in the alley and was suffering from a bad concussion. Didn't that disorient you?

That possibility prevented her panic from spiraling completely out of control.

"I heal fast," he told her.

She frowned. Maybe the concussion made her see something that wasn't real?

"Go ahead, say it," he dared her.

"Are you . . . a vampire?" she whispered.

"And if I am?"

"So you think you're a vampire."

"I *know* I'm a vampire. Now you know it, too."

He had to be teasing her. Nothing else made

sense. "No way!" She socked his arm before leaning back. "I'm sorry. I shouldn't do that."

"It doesn't hurt."

"No, I mean socking a guy who thinks he's a vampire isn't the smartest thing to do. It might aggravate you."

"Believe me, you're already aggravated me more than any human has in ages," he noted drily.

"I don't believe any of this," she confided to him. "I must be dreaming it all. The Hummer coming at me and you rescuing me. Yes, this must all be a weird dream. Or maybe the accident really did happen and I not only suffered a concussion, but I'm actually in a coma. How would I know if I'm in a coma or not?" she wondered aloud.

"I'd know."

"Says the man who thinks he's a vampire."

"I *know* I'm a vampire."

"Show me your fangs. No, don't do that. Horror movies scare me."

"Yet you saw *Twilight*."

"Suz rented the DVD and I closed my eyes for the fight scenes near the end," she said. "But let's get back to you. You really are . . . ?"

He nodded.

"Then I *definitely* have to be in a coma. Because there's no such thing as vampires."

"That's what we want humans to think. We don't want you going all Volturi on us." At her blank look, he said, "You didn't see the sequels to the *Twilight* movie?"

"No. I am a cupcake maker. A damn good one. I don't do vampires."

He raised a perfectly shaped dark eyebrow.

She blushed and put her hand to her cheek, then gave him a startled look. "Is blushing bad? Does that make you want to do stuff?"

"Oh yeah. It definitely makes me want to do stuff."

Her eyes widened, and her heart beat faster than a race car.

"Calm down," he said. "I'm not going to bite you."

"But don't you need blood to like . . . live or something? You don't hurt animals, do you?" She glared at him. She realized she was being totally illogical here. But she couldn't stand the thought of animals being hurt. Even in natural disasters, she felt terrible for the people affected—but it was the animals involved that brought her to tears every time. Besides, this conversation wasn't real. She was in a coma.

"Stop looking at me like I drain puppies and kittens of life. I do not hurt animals. And I'm not going to bite you. At least not that way."

"What do you mean, *that* way?"

"You tempt me for sex, not as a dinner."

"How can you think of sex at a time like this?" she said.

"You're thinking of sex at a time like this."

"How do you know?" she demanded. "Can you read my mind?"

"A lucky guess."

She reached out to touch him. If the accident had knocked her out, she might as well enjoy the experience. Yes, she was definitely going with the coma thing. "I thought vampires were cold to the touch."

"They can be. I'm not."

"Yes, I noticed that." She slowly dropped her hand from his chest. "What about sunshine? I thought daylight is deadly for vampires."

"It can be deadly for humans, too. You've heard of skin cancer, right?"

"But I thought vampires couldn't be exposed at all to sunlight."

"Most can't. I can."

"How?"

"That's my secret."

The questions hit her fast and furious. "Where do you live? In a coffin?"

"No. I live in a loft. And no, I don't hang upside down from the rafters in case you were wondering."

"I wasn't."

Nick sighed. "You still think you're in a coma, don't you?"

"You never answered my question earlier. Can you read my mind?"

"Not yours, no."

"But you can read other people's minds? What about the person who tried to run me down? Could you read their mind?"

"That wasn't a person. That was a vampire."

"A vampire tried to run me down?" She frowned in confusion. This coma was getting complicated. "How many vampires are there out there?"

"Trying to run you down? I'm not sure," he said. "One for sure."

"So there's only one other vampire aside from you in Chicago?"

"That would *not* be an accurate assessment."

She narrowed her eyes at him. "How many vampires are there in Chicago?"

"We don't do a census or anything, but there are probably a few hundred."

"I'm only asking you all this because none of this is real. I'm in a coma right now."

"I'm positive you're not in a coma." He reached for his cell phone.

Like he'd know. Which option was less terrifying? The one where she was in a coma, or the one with him as a vampire? She couldn't pick. They both sucked. Okay, maybe not the best thing to think of when dealing with a possible vampire.

If she was in a coma, she might be on life support. What if someone pulled the plug. What if she died?

What if she wasn't in a coma? Then what?

"What are you doing?" she demanded. Fear and panic were starting to catch up with her once more. It was possible that she was alone with a vampire. One who had just saved her life, granted. But still a vampire.

Could it be true? How else could she explain his wound magically healing over? And his freaky fast speed?

"Coma, coma, coma," she muttered.

"I'm calling in reinforcements," Nick said.

Which meant what? That a bunch of vampires would be camping out in her living room? Were they even called a bunch or was there some special term to refer to a group of vampires? A gaggle? A flock? A coven?

Maybe he was calling in medical help?

A second later there was a knock at her door. How had someone gotten past the buzzer entrance downstairs?

"Relax. It's just Pat," Nick said, opening the door for him.

The sight of the tattoo shop owner was strangely reassuring. "Come in."

"What's going on?" Pat asked with Zenlike calmness.

Daniella pointed to Nick. "He thinks he's a vampire," she said with hyena-like hysteria. "And I think I'm in a coma."

"An outsider vamp in a Hummer just tried to run Daniella over while she was on her Vespa," Nick said.

"I saw it on the surveillance screen," Pat said.

A second later Bruce stood outside her still-open apartment door. "My partner is more empathetic than I am," Pat said. "May he come in?"

As soon as Daniella nodded, Bruce came to squat beside her and pat her hand reassuringly. "Some people are offended when they find out what we are."

"I'm not," she assured him. "I've got several friends who are gay."

"Yes, but do you have other friends who are vampires?" Bruce said.

Her eyes widened. "You're saying you think Nick is a vampire?" she whispered.

"We're all vampires, honey." Bruce said.

"I'm not," she said.

"No, you're not," Bruce said gently. "But we are."

Her rational brain refused to compute what he was saying, yet her instincts told her that he was speaking the truth. Mere minutes ago she'd seen a bloody gaping wound on Nick's left flank and she'd seen it miraculously heal. The good news was that she was not in a coma. The bad news was everything else.

"You're all vampires? How is that even possible?" she said unsteadily.

"It's a long story."

"How did that happen? Did Nick bite you? Did he turn you into vampires?" she said.

"No," Bruce said. "And we didn't turn him into a vampire, either."

It was too much to comprehend and believe. Only yesterday her biggest problem was which flavor cupcake to choose as the weekly special. Now she had a pack of vampires in her living room. Not to mention one Hummer-driving vampire who wanted to flatten her and her Vespa like a pair of pancakes.

Oh my God, ohmygod, omg, omg omg. This *was* real after all.

She couldn't let them see her fear. Couldn't let them know she was panicking. She didn't even realize she was hyperventilating until Pat handed her a small paper bag from her kitchen counter. "Breathe into it."

She did.

"I realize it's a lot to take in," Bruce said. His gaze was so kind and understanding as he continued to squat beside her. "Would you like me to make you some tea?"

She shook her head and removed the bag from her mouth and nose. "I'd like you all to leave." She just wanted them gone so she could figure things out—like whether she should check herself into the nearest psychiatric ward.

"We can't do that," Nick said. "Someone is trying to hurt you."

"You mean some vampire," she said.

He nodded.

"Why?"

"That's what we're trying to figure out. We know that you are immune to mind compulsion—"

"Hold on a minute," she interrupted him, belatedly removing her hand from Bruce's comforting hold. She moved so quickly that he fell back onto his butt.

"Vamps can be klutzy, too," he said cheerfully as he got up.

Daniella returned her attention to Nick. "What do you mean I'm immune to mind compulsion?"

"Exactly what I said."

"You can compel people to do things? Things they don't want to do?"

"Yes," Nick said.

"Not that we do that," Bruce hurriedly inserted. "Not very often. Not if we can possibly avoid it. Only in dire emergencies."

"Is that why you told me not to open my shop the first time we met?" she asked Nick. "You were trying your mind compulsion thing on me?"

"Yes," Nick admitted. "But it didn't work."

"It didn't work when I tried it, either," Pat said.

"Same here," Bruce said.

She stared at the three of them, at a total loss for words. The fact that they were vampires wasn't weird enough? Now she learned they'd tried to compel her? "What else have you tried to do to me?"

"Nothing."

Daniella pointed to Nick again. "You tried getting me into bed with you."

"You responded out of your own free will and your own desire. I didn't make you do anything," Nick said.

"Would you two rather be alone?" Bruce asked.

"No," she said.

"We have to figure out why you are different," Nick said.

"Listen, dude, *I'm* not the one who is different.

You three are. And not because you're gay," she hurriedly assured Bruce.

"Understood." Bruce nodded. "It's the vampire thing."

"That's right," she said.

"Everyone is after you because you are the only human we know of who's immune to vamp compulsion," Nick said.

"So they want to kill me?' she said.

"They were trying to take you."

She frowned, not understanding what Nick meant. "Take me?"

"Abduct you."

"By running me over?" she said.

"They don't have much experience with abductions," Bruce said. "Unlike aliens from outer space. Abduction is their specialty."

"There's no such thing as space aliens," Pat said. "You can't believe anything you read in those tabloids."

Daniella couldn't believe she was sitting here listening to a bunch of vampires discuss the reality of alien abductions. Talk about falling down a rabbit hole. What was next? An appearance by the Cheshire cat?

Vampires were dangerous. Even vampires who had kind eyes like Bruce. And especially sexy vampires like Nick who made her want to have sex with him despite not being able to manipulate her mind.

"Daniella needs a bodyguard," Nick said.

"And I suppose you're going to say that you're the man for the job?" she said.

"No, I'm telling you that I'm the vamp for the job."

"No, you're not," she instantly said. "Why can't Bruce be my bodyguard? Doesn't he have the same vampire skills you have?" Okay, now she knew she was losing it, talking about vampire bodyguarding skills.

"Bruce used to be a circus clown. I used to be a warrior," Nick said.

"He still has the heart of a warrior," Pat said. "Nick is definitely the one who should take care of you."

"I thought vampires didn't have hearts," she said.

"It was just an expression," Pat said.

"We're not here to talk about a vampire's anatomy," Nick said. "I can satisfy your curiosity on that subject later."

Nick made it sound like Daniella was talking dirty. Vampires might not have hearts but she sure did, and hers was just about leaping out of her chest. Why did she want to rip off his clothes and have her way with him? The first time she met him, she didn't even find him attractive.

Okay, she'd known objectively that he was physically attractive back then, but he hadn't done it for her personally. Not in a big way. Not in a humongous way. Now he did. What was that about? What had he done to her?

"Can Nick do stuff that I don't know about?" she asked Pat. "I mean you say that I can't be compelled, but what else could he do?"

"She wants to know if I can make her want to have sex with me," Nick translated.

"I'm not sure how to answer that question," Pat began.

"I knew it!" she said.

"Wait." Pat held up his hand. "He has no vampire skills or supernatural skills to do that. But Nick has always been popular with the opposite sex."

"Was he that way before he became a vampire?" she asked.

"Yes," Nick said with what she considered to be a smirk.

"I didn't know him back then," Pat said.

"How long ago was back then?" Daniella asked.

"Don't you know it's rude to ask someone about their age?" Nick said.

"I didn't know if that rule applies to vampires, too," she said.

"It does."

"I'd just say that we all look good for our age," Bruce inserted. "Vampires don't age once we are turned." He cleared his throat. "We'd appreciate it if you didn't tell anyone about any of this."

"Screw that," Nick growled, showing her his angry face. "You are forbidden from telling anyone else or there will be hell to pay."

"No one would believe you anyway," Pat pointed out. "We'd use mind compulsion on them. You don't want to put others at risk, do you?"

She shook her head. "Don't tell my brother about the accident. He'll tell my dad, who'll just worry or try to cut his trip short. He hasn't had a vacation since my mom died and I don't want to do anything to ruin it."

"That's noble of you," Bruce said.

The truth was that Daniella wanted to tell her dad that a vampire in a Hummer tried to ram her. She could only imagine what his response would be. What would he say? *Don't worry, honey. It'll be okay?* That might have worked when she was a kid and skinned her knee after falling off her bike, but she doubted its effectiveness regarding vampires living next door. Or maybe *living* wasn't the right way to put it. Existing next door? Sucking blood next door?

"Don't worry, we won't tell your brother." Bruce's reassuring tone was similar to her dad's, but her father didn't have fangs.

"Right," Nick said. His voice held no reassurance whatsoever. Instead it held the promise of an impending threat. "We won't tell your brother and you won't tell anyone about what you've learned today."

"You mean about the vampire thing. I understand." Daniella nodded to emphasize that point. "I get it. I won't say anything."

"To make sure of that, we will need some insurance," Nick said.

Daniella didn't like the sound of that. "What kind of insurance?"

"Your brother."

"What about him?"

"Swear on your brother's life that you won't reveal our secret to anyone, and that includes your family and friends."

"Swear on his life? Or what? You'll kill him? Turn him into a vampire?"

"No," Nick said. "I'll compel him to gamble until he loses everything. It wouldn't be difficult to do. He gambles already and wants to do more."

"How do you know?"

"I read his mind."

"Why would you do that?" Her mouth dropped open as realization hit. "OMG. Vampires, funeral home, blood. What are you doing with the funeral home?"

"It's better you don't know," Nick said.

"Better for who?"

"For whom," Nick corrected her. "Better for us all."

"Not for me. Not for my family," she said. "The Evergreen Funeral Home has been in the family since my grandfather's time. Have you been messing with it since then?"

"No," Pat said. "It's been more recent than that."

"How recent?" she demanded.

"The past dozen years."

"Since my mother died." Her heart froze as she stared at them in horror. "Oh my God! You killed her!"

Chapter Thirteen

Daniella leapt from her chair and frantically looked around her apartment. Vampires. She was surrounded by vampires who had lulled her into a false sense of security and may have killed her mother. How stupid was she to let down her guard?

Where was a silver crucifix when you needed one? Wait. She had a sterling-silver tea strainer in the kitchen that she'd gotten at an antiques shop on a trip to London. Maybe that would do?

The problem was, she had to get past three vamps to get to the kitchen. And they moved faster than she could. *Much* faster. She couldn't believe how fast Nick had raced to save her from getting mowed down by that Hummer.

"Calm down," Nick said. Sure, *now* he used his reassuring voice. "We had nothing to do with your mother's death."

"Right." She stood swaying just a bit from fear and adrenaline. "Like you'd admit it if you did."

"She has a point," Bruce said.

Nick glared at him. "Not helping."

"I never saw you around the neighborhood twelve years ago," she said to Nick. "Why is that?"

"Because I didn't live here then. I was in Boston."

"And I was in Florida," Bruce said.

She focused her attention on Pat. "You were here then."

Pat nodded. "True."

"Then it was you." She pointed an accusing finger at him, hoping he didn't notice the slight tremble. "What did you do to her?"

"Nothing."

Daniella needed to protect herself. Who knew what these vampires might do? What about a wooden stick? Or a stake? How big did a stick have to be to earn the description of a stake? She had a wooden yardstick in the closet. Would that work?

"Calm down," Nick repeated.

"Do not try to compel me," she growled.

"I already told you that you can't be compelled," Nick reminded her. "None of us can compel you."

"Good thing, too," she said.

"Although being able to compel you would make life more convenient for us," Bruce said. "Not that the world is all about us," he hurriedly added, given her acidic glare at him.

"You're freaking out for no reason," Nick told her.

"Right," she scoffed. "Discovering your neighbors are vampires is no big deal."

"How do we convince you that vampires had nothing to do with your mother's death?" Pat said.

"A lie detector test," she said.

"We don't exactly have a normal pulse," Pat said.

"Of course you don't," she said. "You drink blood. Blood that you steal from my family's funeral home."

"We don't steal it. We pay good money for it,"

Bruce said before clapping his hand to his mouth. "That wasn't a secret, was it?"

"No." Pat gave his partner a smile.

"So how can I be sure a vampire is telling the truth?" Daniella demanded.

"By trusting us," Nick said.

"Like that's going to happen. I could have you swear on a Bible or something." She paused, unsure of the protocol. Weren't religious objects a problem for vampires? "Okay, maybe not a good choice."

"You want us to swear on a copy of *Twilight*?" Nick mocked her.

"I want to pretend none of this ever happened," she said.

"I could make that happen if only I could compel you," Nick said.

"Not gonna happen, Count Chocula," she shot back.

"Let's be logical here," Nick said.

"By all means," she said sarcastically. "Let's logically examine why vampires may have killed my mother."

"You're basing that accusation on what? The fact that I lived in the neighborhood and I'm a vampire?" Pat said. "Did she die under unusual circumstances?"

"She was killed in a car accident involving a drunk driver."

"Look at me." Nick turned her to face him. "Trust your instincts. I'm telling you the truth when I tell you that no vampire had anything to do with your mother's death. I'm sorry for your loss, but it was a human who caused that accident."

"There would have been fang marks on her throat," Pat said, trying to stay logical. "There weren't."

"Maybe there were and you compelled people to

forget." But her words were weaker now as her instincts strongly told her that Nick was not lying. "I want to believe you." Her voice was thick with emotion.

"Then do." He gently pulled her into his arms and rubbed his hands up and down her back in a motion that was incredibly soothing.

She briefly rested her forehead on his shoulder. This was the man who'd saved her life. The *vampire* who'd saved her life. She had the feeling that had he wanted her dead, she'd be dead. She also had the feeling that Pat was telling the truth. Human stupidity had caused her mother's death, not supernatural beings.

"Better now?" Nick asked her.

She nodded and stepped away.

"We've been trying to figure out why you are immune to compelling," Bruce said.

"Because I'm stubborn," she replied. "Cheerful but stubborn. Or so I've been told."

"Plenty of humans are stubborn. They can still be compelled. But there's something special about you."

She saw the three of them share a look. "What? What was that about?"

"Maybe you should ask your dad when he comes back in a few days," Nick said.

"What? Ask him why I can't be compelled by the neighborhood vampires? Sure, that makes perfect sense. *Not.* You just swore me to secrecy and now you want me talking to my dad?"

"Not about us. About *you.* About your past."

"What about my past? Do you three know something I don't?" she demanded.

"I'm sure we know a great deal more than you do," Nick mocked.

"Very funny. That's not what I'm talking about and you know it. There's something else you're keeping from me."

"We've told you what we can. More than we've told any other human," Nick said.

"Then why stop now?" Daniella said. "Especially if this secret concerns me. I have a right to know."

"Give your father a chance to tell you first," Nick said.

"To tell me what?"

All three remained silent.

Sensing that Bruce was the most empathetic of the group, she focused her attention on him. "Please. I have to know."

Bruce shook his head regretfully. "I'm sorry."

"Fine. Be that way." She'd had it with the bunch of them. "It's time for you all to leave."

"Actually, that's something else we need to discuss," Nick said.

"Pardon me if I've had enough exposure to vampires for one day." She directed her sarcasm at him. "I want you out. Now."

"The incident today indicates that our rival vamp clan is ramping up their efforts to get you. Therefore, we need to ramp up our security," Nick said.

"I've already got security systems."

"You need a full-time bodyguard," Nick said.

"You're volunteering for the job."

"I wouldn't call it volunteering, exactly," he said.

"Then what would you call it?"

"Filling a need," he said.

She was sure he deliberately made his voice go all husky and sexy. "I don't want you filling my needs."

"Don't you?

"No. Absolutely not."

"You'd rather be attacked by a rogue vampire than be protected by one who will put your safety first?" he said.

"I'd rather not have to deal with vampires at all," she retorted.

"That's no longer an option," he said.

"It really is for your own good," Bruce said.

"Better the vampire you know than the one you don't," Pat said. "It's in our own best interests to keep you safe."

"Not all vampires are created equal. Some are stronger than others. Some are more evil than others," Nick said. "More violent."

"And where do you guys fall within that spectrum?"

"Strong," Nick said. "Not evil. Not violent unless we have to be."

She sank back into her chair. "So what exactly are you suggesting?" she said.

"That I'm with you twenty-four/seven," Nick said. "That I go where you go."

"And how am I supposed to explain why you are in the cupcake shop at five in the morning while we're baking?"

"You won't even know I'm there."

"How do plan on accomplishing that?" she demanded. "Do you have a cape that makes you invisible like Harry Potter?"

"No."

"And what about after work? What about at night?"

Nick tilted his head toward the other side of the room. "Your couch looks comfortable."

"It's not. Even if it was, there's no way I'm having you in my apartment while I sleep."

"Why? Because I'm a vampire?"

"Because you're you."

"So you've said before. I still don't know what that's supposed to mean," he said.

She ran her hands along the arm of her favorite chair. The soft linen felt surprisingly comforting against her skin. She needed comfort now because she was becoming overwhelmed with this all. "What about when you're asleep?" she said.

"Vampires don't need much sleep," he said.

"I thought they spent half their time in coffins and stuff," she said.

Bruce rolled his eyes.

"Excuse me if I don't know the sleep protocol for vampires," she said sarcastically.

"You're excused," Bruce said. "There are a lot of urban myths out there about vampires."

"Like the fact that you exist?"

Bruce frowned. "Of course we exist."

"She may be trying to convince herself again that she's in a coma," Nick told Bruce.

"Don't be silly, Daniella," Bruce said. "Of course you're not in a coma. Why would you think that?"

"Because I'm talking to vampires," she said. "And they're talking back to me."

"Would it be better if we didn't talk back?" Bruce asked.

She shook her head.

"Do you at least believe now that we didn't have anything to do with your mother's death?" Bruce said.

"I don't know." She eyed them all warily. "And I am not approving that overnight plan, either. Besides, you have businesses to run."

"We have staff for that," Nick said.

"Do they know you're vampires?" She saw the answer on Bruce's face. "No way! Your staff are all vampires, too?"

"We tend to stick together in small groups," Bruce said.

"How small?"

"Two or three dozen."

"I don't get it. How have you stayed under the radar?" she said.

"We've vampified the neighborhood. Not many humans hang out here."

"This is too weird for me," she said. "I can't process this." She put her hand to her head. "I'm getting a headache."

Nick gently moved her hand aside and checked her for bruises. "Did you hit the pavement? I thought I caught you in time."

His touch was so gentle, so human, so sexy. She stared at his face, searching for some sign that he was different.

"Looking for my fangs?" he said.

"To quote your friend Pat, let's be logical here," she said. "First you inform me that not only are you a vampire, but most of the neighborhood is as well. Then you tell me that not only do vampires exist, but some of them are trying to harm me. Yet I'm supposed to just say *Sure, move on in, Nick. Let's have a sleepover pajama party. No problem.*"

"Of course there will be problems. But they won't be as bad as you falling into the wrong hands and being taken. This wasn't the first time they tried to grab you. Remember those guys in the alley?"

"The gang members?"

"They were vampires. Outsiders."

"From the Gold Coast clan," Pat said.

Her eyes widened. "Gold Coast? You mean like ultra-wealthy bankers and brokers? Vampire bankers and brokers?"

"The vamps in the alley were hired help," Bruce said. "The Gold Coast clan wear much better clothing. Armani suits. I'll never forget the first time I saw their leader, Miles. He's over six feet tall, and was wearing a very natty pin-striped suit with a purple tie and matching pocket square. He has excellent posture, silver hair, and a dapper mustache."

"You're saying vampire bankers and brokers are after me?" Daniella said.

"They are cutthroat dangerous," Pat quietly said. "Especially Miles the Mustache. Do not underestimate the havoc they can create."

She could believe that. Just look at what they'd done to the economy with their greed. "Did vampires cause the global recession with the mortgage derivative thingies?"

"They weren't all vampires," Bruce said. "Most were human. You can't blame everything bad on vampires. That's racist. You shouldn't do that." He paused before admitting, "That wasn't easy for me to tell you. To quote Len Goodman, the *Dancing with the Stars* judge who says he's misquoting Churchill— 'The three hardest things in the world are to climb a wall that's leaning toward you, to kiss a girl who's leaning away from you, and to criticize someone who's looking at you.' I'm not good about criticizing someone when they're looking at me," he told Daniella.

"If we can get back to the matter at hand," Nick said impatiently.

"Nick was in the British army," Bruce said. "Therefore he likes giving orders and doesn't care for chitchat."

"We can't all be former clowns," Nick growled.

"Once a clown, always a clown," Bruce said proudly.

"You were in the British army?" she asked Nick, who nodded curtly.

"Which is why he's an excellent bodyguard," Bruce said.

"You mean like James Bond or MI5? That kind of British army?" she asked.

"Close enough," Nick said.

She wanted to know more about Nick. Clearly the only way she'd find out was to ask questions. "Why don't you have an English accent?"

"Because I've lived in this country a long time."

"How long? I'm not just being nosy. I need to know more about you before I can decide whether to let you protect me."

"She's right," Pat said.

"How about I'll tell you more about me if you behave and go along with the bodyguard plan?" Nick countered.

"Behave? You mean I should just be a good little girl and go along with what the nice vampire wants?" Her outrage came across in her curt voice as she stood to face him.

"Right."

She glared at him. "Wrong!"

"He's already saved your life twice," Pat quietly pointed out. "You really don't want to risk a third time, do you?"

"Isn't there something I can do to protect myself from vampires?" she said. "What about garlic?"

"Smells bad but doesn't bother us," Nick said.

"A crucifix? A Bible?"

"Keep them handy if they make you feel better," he said.

"Will they keep vampires away?"

"No."

"What does?"

"Fire," he said bluntly.

"So you're saying I should sleep with a flame-thrower in my bed?" she said.

Nick actually grinned. "It sounds sexy when you put it that way."

She socked his arm before she could stop herself. Hitting a vampire may not have been the smartest thing to do, but she couldn't resist. "So we're back to me trusting you on blind faith."

"Trust your gut," Nick told her.

"How do I know you won't suck out my gut?"

"Zombies do that, not vampires."

"My instincts never told me you were a vampire," Daniella pointed out.

"What did they tell you about me?" he said.

"That there was something strange about you."

"Exactly," Nick said. "Your instincts were correct."

The problem was that her instincts warned her that while he might not want to physically harm her, he remained a powerful temptation. Instead of being turned off by his admission of being a vampire, she was strangely honored that he'd trusted her enough to share his deepest secret with her.

Not that she could be sure being a vampire was his deepest secret; she just couldn't imagine anything else that would be as big a headline. And he hadn't exactly trusted her. He had threatened her brother if she told anyone. But at least he hadn't threatened to suck Gordon's blood. He hadn't threatened to suck her blood, either.

She should not be finding him sexy at this point. No way. She wasn't into the vampire lust stuff. Really, she wasn't. At least she never had been in the past, although the canceled TV show *Moonlight* was a guilty pleasure of hers.

Okay, maybe she *was* more into vampires than she realized. Did that explain her attraction to Nick? Was it because she'd somehow sensed that he was a vampire?

She supposed that made as much sense as anything else she'd seen or heard today. It was all pretty outrageous stuff. So how would Nick staying with her 24/7 work out? She wasn't about to sleep with a flamethrower, despite him thinking that sounded a little sexy.

She did have a small butane torch that she used to brown the top of crème brûlée. She supposed she could stash that on her bedside table. Along with condoms.

Whoa, where did that thought come from? No way she was having sex with a vampire. It probably wasn't even possible . . . or was it?

"Okay, you can stay," she told Nick. "For *one* night. After that . . . we'll just have to wait and see."

Chapter Fourteen

"Stiffer. You're not stiff enough." Daniella glared at the contents of the bowl as she spoke directly to it. "You're frosting. You need to be stiffer, not all gloppy." She resumed frantically beating the contents. "Stiffer and stiffer."

Daniella's admonition was enough to make Nick stiff and as hard as her granite countertop. Her focus remained on the bowl of frosting, however. She was clearly in cooking mode.

Bruce and Pat had cleared out an hour ago, promising to secure Daniella's pink Vespa for her. The second they left, Daniella had leapt up and headed for her kitchen. She'd started grabbing ingredients and mixing bowls.

"What are you doing?" he'd asked, still concerned that she might have hit her head when they fell and that her actions therefore could be confused.

"I have to bake," she'd growled. "Do not try to stop me."

"You might want to rest . . ."

She gave him an icy glare.

"Or maybe not," he'd allowed.

Nick was still trying to recover from a day that had gone to hell and back. When he'd seen that huge Hummer heading straight for Daniella, he'd felt a stab of fear. Only now was he able to identify it as such because it had been so long since he'd experienced it.

He'd felt a moment of terror that he wouldn't be able to reach Daniella in time to save her. He'd gone vamp full throttle and in doing so had saved her life but exposed his secret. Not just *his* secret, but the secret of the entire neighborhood.

Looking back and reviewing his actions, Nick couldn't think what else he could have done. He supposed Daniella had taken the news well, all things considered. Once she realized she wasn't in a coma and imagining everything, she seemed to handle his confession without too much hysteria.

Yes, there was the incident regarding her mother's death, but they'd handled that. He hadn't been lying when he'd said that vamps had nothing to do with her mother's tragic accident.

Even then, she'd gotten furious and somewhat scared, but hadn't totally freaked out. No tears or fits of the vapors.

All this logical introspection was intended to distract him from her comment about being stiff. Hearing those words from her lush lips had a ridiculously powerful effect on him. Even now, his attention was drawn again and again to her mouth.

She paused in her vigorous beating of butter and sugar to stare at him. "Can vampires eat? Real food I mean."

"No."

"So you lied when you said you'd sampled my cupcakes."

His mind flew back to their first meeting, when she'd tried to coax him to sample her wares. He'd known then that she'd be more than he'd bargained for. But he'd been confident in his ability to manage her.

"Yes, I lied."

She slid a batch of chocolate cupcakes into the oven before turning to face him. "That must be hard. Not being able to eat food. Don't you miss it?"

He shook his head. Another lie but he was good at that. He'd had centuries of practice.

"So how ancient are you?"

He took her hand and placed it on his chest. "Do I feel ancient?"

He could hear her heartbeat increase, and her voice sounded husky. "I thought vampires were supposed to be pale and skinny."

"Some are."

Nick knew he was playing with fire but he couldn't seem to stop.

Daniella knew she was playing with fire but she couldn't seem to stop. She could feel the warmth of Nick's muscular chest beneath the thin cotton of his Henley T-shirt but she couldn't pull her hand away.

Would it be easier to cope with all this vampire stuff if she wasn't so darn sexually attracted to him? She wished she could go back to that first day in his bar before she'd fallen under his spell—*spell* being the operative word here. "You're sure you can't compel me?"

He nodded. "I tried really, *really* hard."

"And you're not compelling me right now?"

"Compelling you to do what?"

"Anything."

He squeezed her hand gently. "Why? What are you feeling?"

"More affectionate than I should with a vampire," she muttered, pulling her hand away.

"Have you heard of Waterloo?" he abruptly asked.

She nodded. "The song by Abba."

"No," he said curtly. "The Battle of Waterloo. Napoleon versus the Duke of Wellington."

"Yes, I've heard of it."

"I fought in it."

Her eyes widened. "Really?"

"Fought and died. To be more precise, I fought and was mortally wounded, on the verge of death. Then I was turned."

"Turned into a vampire?"

He nodded.

"Did it hurt?" she asked hesitantly.

"Being hit by a cannonball? Yes. It hurt like the hounds of hell had devoured me."

She gulped. "And being turned? Did that hurt?"

"I was surrounded by corpses and the stench of blood when I heard this voice ask if I wanted to live. I thought she was a nurse or something."

"She?"

Nick nodded. "Her name was Magdalene Dolyn. Not that I knew it at the time. Or knew she was a vampire. She asked me if I wanted to live and I whispered yes." He paused to look at her pale face before saying, "You don't want to know the details."

She kind of did. Not because she was into bloody gore or anything. But because she wanted to better understand Nick, if that was possible. "Please tell me."

He paused as if he was going to refuse her request. Then he said, "She drained me of what little blood I had left."

"She bit your neck?"

Nick nodded. "Then she cut her own wrist with her fangs and put her wrist to my mouth. She had me drink her blood, replacing my blood with hers."

"Her vampire blood?"

"That's right."

"And that was it? That turned you into a vampire?"

"Yes, but the entire process is not an easy one. The transition period is hell."

She could tell by the look on Nick's face that he was not going to say more than that about the process. "Did she turn a lot of wounded men on the battlefield into vampires that day?"

"No. Only me."

"Why?"

"Because dealing with a fledgling vampire once you've turned them is a full-time job. Like I said before, it's complicated. There's a lot to learn. She taught me everything."

Daniella couldn't decide if it was a little twisted that she felt jealous of Magdalene. "Why did she pick you out of all the dead bodies that day?"

"*Nearly* dead," he reminded her. "If I'd died it would have been too late. You can't turn a dead human into a vampire."

"Did you ever ask her why she picked you?"

His sudden smile was wolfish yet charming. "She'd only say that she thought I was very handsome. She liked the look of my face."

So Nick looked sexy even with a cannonball shot through his body. Why was she not surprised?

Daniella redirected her questioning slightly. She'd

heard enough about Magdalene for now. She didn't want to hear any details about what exactly she'd taught him.

"So you were alive during the Regency period? What was that like? I love reading Regency romances," she confessed. "Jane Austen, Georgette Heyer, Amanda Quick."

"I don't read them."

"You don't have to read them. *You* were there. The regent was known as the Prince of Pleasure."

"A nickname of mine also," Nick said with a slow grin.

Daniella's imagination went wild with that bit of information. The rarity of Nick grinning at her again also had a huge impact. She could easily imagine him as a rake or a rogue or both. Closing her eyes, she could envision him loosening his cravat, undoing her stays, lifting her petticoats . . . oh *yeah*.

She already knew how talented Nick was at the art of pleasuring a woman. Her head was filled with the image of him carrying her to a huge bed in some drafty castle or elegant manor house.

Or maybe he'd take her on his mahogany desk in his library the same way he'd lifted her onto her stainless-steel worktable in her shop. Only in her ongoing fantasy he continued his seduction, loosening the fastening of his ultra-tight Regency buff breeches and freeing his manhood before sliding into her slick vagina. No, her slick womanly passage that tightened around him with each powerful thrust.

The kitchen timer going off abruptly brought her back from her fantasy. She could feel her body responding to the seductive images of her fertile imagination. If her response was this powerful without him being able to compel her, she was afraid to think what it would be like if he could intensify her urges and make them reality.

Hell, the cupcakes could burn. She needed to kiss him. Just one kiss. She deserved it after the day she'd had. Just one kiss.

She pulled him to her. She could see the surprise on his face and in those sexy gray eyes of his. Then she closed her eyes and parted her lips. Lips that she pressed to his.

Despite being startled, Nick responded quickly and intensely. Tongue-to-tongue, he welcomed her and beckoned her to further intimacy. Their kiss was raw and elemental. He quickly took control, doing things to her that made her want to beg him for more.

He gave her more. He cupped the back of her head with one hand while sliding his other hand down to cup her bottom and squeeze. His touch was hungry and desperate. She could feel his arousal against her. He clearly wanted her as much as she wanted him.

The piercing wail of the smoke detector above them made her ears ring and was the only thing that could make her step away from him. She rushed to the kitchen and the oven, but there was no saving the crispy cupcakes. She turned on the vent fan over the stove to get the smoke out.

She welcomed the baking disaster as a distraction. Otherwise she could be having sex with a vampire right now. Was that even possible?

It had certainly felt possible. In fact, it had felt downright probable.

Okay, the truth was that it had felt inevitable, out-of-this-world meant-to-be kind of stuff. She was talking fireworks and exploding stars with the tantalizing promise of the best orgasm *ever*.

Instead piercing alarms had gone off over her head. It was fate's way of telling her to step away from the sexy vampire before she did something she'd regret.

Daniella tossed the blackened cupcakes into the trash, which was where she should be dumping her naughty thoughts about Nick as well.

If only it was that easy.

"So how are we going to handle this bodyguard stuff?" she said, rather proud of how matter-of-fact her voice sounded considering the R-rated thoughts recently racing through her mind.

"You just go to bed like you usually would," he said.

"And forget there's a vampire in my living room?"

"That would be good."

"That would be impossible," she said. "You must have a plan."

"Of course I have a plan."

"Okay." She waited. Nothing but silence. "So what is it and why are you so reluctant to tell me about it? It's because I'm not going to like it, right?"

"No, not right. You go to bed in your bedroom and I stay here in the living room," he said before adding, "You keep your door open."

"In your dreams."

"Partially open."

"Why? So you can spy on me?"

"So I can detect the scent of a vampire before he enters your bedroom through a window," he said,

Daniella sank into a dining room chair before reaching for her laptap on the table.

"What are you doing?" he said.

"Googling. I thought I heard someplace that vampires can only go where they are invited. I realize I invited you and Pat and Bruce into my apartment. But I don't intend to invite any other vampires in," she said, before adding, "No offense."

"None taken."

"Here, look." She pointed to the screen of her laptop. "It says right here that one of the old folklore legends is that a vampire has to be invited across a threshold to enter a house." She paused to look at Nick. "Is it true and does an apartment count?"

"Yes to both questions. But a window isn't a threshold per se. It's a gray area for some clans."

"So what am I supposed to do?"

"You're supposed to let me protect you," he said.

"For how long?"

"For as long as needed."

"I can't deal with that," she said, trying not to hyperventilate. "I can only deal with one night at a time."

"Fine. We'll start out with that."

"Do vampires leave the toilet seat up?" She had no idea where that came from, but the words tumbled out of her mouth before she could stop them. "Never mind, I don't want to know. But I do not want to be falling into my john in the middle of the night."

"Understood." His lips lifted just a smidge in what she could only describe as a wry smile.

"I'm serious."

He nodded solemnly. "I know you are."

"I'm not ready for bed yet." She plunked herself onto the couch. The truth was, she wasn't ready to leave herself vulnerable with him so nearby. She needed to rebuild her resistance, brick by brick.

"Okay," he said. "What do you normally do when you can't sleep?"

She hadn't said she couldn't sleep, exactly, but she

didn't correct him. Instead she said, "I'd watch a DVD of a movie."

"Go ahead and do that then."

Daniella shook her head. "You wouldn't be able to cope with my choice of movie."

He lifted a dark eyebrow. "And why is that?"

"Because they are all chick flicks." She pointed to the slight grimace that crossed his face. "I saw that."

"You saw nothing."

His words aggravated her. So did the way he said them, as if she were a silly child. "Don't tell me what I saw. I saw you move at freaky fast speed, I saw your bloody wound heal at the speed of light, and yes, I just saw you make a face at chick flicks. Don't even bother denying it."

"I don't watch many movies."

"You will if you stay here," she said. She did experience a brief pang of guilt at being an unwelcoming hostess. After all, he was only acting in her best interest. Or so he said.

Nick was trying to protect her from evil banker vampires. She should be grateful. That could happen, but emotionally she wasn't there yet.

"I also watch shows on the Food Network," she added for good measure.

"I've experienced worse."

His words made her curious about his past. "What's it like?"

"Being a vampire?"

She nodded.

"It's no piece of cupcake. Not that I've ever had a cupcake."

"Never?" This news shocked her nearly as much

as the fact that he had fangs. "I can't imagine that." She got up and retrieved her laptop before returning to the couch.

"What are you doing now?"

"Googling the history of cupcakes." She paused to read what was on the screen. "You're right. They don't think cupcakes were around until perhaps the 1820s. That's really close to your time, though."

"Close but no cigar." Seeing her look, he added, "Do not ask me what that means as I have no idea."

"Do you want me to Google it for you?"

"No." He sat on the couch beside her.

"What else can you tell me about your time? Did you have parents? Well, obviously you must have had parents. You were human once, right?"

He studied her closely for a moment before slowly saying, "I had parents. I was adopted." He seemed to be eyeing her expectantly.

She was hesitant to confess that she, too, was adopted. Some instinct inside her warned her to wait.

Keeping the focus on him, she said, "What were your adoptive parents like?"

"They were good people."

That was rather vague in her opinion. "Was your father in the army?"

"No."

"What did he do for a living?"

"He ran his estate. Marchmore in Gloucestershire."

For the first time, she detected a hint of an English accent in his voice. "Was he a duke or an earl or something?"

"Or something."

"Was he a vampire?"

"No." He sounded outraged by her question. "I

told you, I had no idea about vampires until I was mortally wounded on the battlefield at Waterloo."

"Right." She looked at his face. That much of his story she believed. "You really were adopted by British royalty?"

"It's not as if the Prince of Wales adopted me, although he was rumored to have several illegitimate children."

"I didn't know that."

"You can Google it if you don't believe me," he said.

"No, I do believe you." She closed her laptop and turned to face him. "So you were an aristocrat?"

He nodded.

"Did you always know you were adopted?"

A cryptic look crossed his face . . . part pain, part something else. "No."

It was that expression and the conflict in his stormy eyes that made her say, "I'm adopted, too."

He leaned forward. "You are?"

She nodded.

He repeated her earlier question back to her. "Did you always know you were adopted?"

"Yes."

"You never mentioned it to me before."

"You never mentioned you were a vampire before."

"You know the reason for that. Is there a reason you keep the fact that you're adopted a secret?"

"I don't keep it a secret."

"What do you know about your birth mother?" he asked.

"She died when I was born. She was a cousin of my mom's." Daniella yawned. "I'm sorry. It's just been a long day, you know?"

Nick nodded. "You should go to bed."

She shook her head. "I'm not ready yet."

"Then at least lie down here on the couch." He moved to a nearby chair.

She reached for the remote before stacking the throw pillows in the corner of the couch and getting horizontal. A moment later, the opening credits for the movie *The Proposal* filled the screen.

Two hours later, or one hour and forty-eight minutes to be precise, Nick watched the end credits roll for the movie. Daniella had been right. Chick flicks weren't his cup of tea, although he did enjoy the lead actress's nude scene when she ran into the hero.

Perhaps something like that would happen while he protected Daniella.

She'd fallen asleep on the couch about twenty minutes ago. The truth was that he'd spent more time watching her than he had the end of the movie. She was curled on her side, her hand tucked under her cheek, a strand of her hair sliding down over her face.

Reaching out, he smoothed the silky strand away before yanking his hand back as if burned.

Shit, he was getting too emotional about all this. About *her*.

Hell, yes, the truth was that he'd kept his eyes on her instead of the flat-screen TV—but the truth also was that he'd lied to her about being adopted. It had been a deliberate move on his part. He didn't expect the slight pang of guilt as he got out his smartphone and he texted the info about her birth mother to Neville on a secure vamp account.

He'd done what he'd done to protect his clan. Yet now his job was also to protect Daniella.

He set the smartphone aside and reached for a soft throw from the arm of the couch. Tucking it around Daniella, he wondered if he should carry her to bed. Would it freak her more to find herself in her bedroom or still on the couch?

Why did he care how freaked she got?

Because a calmer Daniella meant a more obedient Daniella, and that would make his bodyguarding duties easier. If she'd been fifty years older and not had this hold over him, that would also have made his duties easier.

Vampires and humans having sex never worked out well. In fact, it often resulted in dangerous if not deadly results. Vampires experienced everything with heightened senses, including desire. Nick wanted her more than he wanted blood, and that was saying something. What it said was that he was in deep shit here.

Chapter Fifteen

Six days later, the day before Halloween, Daniella was in her cupcake shop mixing, baking, and frosting before daybreak as usual.

What wasn't usual was that she had a vampire living with her. She'd survived six long days and nights with Nick in close quarters. She'd been careful not to kiss him again. He'd shown similar restraint. But the sexual tension between them continued to grow despite the fact that neither one of them acted on it . . . or even talked about it.

Daniella had ditched the romantic comedies and instead chosen the Food Network for late night viewing. After falling asleep that first night on the couch, she'd stuck to her bedroom, going into her bathroom to change into a pair of cotton flannel pajamas that weren't at all sexy. She continued to have sex-ridden Regency dreams every night and may even have moaned in her sleep although she sure hoped not. If he heard her, maybe Nick thought she was having a vampire nightmare instead of a vampire wet dream.

"I think it's so awesome that your man can't stand to be away from you for a minute," Xandra said as she frosted a batch of mocha latte cupcakes.

He's not a man, he's a vampire, was Daniella's first thought. A Regency vampire with the nickname *Prince of Pleasure.*

He even looked like a Regency rake at the moment. His dark hair tumbled over his forehead with Byronesque flair. All he needed was a cravat. Or to walk out of a pool the way Colin Firth did as Mr. Darcy in the BBC production of *Pride and Prejudice* all wet and sexy.

Daniella had actually seen Nick wet and sexy in the shower. Well, not actually *in* the shower but just out of it, with a towel hanging low on his hips—very low and just barely hanging on as she'd just barely hung on to the door frame when he'd emerged from her bathroom with droplets of water meandering down his bare muscular chest.

No one, human or vampire, had the right to look that good.

She vigorously beat the batter for the next batch of cupcakes, a new maple bacon spice version. Business had continued to be brisk all week, with several foodie blogs listing their approval of her cupcakes. A reporter with the local ABC affiliate had emailed her to set up an appointment to interview her next week. She had no idea how she would explain her vampire boyfriend's appearance at her side.

Not that Nick was her boyfriend. She shouldn't think of him that way. He was her vampire bodyguard, and that was all.

Yeah, like that sounded any better.

She glanced over at him, where he sat with his

smartphone in his hand, texting away, taking care of business. He certainly had adapted to modern technology well. He'd adapted to everything well, including sleeping on her couch and using her shower.

"I'm totally stoked about Halloween," Xandra was saying. "I can't wait to see Lois's fangs. I know mine are going to be better."

"I don't know. I think Lois is going to be a strong contender," Daniella said. What she couldn't say was that Lois was a vampire. When she'd pressed, Nick had admitted as much. Not that Lois had actually talked to her about it herself or that Daniella had brought the topic up when the two of them were alone—or rather alone with Nick—at Heavenly Cupcakes. Daniella still had a hard time seeing the maternal-looking Lois as a vampire.

"When are you going to put on your costume?" Xandra asked.

"When we're done baking."

"Is Nick going to come in costume, too?"

"I don't think so," Daniella said. "He's not a big fan of the holiday."

"Trashy and tasteless" had been his exact words. Oh, and "insulting," too. He particularly didn't like the way vampires were portrayed with stupid black capes and slicked-back hair like amateur magicians in a carnie show.

"That's a shame," Xandra said. "He would look good as a pirate like Jack Sparrow. Minus the eye shadow."

"Definitely minus the eye shadow," Daniella agreed. While she could picture Nick as a pirate, she couldn't imagine him in makeup. Besides, his eyes were expressive and captivating enough as they were.

And those dark, thick eyelashes of his . . . no, Nick definitely didn't need anything to make him appear sexier.

He looked up and caught her staring at him. "Everything okay?" he said.

Not really, but what could she say? *No, nothing is okay? My life is a mess and so am I? Banker vampires are after me and I don't have time for any of this? I especially don't have time to lust after a hottie vampire.* There was no question about that.

Since she couldn't say any of that, she smiled politely and said, "My dad comes home tomorrow."

It was a friendly reminder that there was no way she could explain Nick's presence in her apartment once her father got back.

Once the store opened and Xandra was busy dealing with the morning rush of customers, Daniella pulled Nick aside in the back work area.

"You can't still be living with me when my dad returns," she reminded him. Choosing her words carefully, she added, "Can't you and the . . . others . . . call some kind of truce or something?"

"Possibly or something," Nick said. "I'm going to have Bruce watch you for half an hour while I go work on some things. Don't leave the shop, don't invite anyone in, and try to stay out of trouble."

"Never fear, I am here," Bruce announced with a grand flourish as he entered the work area. "Wow, this is quite a production. A cupcake production zone. I'm impressed."

"How good are you with a pastry bag?" Daniella asked him.

Bruce grinned. "Let's find out. After all, I'm a fellow artist. Clowning is an art form, too."

"Don't get distracted," Nick warned Bruce. "I won't be long."

"Long time, no see," Neville greeted Nick as he entered the Vamp Cave.

"I can't believe it's been six days and you still haven't found anything about Daniella's birth mother," Nick growled.

"First off, her mother had twelve cousins, eleven of them females. Six had babies the year that Daniella was born. That's all I discovered before the Gold Coast aka the GC gang crashed our computer system."

"Why can't you use another computer system? It's not like Vamptown has the only gateway to the Internet in the city."

"We're being watched."

"And hacked," Nick said."

"If we leave to use a computer or smartphone outside of Vamptown it definitely will not be secure."

"So it didn't matter that Daniella told me her birth mother's name two days ago. Because you haven't been able to follow up on that, is that right?"

Neville nodded before adding, "But it does mean she trusts you enough to finally share her birth mother's name with you. You never said how you managed that."

"And I don't intend to," Nick said. That stubborn sliver of guilt about telling Daniella he was adopted remained with him, and it aggravated the hell out of him. He hadn't experienced guilt since his early days as a vampire when he'd annihilated those who'd wronged him. After being turned, he'd stayed near the battlefields with Magdalene, who taught him the way of vampires and how to make a quick kill. He hadn't turned anyone but had continued fighting Napoleon's Imperial Guards as retribution for all the good men in his regiment who'd been killed. He'd feasted on a lot of French blood.

But that wasn't how he'd gained his reputation for being ruthless. That had come later . . .

He shoved the memories away. Regret and remorse were luxuries he couldn't afford. As he'd told Pat, he didn't do regret. He didn't think he did guilt, either, but that might not be the case after all where Daniella was concerned.

Daniella's instincts had warned her not to confide in him immediately. He recognized that fact. So he hadn't pressed her but instead had subtly done everything he could to make her believe she could trust him.

"You're sure the Gold Coast vamps aren't able to access the information you'd been researching about Daniella?"

"I'm sure," Neville said. "But our system still isn't up to par. Of course, neither is theirs considering the fact that I crashed their computer systems, too, and messed up their stock bids, day trades, and buy orders."

"Is this what modern vampire warfare has come to?" Pat said as he entered the room. "You hack my computer. I hack yours. What happened to 'you mess with me and I decapitate you'?"

"That may still come to pass," Nick said. "Tomorrow is Halloween."

"That sucks," Neville said.

"It does suck," Pat agreed. "There are additional security issues because of it."

"Not to mention the fact that Daniella's dad is set to return from his cruise tomorrow morning," Nick said.

"I don't imagine he's going to be a happy camper when he discovers you shacking up with his only daughter," Pat said.

"I am not shacking up with her. I'm protecting her."

"From rival vampires. Not something you can tell him, Nick."

"I realize that. We have to crack this mystery about her background." His voice reflected his frustration with the situation. He hoped it didn't reflect his sexual frustration as well. "I'm sure it has something to do with her birth mother."

"I'm doing the best I can," Neville said.

"Do better. And do it faster," Nick growled.

"Is the bodyguard job harder than you thought?" Pat pulled Nick aside to ask as Neville focused all his attention on the computer.

"That's one way of putting it."

"I can step in if you'd prefer."

"I'd prefer that we get this entire situation rectified."

"And how do you propose to rectify the situation with Daniella?" Pat asked. "You know that sex between a vamp and a human—"

"Is a disaster. I know."

"Yet you find her hard to resist," Pat said.

Again with the "hard." Glancing at the surveillance screens, Nick saw Daniella showing Bruce how to ice cupcakes. Hardly a sexy scene. Yet the mere sight of her was enough to arouse Nick.

"You're sure the Gold Coast clan didn't hack into our surveillance camera system?" Nick asked Neville.

"I've checked it numerous times."

"Check it again," Nick ordered.

The idea that Miles was seeing the same scene with Daniella that Nick was viewing was enough to get his vamp blood boiling.

Pat could sense Nick's anger. "You can't afford to lose control. You are exposed to the human customers at the cupcake shop. They can't see you with your eyes glowing and your fangs exposed."

"I know that."

"Has Daniella seen you that way?"

"No."

"Maybe she should," Pat said thoughtfully.

"Why?"

"To instill more fear into her. I'm not sure she fully realizes the danger of this situation."

"I've told her . . ."

"Showing her may be more effective. Or are you afraid she'll find you disgusting? Has she talked to you about you being a vampire?"

"She asks questions," Nick said. "A lot of questions. The other night she wanted to know why a vampire who can't eat would own the All Nighter Bar and Grill."

"What did you tell her?" Pat asked.

"That our customers are vampires. No fangs, no service."

"She hasn't been in the bar since that first day, has she?"

"No. And I plan on keeping it that way."

"Yes, but does *she* plan on keeping it that way?"

"The inability to compel her does make life more difficult," Nick acknowledged. "But I expected that."

"Did you also expect to be so sexually attracted to her?"

"She's a good-looking woman."

"She's not that good looking," Pat said.

Nick glared at him.

Pat laughed softly. "Look at you, all protective."

"My job is to protect her," Nick said.

"As long as you don't forget your main job, which is to protect your clan," Pat said.

"You're really good at this," Daniella praised Bruce.

"It's all in the hands," Bruce said before adding candy corn atop the frosting of the cupcake he was decorating. "Steady hands." Looking up, he smiled at Nick. "Welcome back."

Nick didn't smile back. "Thanks for taking over for a few minutes," he said curtly.

"No problem."

When he left, Daniella asked, "Is something wrong?"

He shrugged, despite knowing how much that move aggravated her. But she didn't have time to call him on it because she had two special orders to finish today.

So she concentrated on the batch of mini Thriller Killer Chocolate cupcakes for a *True Blood* fan party. They wanted the series name written out with one letter on individual cupcakes; the rest were supposed to have white fondant fangs with dripping blood.

It was hard not to imagine Nick and his fangs while she was creating her decorating magic. She never used to think there was anything the least bit sexy about vampires and blood and fangs. Now she wasn't so sure. There was definitely something sexy about Nick. She found a number of things sexy about Nick. Granted, fangs would not be her first choice, which got her thinking . . . what would be her first choice?

His body? His fiercely sensual mouth? His long lean fingers?

Did it make her shallow if she picked his body? Because he truly did have an awesome body. Not overly muscular like someone who hung out at a gym and was totally self-centered. No, his body was more . . . hmmm, she couldn't find the words and in trying to do so managed to mangle the fangs on the cupcake.

Nick glanced over at her and shook his head in disgust.

"This wasn't my idea," she said defensively. "The client picked the design."

Xandra joined them for a moment. "I posted on our Facebook page that anyone who comes in a costume between noon and one in the afternoon today and says the secret code word gets four cupcakes for the price of three."

Daniella checked the time and set down her pastry bag filled with chocolate frosting. "I'd better go get changed into my costume."

Nick accompanied her up to her apartment. He was not a happy camper or, in his case, a happy vampire. "You didn't clear that costume thing with me first."

"I fail to see why you need to know what my costume will be."

"I'm not talking about that. I'm talking about the post on the shop's Facebook page. That's a huge security risk."

"It's only for an hour."

"It takes less than a second for a vampire to grab you and be gone."

She gulped. "The offer is already out there. I can't take it back now." Her frustration and fear mounted. "I'm trying to start a new business here. Do you have any idea how difficult that is in this economy? I do not have time to deal with feuding vampires right now. I really don't!"

"Are you going to cry?" he asked suspiciously. "You're not going to cry, are you?"

"I might," she growled. "Do you have a problem with that?"

He remained silent.

"This has not been easy for me. It's hitting me that I've opened my cupcake business in a neighborhood where no one eats. Do any humans live around here or are you all vampires?"

"There are some humans," he said.

"How many," she instantly demanded.

"Enough." He sounded crabby.

If anyone had reason to be crabby, it was her. She needed a hug and not from a sexy vampire. She missed her best friend Suz who'd been gone for the past week at a professional conference in Rome. Suz had called her a few times but the cell connections had always been bad and their conversations brief.

"You still haven't told me what kind of costume you're going to wear," Nick reminded her.

"You'll see soon enough." She closed her bedroom door in his face. He immediately opened it a crack. "No peeking," she ordered him. "You can't see around corners, right?"

"Right."

She didn't take long to get out of her jeans and Heavenly Cupcakes T-shirt, but getting her costume on took some doing. The dress was a replica of the

gown worn by Billie Burke as Glinda the Good
Witch of the North in the film version of *The Wizard
of Oz*. The tulle underskirt nearly poked Daniella's
eye out as she tugged it over her head. Maybe she
should have stepped into it instead. Too late now.
She slid her arms into it and pulled the costume on.
Try as she could, she was not able to reach around to
zip it up in the back.

"What was that noise?" Nick demanded.

"That was me growling in frustration," she said
as she yanked the door open. "I could use some help
here." She turned her back to him. "Please zip me
up." She turned her head to look at him over her
satin-covered shoulder. "You know how to use zip-
pers, right?" Her eyes lowered to the placket of his
jeans. "Of course you do. Never mind." She turned
to face away from him. "Stupid question."

"It's been a while since I've helped a woman get
dressed," he murmured, his breath warming the nape
of her neck.

"You're more used to undressing them, right?"

"Perhaps." He seductively trailed one finger down
her spine.

Daniella kept her gaze downward, focusing on
the gorgeous sandy pink color of the satin bodice of
her gown. The full skirt was embellished with
crystal-like stars and rhinestones to match the star
wand she'd left in the bedroom. Focusing on her attire should have kept her and her hormones from
flying out of control. It didn't.

"It's a beautiful dress," he said softly.

"A friend of mine used to be a costume designer
for the Steppenwolf Theatre here in Chicago. She
made it for me."

He made no verbal reply. Instead he skimmed his

finger back up her spine, pausing over the delicate ridge of each vertebra to add a delicately erotic caress with the pad of his thumb. She bit her lip to refrain from moaning aloud in pleasure. How could such a simple touch make her go weak at the knees and damp with desire?

Nick moved closer and used his other hand to lift her hair out of his way. His breath was warm against her nape. Was he going to sink his fangs into her? She should step away but couldn't break the contact. He placed a string of kisses starting at the back of her neck and moving around to the side until his lips pressed against her pulse. Once there, his tongue darted out to lick her skin.

His hand shifted from her back to the drooping bodice of her dress, where he cupped her breast in the palm of his hand. The satin material provided little protection and instead amplified the pleasure of his caresses. Her nipples tightened, and the rest of her melted.

Having a vampire this close to her carotid artery should make a girl nervous at the very least, and downright freaked-out hysterical at the worst. Instead she welcomed his touch, tilting her head to the side to allow him better access. She tried to abandon her hold on her dress's bodice for the same reason but instead inadvertently tangled her hand with his.

To her surprise, he lifted her hand to his mouth. His tongue darted out to tease the ultra-sensitive web between her fingers. The sexual heat of his touch seared her.

She leaned her head back against his shoulder. His body was pressed against hers, and she could feel his arousal.

"You . . . I . . . ," she whispered with husky incoherence.

A mere two words, yet they were enough to shatter the spell between them.

Chapter Sixteen

Nick released her hand and shifted both of his hands to do up her zipper with efficient haste before quickly stepping away.

Actually he moved clear to the other side of the living room.

Daniella stood there bereft, momentarily unable to speak, move, or think. She didn't even know what she'd been trying to say when she'd uttered those two words. A protest, or a plea for more?

"We need to get back downstairs," Nick said curtly.

She nodded her agreement and gathered her scattered wits together.

Getting down the stairs was a little tricky with her costume but it was nothing compared to trying to cope with what had just happened with Nick. Or hadn't happened. Or had almost happened. Or all of the above.

The moment Daniella walked into the shop, Xandra started playing "Defying Gravity" from *Wicked*. "Defying Logic and Caution" was more in tune with

Daniella's mood, but because she'd told Xandra about her costume, the song selection was appropriate.

Lois joined Xandra behind the counter. "You look lovely," she told Daniella. "You look nice, too," she told Xandra, who'd exited the shop's employee bathroom in Goth attire complete with spiky dog collar around her neck before playing the music.

"You didn't enter in a bubble," Xandra said. "That would have been sweet. Did I tell you I've seen *Wicked* six times?"

"You may have mentioned it," Daniella said with a smile.

"I love its message. It never fails to get me totally stoked. Have you seen it?" Xandra asked Lois.

"No."

Xandra eyed Lois's outfit of a tweed skirt and white cotton blouse with a discreet scarf tied around her neck. "Did you forget to put on a costume?"

"Can't you tell who I am?" Lois countered.

Xandra shook her head.

"What about you?" Lois asked Daniella.

"Well, uh, you look a little like Mrs. Cunningham from the classic TV show *Happy Days*," Daniella said.

Lois nodded happily. "That's what I was aiming for. I've been told I look like her."

"Okay, everyone. It's noon," Xandra said.

Daniella viewed the three customers who were already waiting at the counter. "Nice music," the first person in line, dressed as a cowgirl in jeans and a checked shirt, said. "Great costumes, too. I could tell you were Mrs. C," the woman told Lois. "I'll have a Whipped Scream Delight, a Devil's Feud, plus a Black Magic Banana. And a Thriller Killer Chocolate for my free cupcake."

Eyeing Nick's frowning face as the song's finale came, Daniella decided that like Elphaba from *Wicked,* she was not going to let anyone bring her down. Including vampires.

Nick was not amused. He stood by Heavenly Cupcake's front door to check each person as they walked in to verify for himself that they were human. He should have spent their time upstairs ordering Daniella to refrain from having any more of these spontaneous marketing events. No flash mobs, no costumes, and no open invitations on social media sites.

Yes, that's definitely what he should have been doing instead of fondling her back and her breasts.

This all had to be coming to a head soon. His arousal sure was. But also the situation.

He lost count of how many humans came through the door in the next fifty-five minutes. They all passed the sniff test, although several could have used a shower. His vamp's heightened sense of smell was definitely getting a workout.

A familiar and unwelcome scent caught all his attention as Nick recognized vampire Andy's smell.

Grabbing hold of him before he could enter the shop, Nick told the few remaining in line, "We're out of cupcakes. Sorry."

The humans started grumbling. He had to disperse them. "Come back tomorrow."

"You're closed tomorrow," someone said.

Nick quickly went down the line of ten remaining customers, confirming all were human and that none had been compelled by Andy. Humans had a certain scent while being compelled. Once that was done, Nick opened the door and allowed them into the shop before closing it again. It was one o'clock, so the special offer was done anyway.

Now he could focus his entire attention on Andy. Nick held the vamp's arm in a bone-crunching grip. "I thought I told you not to show your face around here again," he said with flinty menace.

"I'm not showing my face," Andy said, his voice muffled by the mask he wore. "I'm wearing a George W. Bush mask so my face doesn't show."

"I'm not amused," Nick said. "This is your final warning. Do not enter our territory again."

"My sire wants you to know that he considers the truce broken by your hostile actions of hacking our computer system."

"Your boss broke the truce when he first sent you here. And again by having you come to the flash mob. If I find out that you were behind the wheel of that Hummer that tried to mow Daniella down, then you will wish for a death by decapitation."

"I wasn't trying to kill her. That Hummer is hard to drive. Besides, I'm not afraid of you," Andy said, despite his trembling voice. "You haven't killed any vamps or humans in over a century. Your reputation is based on stuff that happened ages ago."

"I haven't killed any vamps or humans *that you know about*," Nick said. "Unlike your boss, I don't brag about my work."

"You're lying."

Nick tightened his hold. "Am I?" He would have stared him down as well but Andy's mask was in his way, so Nick yanked it off.

Andy automatically put his arm up to block his face from the sun before lowering it to defiantly stare back. "You aren't the only ones who can take the sunshine," he said. "We can do that now, too.

You no longer have any advantage over us." A moment later he winced and then started to sizzle. Yelping, he leapt to some nearby shade beneath a small tree that had lost all its autumn leaves. Realizing his mistake, Andy rushed a bit farther down the block.

"Looks like your sunblock doesn't work as well as you thought it did," Nick noted.

"My sire knows as much about the cupcake maker as you do," Andy shouted as he huddled beneath the dental clinic's awning.

"Having trouble out here?" Doc Boomer asked. He'd gotten his nickname from his booming voice and his overwhelming physical appearance. He was a mountain to Andy's skinny aspen. "Shall I escort this specimen out of the area?"

Nick nodded, keeping one eye fixed on Daniella in the shop. "But be discreet." There were no humans on the street at the moment, but there would be in a second.

"Understood. I do believe he needs some dental work." Doc Boomer hauled Andy out of the shade and disappeared with him.

The instant Nick returned to the shop, Daniella pulled him back into the relative seclusion of the work area. "What was that all about?"

"I'll tell you later."

"You'd better," she warned him before flouncing off. Or maybe she stomped off and it was just her pink fluffy costume that made it seem like she'd flounced. Her attire reminded him of women in his own time.

What if he'd met her back then, when he'd been a decorated war hero, before he'd been turned? Would their relationship be as stormy if he was human? It definitely wouldn't be as dangerous, that's for damn sure.

Caressing her as he had in her apartment earlier was a risky move on his part. He'd restrained himself for days. If called upon, he could even list the number of hours he'd spent with her. Hell, he could list the minutes. And the touches. They'd mostly been accidental. A brush of his hand against hers as she reached for the remote control.

Then today she'd turned her back to him and asked for his help. He'd been unable to resist.

But he had to resist . . . or risk her death.

Daniella knew that Nick had been involved in vampire business. She might not know the details, but she knew that much.

She couldn't dwell on it because she had to focus on taking new special orders. Of course, it was too late for Halloween orders because the holiday was tomorrow. But she had several special orders for as far out as Christmas.

Business was so brisk that they ran out of cupcakes and had to close early. All the special orders had been picked up earlier, including the *True Blood* party cupcakes. The hostess was pleased with the results even if Nick wasn't.

"Let's call it a day," Daniella said. Things had gotten so hectic that she hadn't even had a chance to change out of her Glinda dress, which was not designed for easy movement. She'd already almost knocked Xandra off her feet several times and had nearly poked her own eye out with the star wand she waved. Well, she'd waved it for the first few minutes. After the eye incident, she'd stored it safely out of the way.

"Aren't you forgetting something?" Xandra said. At Daniella's blank look, she added, "The fang contest." She showed her teeth and her online purchased fangs before turning to Lois. "Now let's see yours."

Lois turned her back to them before facing them again, fangs bared.

"Those are totally legit," Xandra said, clearly impressed.

"Yes, they are," Lois modestly said before turning away for a moment.

"Let's call it a tie," Daniella said.

"No, Lois wins," Xandra said. She hugged Lois. "Congratulations."

Once Xandra was departed, Daniella was left alone with Lois and Nick.

Daniella turned to face Lois and said, "So I'm guessing Happy Times Dental Clinic also has the policy of no fangs, no service?"

"We used to take some human walk-ins," Lois said. "But it got too . . . complicated. They'd bleed and we'd be tempted."

"I thought you were just the receptionist so you wouldn't be in the room with the patients."

"I help out where I can."

"Like working here," Daniella said. "I'll bet Nick came up with that idea."

"Actually I was against it at first, if you recall," Nick said.

"Because you knew that your saying that would make me want to hire her all the more," Daniella said. "You saw the advantage. Lois could spy on me and report back to you."

"That may have been the case in the beginning," Lois said. "But once the surveillance cameras were installed—"

"Wait," Daniella interrupted Lois. "What cameras?"

"They're all over Vamptown. Didn't you tell her that, Nick?"

"No," he said curtly.

"You should have," Lois said.

"Damn right, you should have." Daniella was furious. She felt violated. "So in addition to being a vampire, you are also a Peeping Tom pervert." Looking around, she demanded, "So where are they?" She yanked open the bathroom door. "Are they in here, too?"

"Calm down." Nick was using his soothing voice, although it did have a crabby edge to it. "There are no cameras in any bathrooms."

"What about my bedroom?" Daniella said.

"Not there, either."

"But here in this room? And in the rest of my shop?"

Nick nodded. "And in the rest of your apartment as well. It's for your own safety."

"I am so sick of this!"

"You poor dear." Lois patted Daniella's shoulder.

"If you have cameras everywhere, why can't you find the person driving that Hummer that almost hit me?" Daniella challenged Nick.

"He was taken care of."

Nick's words sounded ominous. Her squeamish self didn't want to hear the details. Maybe they just put the driver in vampire jail or something.

She'd checked her Vespa and it wasn't damaged. She wasn't hurt, and Nick's injury had healed. What if they planned on chopping the vampire driver's head off? Or frying him? She didn't want to be responsible for a vampire's death. "Maybe it was just an accident . . ."

"Doesn't matter," Nick said.

"Of course it matters."

"He was trespassing on our land."

"Actually the alley belongs to . . ." She stopped when she saw Nick's flinty yet fiery glare. "Never mind."

"If you don't need me any longer, I'll let you two continue this conversation alone," Lois said.

Daniella prepared the shop for closing. A quick glance out the front window let her know that the sun was setting. Not that she could see it with the surrounding buildings, but that special buildup in the sky had a certain glow. Of course, it could just be the streetlights going on.

Daniella had been consumed with her shop's grand opening and, more recently, coping with her vampire bodyguard. So she hadn't really been paying much attention to the weather, which fluctuated between Indian summer and chilly fall this time of year. Soon it would be November. The time had gone by so quickly.

She only met Nick earlier this month yet it felt as if it had been ages ago that she'd walked into his bar. She'd never dreamed she'd be held captive in her own building. Well, her father's building to be exact. And it wasn't as if she was bound and gagged or anything. But her independence had been compromised. The discovery that cameras were following her every move did not improve her mood. Because now her privacy had also been compromised.

After she set the security alarm, Nick held the door open for her. He always did things like that.

Courteous things. And then he went and chopped the head off some vampire.

Okay, so she didn't know for sure he'd actually done that, but she wouldn't put it past him.

She remained silent until they entered her apartment. Then her temper blew. "I want to know exactly how long you have been spying on me."

"It wasn't spying."

"The exact date." She was scrambling to remember what she and Suz had talked about in those early days before the opening. She was sure they'd talked about Nick. "Before my grand opening?"

"I believe so."

"You *believe* so? I can't even tell you how upset I am. I am so mad at you!"

"I can tell," he said. "Want me to unzip your dress for you?"

"No, I don't want you to, but I don't have a choice. I can't get it off myself without ripping it or dislocating a shoulder. But no extracurricular activities this time. You keep your hands on the zipper and not on me."

He obeyed her command for the most part although his fingers did brush against skin. "Sorry," he murmured.

"Are you? I doubt that." Gathering the drooping bodice, she headed for her bedroom, where she grabbed jeans and a white shirt and then kept going to the bathroom where she slammed the door shut.

Then she looked around the medicine cabinet, the mirror above the sink, searching for a camera.

"It's not in there," Nick called out, startling her.

"What isn't?"

"A camera. I already told you that."

"You've told me a lot of things, not all of them true."

She kept searching until she'd convinced herself that there was no camera or any kind of a nannycam device. Only then did she remove her costume and place it on the hanger on the hook at the back of the door. The dress was really beautiful. It deserved a better occasion than it got.

Daniella quickly donned her jeans and shirt. She'd forgotten to wear the tiara with the costume, distracted as she was by Nick's earlier exploration of her spine. The memory of his caresses was seared into her brain.

Lowering the lid on the toilet, she sat down and tried to regain her perspective and defuse her anger. Instead she was distracted by the peeling pale pink nail polish on her toes.

This was something she could rectify. Reaching over her shoulder, she grabbed the plastic bottle of nail polish remover and a bunch of toilet paper. She was out of cotton balls. So sue her.

She set to work then, when she was done with that job, she spent another five minutes trying to decide between O • P • I's nail polish colors Diva of Geneva hot pink and From A to Zurich deep raspberry. In the end, she selected the Diva color. Propping her foot on the edge of her tub, she started brushing the polish on.

This felt normal. She hadn't felt normal since Nick had saved her life. She worked slowly and carefully and then waited another ten minutes until the polish was dry for sure.

Admiring her diva-ish toenails, she tidied up and took a deep breath before reluctantly abandoning the bathroom and walking in her bare feet into the living room.

Despite the sort-of-pedicure she'd given herself, her feet still ached from being on them all day. The Cinderella-type flats she'd worn to go with her Halloween outfit hadn't helped matters any.

Beauty before comfort usually was not her philosophy because . . . well, because she wasn't beautiful.

Daniella plopped onto the couch and lifted her feet onto the pillows. Nick remained silent but he came and sat at the edge of the couch. She deliberately didn't leave him any room, so he had to lift her feet to sit. He tucked her feet onto his lap.

"I'm still mad at you," she warned him as he started slowly massaging the sole of her right foot.

"I know," he said. "But it feels good, right?"

Almost everything he did to her felt good. Except spying on her and lying about it.

She yanked her feet away.

Nick gently returned them to his lap.

"You're taking a big risk," she warned him. "I could kick you in your family jewels."

"You're too nice to do that."

"Am I?" She shifted her foot so that she was pressed against the placket of his dark jeans. She exerted just enough pressure to let him know she meant business.

The problem was, what kind of business. Retribution or seduction?

"Still think I'm too nice?" Her voice was silky as she rubbed her foot against him.

"Uh, I hate to interrupt," Cookie said from Daniella's laptop, which was on the coffee table aimed at the couch. "Did you forget you had our Skype session set up?"

She had.

"I opened the laptop for you," Nick said. "I remembered you saying that you moved your Saturday Skype session to tonight."

Daniella had been so consumed with admiring her Diva of Geneva painted toenails that she hadn't even noticed the presence of her slim laptop.

That's how bad off she was.

But Nick had known. Her glare at him warned that he'd better take that smirk off his face or he'd pay the price.

"You have company, obviously," Cookie said. "Do you want to introduce him?"

"This is Nick," Daniella said. "Nick, this is Cookie."

"You must be the mentor," Nick said to Cookie.

"And you must be the new boyfriend," Cookie replied. "Well, I can tell you two are busy, so let's shelf this session and we'll touch base next Saturday as usual. Unless Saturday nights no longer work for you, Daniella?"

"They work just fine," Daniella said firmly. "I'll see you then."

After disconnecting the videocam, Daniella snapped her laptop shut and turned to confront Nick. "What is it with you and video cameras?"

He shrugged.

She wanted to hit him but didn't. He knew his shrugs aggravated the hell out of her but he did it anyway.

"I was just trying to be helpful," he said.

"Sure you were. Well, let me tell you, buddy, I don't need that kind of help."

Nick lifted one dark eyebrow. "Buddy?"

"It's not a term of endearment and it doesn't mean we are BFF. Best Friends Forever."

"Right. I'll be sure to note that in my tweet."

"You're on Twitter?"

"No, but that reminds me. No more marketing specials on social media until we get this situation resolved. You cannot go around making open invitations. It's much too dangerous."

"Is that what happened today? A vampire came into the shop?"

"Tried to come in and failed. The costume idea didn't help, either. So tell Xandra to stop. Tell her now." He handed Daniella her smartphone. "Text her. No more special promotions. No more inviting everyone to come on down to try your cupcakes."

"I'm trying to run a business here, you know."

"And I'm trying to protect your life here, you know," he retorted.

"Fine." She sent off the text. "I'm going to bed now."

"But it's only six PM."

"It's been a long day. And remember, my dad is back tomorrow morning. You cannot be here then."

"I cannot leave you unprotected. That vamp's appearance today proved you are still in danger."

"Then you'll have to stay out of sight." Her voice was curt as she turned and walked away.

"Wait."

Something in his voice made her stop.

"That night-light you always keep on in your bedroom. Is that because of me?" His voice was gruff.

"It's because I'm afraid of the dark," she admitted a bit self-consciously.

"I didn't know if you were using it because you're afraid of me," he said quietly.

"No, I've been afraid of the dark since I was a little girl."

"Any particular reason?"

"The usual ones. Monsters under the bed and the fact I grew up above a funeral home." She was not about to reveal her unspoken fear, a sense of menace that someone or something was out to get her. "Good night."

"Don't let the bedbugs bite," he teased her.

"Or the vampires, either," she said before walking away.

Daniella was up early the next morning despite the fact that her shop was closed and this was her day off. Nick remained unusually quiet, his attention focused on his smartphone and whatever he was doing on it. Her dad showed up by eight. Nick heard him coming in plenty of time and stepped into her bedroom, partially closing the door.

"Welcome home, Dad." She greeted him with a big hug. "It's so good to see you."

"I missed you." He gave her a pair of his customary bear hugs because two hugs were better than one.

"How was your trip? You look great. Tanned and fit."

"The trip was life changing. In fact, I have some news for you," he said.

She had news, too, but she was sworn to secrecy.

"I asked Franny to marry me and she said yes."

Daniella was speechless.

"I can't wait for you to meet her. I thought we could have dinner tonight."

"It's Halloween."

"I know it is." He reached into his jacket pocket. "I have something for you." He handed her an envelope.

"What's this?"

"You mother made me promise to give this to you Halloween morning the year you are twenty-nine."

She stared at the sight of her name written in her mother's perfect handwriting. "You held on to it all this time?"

"Of course. You know I don't break promises." He glanced at his watch. "I'm sorry but I have to get back to the funeral home. I'll let you read your letter alone." He hugged her again. "We'll talk later." Then he was gone before she could say anything further.

"You can come out now," she told Nick, who sauntered out of her bedroom.

"Aren't you going to read that?" Nick asked when she set the letter on the table.

"Not now."

"Why not?"

"It's waited over a decade. It can wait a little longer."

He studied her face. "You have a feeling about it, don't you? A premonition. Do you think it's bad news? Are you afraid what it might say?"

"I've got big bad vampires chasing after me," she said. "Being afraid of a little letter after that seems silly."

"Silly, perhaps, but true."

"Not true," she said. "I'm not afraid."

"Then open it."

"Fine. I will. But don't expect me to read it out loud to you or even share what it says with you. Some things are private."

He made no comment.

She carefully opened the envelope and removed the page.

The sight of her mother's handwriting brought sudden tears to her eyes. Seeing her name on the outside of the envelope was one thing, but to see it on the page was incredibly powerful.

"Dear Daniella, If you are reading this it means that I have passed on before Halloween on your twenty-ninth year. I had hoped to be there personally to share what I'm about to share with you. I'm not sure how to put it so I will just be direct. You know I always told you how special you are. It's true. More than you know . . ."

As she kept reading, Daniella gulped and sank onto her chair, stunned by the words blurring before her eyes. "No," she whispered unsteadily. "It can't be true."

Chapter Seventeen

"What is it?" Nick's voice was laced with concern.

Daniella was too stunned to answer. She was hit by so many conflicting emotions that they were a tangled mess as she continued reading the rest of her mother's letter.

Your birth mother was my cousin Morgana. It's true that she died when you were born. I was there. It's also true that she was special. She was a druid and so are you. Actually you are a blend of druid and human. She claimed there was a tinge of vampire blood as well in your heritage, but I'm not sure about that. I find that hard to believe. Silly, I know, to believe in druids and nothing else. What can I say? I so wish I could be there to help you cope with this news. I can only imagine how difficult this is to comprehend. Believe me, I found it difficult, too, in the beginning. But Morgana always knew things about the future before they happened. She made me swear on

her deathbed to tell you, but not until Hallow-
een on your twenty-ninth year. I'm hoping
you'll know what to do with this information.
Morgana said you would. She said that to tell
you earlier would have dangerous conse-
quences and I believed her. I hope you forgive
me for keeping this secret. It never changed
how I feel about you. Always remember that I
love you.
Mom

Daniella had no idea how to deal with this. She tried to make sense of it all. But that didn't seem possible at the moment. "It's about my birth mother."

"What about her?"

"This must be some kind of sick Halloween joke," Daniella said. "There's no way *this*—" She waved the letter in the air. "—can be true."

"What are you talking about?"

"I'm talking about the fact that this letter claims I'm some sort of weird druid–human hybrid with just a smidge of vampire blood in me."

He stepped closer and sniffed. "You don't smell like a vampire. You've never smelled like a vampire."

"Excuse me?" She reared back.

"Vampires have a certain scent that is only discernible to other vampires."

"Wait a second. Is that why you sniffed me the first time we met?" she said.

"Yes."

"Of course I don't smell like a vampire—or a druid, either, for that matter. Because this is all ridiculous. I'm just a girl who loves to make cupcakes."

"A girl who loves to make cupcakes who is also immune to being compelled."

"That doesn't make me a druid."

"It makes you special."

"That's what my mother says in this letter," Daniella said unsteadily, handing it to him. "It's what she told me my entire life until the day she died." Her throat closed up and she couldn't speak for a moment. "I don't understand any of this. Why wait so long to give me this letter?"

"Maybe it's a druid thing," Nick said. "I'll check it out."

"Don't bother," she said, "I am *not* a druid. There is no such thing. Druids do not exist."

"That's what most people say about vampires."

"That's different."

"Is it?"

"Do not tell me to be logical right now," she warned him.

"I wouldn't dream of it," he said drily.

"I need answers."

"Wait. Where are you going?"

"To talk to my father."

"Remember, you cannot tell him anything about us."

"No vampire talk. Got it." She held out her hand for her mother's letter, which he returned to her.

"I'm serious," Nick said.

"Believe me, so am I."

"I'm going with you."

"I need to talk to him alone. You may accompany me, but that's it. And not into his private office."

"You may want to calm down first. Or not," he said as she marched out of her apartment. He followed her, delivering a serious warning as he did so. "If you get upset, you may say something you shouldn't. If you do, I am going to have to compel your father to forget and you will have broken your oath to us—which puts your brother at risk."

"I've got news for you." She paused to jab her finger at Nick's black-T-shirt-covered chest. "This isn't about you. Everything is not always about *you*."

Nick took her hand in his and gently squeezed. "I know."

"Are you trying to be nice to me now that you think I'm a druid? You believe it, don't you? Well, don't, because it is not true."

"Trust your gut," he said quietly.

She yanked her hand away. "Keep my gut out of it. And respect my privacy." She headed into the funeral home's back entrance but stopped as another thought occurred to her rattled mind. "Wait, do you have surveillance cameras in my father's office?"

"Yes."

Daniella muttered under her breath. Angry as she was, she knew better than to order him to turn them off. So she bit her tongue and walked into her father's office.

Rattled as she was, now she had to be aware of the camera and the fact that she was being watched, which sucked. She supposed it was better than being taken in the blink of an eye by a hedge fund Gold Coast vampire.

She sat in the same brown leather wing chair she had as a little girl offering her dad a lopsided cupcake. His tan stood out in the indoor lighting, but he didn't appear surprised to see her.

"We need to talk," she said.

"You're upset."

"Damn right I'm upset. What did you expect?"

He sighed. "I realize the news about my engagement probably comes as a surprise."

"You know what comes as a bigger surprise? The fact that my mother thinks I'm special. That I'm part druid."

Her father's eyes widened. "What? That's just what her wacky cousin Morgana told her. Morgana was your birth mother and the seventh daughter of a seventh daughter or something strange like that."

"So it's not true?"

"Of course it's not true," her father said. "What even made you think it was?"

"A lot of weird stuff has been happening lately," she muttered.

"Like what?"

Daniella shook her head. "I can't talk about it."

"Sure you can. I'm your father. You can tell me anything."

Trust your gut. She heard Nick's words in her head.

The ironic thing was that she'd always had a feeling that she didn't quite belong. That she was different. She used to confess as much to her mom, who had always reassured her while telling her that she was special.

Daniella had chalked up her feelings to the fact that she was adopted, but now she wasn't sure if that was truly the reason. She'd also chalked up the fact that she had occasional premonitions of the future to ordinary visualization techniques. She saw her cupcake shop as a success in her mind's eye. Plenty of business owners had the same experience. Perhaps not as many actually saw their logo down to the smallest detail. The challenge had been making reality match her vision.

She always considered herself to be more of a planner than a free spirit. Yes, but was the druid stuff true? That's what Daniella wanted to know. What kind of blood did she have?

Sure, she knew that medically she was type O, the most common type of blood. But what about this other stuff? The druid stuff? Not to mention that bit of vampire mixed in. Did that mean that at some point she was going to start craving blood? And if she did, would it be type O blood?

Overwhelmed by it all, she latched onto something else. "Did you know what was in the letter?"

"No, I never opened it."

"Why give it to me today?"

"Your mother said it had to be today, Halloween the year you were twenty-nine."

"Did she say why?"

"No. I assumed she explained why in the letter."

Because Morgana told her not to let Daniella know until today or there would be "dangerous consequences."

"I'm sorry if the letter upset you," her dad was saying. "I had no idea your mother was repeating the make-believe woo-woo stories that her cousin told her. That really isn't like your mom. She was a very practical woman."

"You always told me mom was your soul mate," Daniella said quietly.

"She was."

"Yet you come home from a cruise, hand me a letter saying I'm a druid, and then tell me you're engaged. You've only known this woman a few months."

"I knew as soon as I saw her again. It was magical."

Daniella didn't want to hear about magical. She was sick of magical. Give her a recipe anytime with specific measurements, ingredients, and baking temperatures. Sure, you could tweak those things a little. But then you made a new recipe. It wasn't all spooky strange hocus-pocus stuff.

She was still finding it difficult to cope with the fact that she lusted after a vampire who was her bodyguard. People who posted "It's complicated" under relationships on their Facebook page had nothing on her situation.

And then there were the Gold Coast vamps after her. And the fact that the funeral home was some kind of fast-food outlet for the neighborhood vamps. It was all too out there for her.

She didn't want to be special. She wanted her old life back. The life she had before all this chaos. The life where "Normal" was her default setting.

"When you meet Franny, you'll see what I mean," her father was saying.

She wanted her father to be happy, she really did. But this was all too much. Seeing her mother's handwriting brought back so many memories.

"I can't deal with this right now," Daniella muttered, jumping up from the chair and hurrying out of the room.

Nick was waiting for her outside.

"You probably had a live feed onto your smartphone from your spy cameras," she said.

He made no comment.

"So you already know that I told him that my mother thought I was part druid. He said it wasn't true. That my birth mother was into that kind of thing but it wasn't real. So forget about pursuing this paranormal stuff about my birth mother."

"I can't do that."

"My father said it isn't true. Are you calling him a liar?"

Nick just shrugged.

That did it. "We need to talk," she growled. "Upstairs. Right now."

Nick appeared amused by her angry order, but he didn't protest. Given the fact that he was rarely far from her side, she supposed it figured that he wasn't going to walk away. But it gave her a momentary feeling of control over the wild situation that was rapidly swirling into *The Twilight Zone*.

As soon as they were in her apartment, she got right to the point. "I do not appreciate you eavesdropping on my private conversation with my father. That was extremely private."

"You know how important this all is. We need to figure this riddle out ASAP. And that letter of yours adds a critical part. While you were talking to your father, I had your birth mother's ancestry checked out."

"After I told you not to. And do not shrug," she warned him, grabbing her silver tea strainer out of the kitchen drawer and waving it threateningly at him.

"That isn't pure silver," Nick said. "It's silver-plated."

"No, it's not." She turned it over. "It's got the nine-two-five stamp on it."

"Which wasn't used until 1906."

"Damn. The antiques dealer in London told me it dated back to the Regency period." She tossed it onto the kitchen counter. "That just goes to prove that you can't trust anybody."

"Now that you know about your tea strainer, don't you want to know what we found out about you?"

"Not really."

He lifted a dark eyebrow.

"Okay, fine tell me," she said.

"It's all true."

"Says the vampire."

"Says the vampire with the plastic fish on the wall of his bar," he noted drily.

The fact that Nick had just teased her brought tears to her eyes. "You're trying to make me feel better, aren't you?"

He nodded solemnly. "Apparently I'm not doing a very good job of it."

"I appreciate the effort."

"Do you?"

She nodded. "But I can't believe anything you're telling me right now."

"Because I'm a vampire?"

"Because it's too weird. Look, I'm still trying to wrap my brain around the fact that I live in a coven of vampires."

"Covens are for witches."

"Witches like me."

"Actually you have druid blood, which is different."

She waved her hands. "Witch, druid, what does it matter? It's all crazy."

"Not really. It makes sense."

"To you maybe. Not to me."

"Morgana's story checks out."

"How do you know that? Is there some kind of druid registry or something?"

"Not that I know of," he said.

"Then how do you know it isn't all just a wild story?"

"What does your gut tell you?" Nick asked.

She clutched her stomach. "It tells me that I am under too much stress."

"You've hinted that you felt different growing up."

"Because I was adopted. Not because I was some sort of weird thing."

"You aren't weird. You're a hybrid."

"Which is fine if you're a car," she retorted. "Not if you're a person. Oh wait, I'm not a person after all. I'm a druid hybrid."

"And damn proud of it, too, right?"

She glared at him. "Not funny."

"Come on." He nudged her lightly. "It's a little bit funny."

"If you have a warped vampire sense of humor maybe."

"Wait, does that mean you think I'm warped or my humor is?"

"I'm glad you're finding this all amusing."

"You're not going to cry, are you?" He eyed her in alarm.

"I might. So just deal with it. Unless you tough vampires can't deal with a druid's tears?"

"I can't deal with *your* tears," he growled. "I can deal with the fact that you're cheerful and chatty but not with you crying."

"What's wrong with being cheerful and chatty?" she demanded, offended by his words for some reason. Maybe because he didn't make those two traits sound like a compliment but rather a flaw.

Instead of answering, he said, "You never wondered about your birth mother?"

"I didn't want to know."

"Why not?"

"My mom said my birth mother died when I was born. She cried when she told me that. My mom didn't cry. Ever. When I saw how distraught she got, I didn't ask about it again."

"What about after she died?"

"My dad was so torn up by her death that I didn't have the heart to upset him further. And then I went away to college and trained in New York City. I was too busy living my life to look back. My parents were my parents as far as I was concerned."

"And your birth father?"

"I was going to look into that someday. When I had time. There was no urgency. I had other things on my mind. The fact that I was adopted didn't seem that relevant. I'd known it for a long time. Even if they hadn't told me, I always sensed that I didn't quite fit in. Not that I wasn't loved a lot, because I was. And not that I was treated any differently, because I wasn't."

"But you had an ability that no one else had."

"It wasn't an ability I wanted. I didn't want to see a vision of my mom dying before it happened. I didn't want to believe it was true." She slapped her hand over her mouth. She'd never confessed that to anyone. Visualizing her company logo was one thing. Seeing the future was another, especially when it involved her mother's death. She'd convinced herself that she'd merely had a dream or something. That image of the car crash had been horrendous.

She should have said something to her mom. Warned her. And the fact that she hadn't filled her with a guilt that had taken her years to recover from. She'd had to shove it so deep inside of her that it couldn't be retrieved. Until today.

She couldn't open that Pandora's box of emotions so intense she was afraid it would destroy her. So she focused on her anger and once again shoved the guilt back into the depths of her mental vault.

"You didn't want to believe you had a special talent just like you don't want to believe what's in that letter now," he said "Why is it hard for you to accept?"

"Aw gee, I don't know. Maybe the fact that we're talking about druids here."

"You already know vampires exist. Why not druids?"

"How many druids do you know?"

He shrugged. "It's unlikely they're going to tell me what they are."

She reached for her iPad.

"What are you doing?" he said.

"Checking out what you said about nine-two-five and the silver mark."

"I lied about that. Your tea strainer is really silver. Not enough silver to bother me, but not a fake."

"What else have you lied about? Never mind. I downloaded *Vampires for Dummies* and I'm checking the index to see if druids and vampires have a history."

"You're not going to find that kind of information there."

"You're right. I should Google it."

"No, don't do that."

But it was too late. She'd already clicked on a link. "Listen to this." She read aloud, " 'Legend has it that Irish druids kept vampires locked in the hollows of ancient oak trees. Twice a year, during their druid celebrations, they'd feed unlucky people to these starving vampires. This practice was featured in Anne Rice's *Vampire Chronicles*.' "

"I never read her books," Nick said.

"Me neither because they are too damn scary.

And now we find out that druids and vampires are not BFFs. More like mortal enemies."

"That's a little strong."

"Really? You don't think that locking vampires up and torturing them was twisted? Not to mention feeding people to them twice a year." She shuddered.

"What are you doing now?"

"Checking the definition of *druid*. It says a druid is a priest, magician, or soothsayer in the ancient Celtic religion or a member of a present-day group claiming to represent or be derived from that religion. And under *soothsayer,* it says a person able to foresee the future." She looked up from her iPad. "Great. That's just great. I always wanted to be a soothsayer when I grew up," she said sarcastically.

"So what does your soothsayer self say about your future?"

"That I'm about to freak out." What if her mother believed that Daniella was able to see into the future? If Daniella had told her she'd had a dream about her mother dying in a car accident, maybe she would have stayed home that day and would still be alive today.

"Do not freak out," Nick said. "There's more to your story."

"I don't want to hear it." She slapped her hands over her ears.

He gently lowered them "You have to hear it."

"Does it involve oak trees or feeding tortured vampires?"

He paused.

"I knew it." She shook her head vehemently. "I don't want to know."

"There's no violence involved. Legend has it that if a vampire mates with a druid hybrid like you, their powers will increase."

"So they can eat more people?"

Before Nick could say a word in response, the afternoon was shattered by the blast of a huge explosion.

Chapter Eighteen

Nick instantly had Daniella in his arms. She could feel the tension in his body as he assessed the situation. There were no flames in her apartment. The explosion had occurred elsewhere, but nearby.

"What . . . what was that?" Her voice was unsteady. The sound of car alarms going off filled the night air. "The funeral home? My dad and brother? My shop?" She frantically tried to get free.

He released her and glanced out the front window. "That was my car."

"Who would blow up your car?"

"Someone who doesn't like black Jaguars."

"You drive a Jaguar?"

"I used to drive a Jaguar," he said.

"But fire is deadly to vampires."

"Which is why it's a good thing I wasn't driving it," Nick noted drily. "It was meant to send a message."

"What kind of a message?"

"That the war has progressed to the next level." His voice was grim.

"So I guess this means the truce talks between your factions didn't work out?"

"I'd concur with that assessment, yes."

"How can you be so calm about all this? Someone just blew up your car!"

"Which is unfortunate. We have some vamps on the police force, but none in the fire department."

"That's understandable," she said. "Fire and vampires do not mix."

"True. But now we know why Miles is so intent on taking you. Because of the legend."

"So now I'm not only dealing with a bunch of vampires and the fact that I may have weird druid blood, but there's also a legend wrapped around the entire thing? Why am I not surprised?"

"Because you're a soothsayer."

"Don't start with me," she warned.

"Mating with you would increase a vampire's powers. That's why Miles wants you," Nick said.

"And here I thought it was because of my sexy smile and sweet disposition," she retorted.

"No, that's why *I* want you," he said with a slow grin. "I care about you."

"You care about getting me in bed," she said. "So this is all my fault."

"Me wanting you? Okay, I'll go along with that. It is all your fault."

"I meant this war between you and Miles. Your car going up in flames. It was a Jaguar."

"I can get another one."

"You realize how this once again points out the differences between us. Not only are you a vampire and I'm supposedly some kind of druid hybrid, but you drive a Jaguar and I drive a Vespa. I didn't even know you owned a car."

"I fail to see what our vehicles have to do with anything."

"We are total opposites. From different worlds."

"And different vehicle dealerships. So what?"

"So what? So people are blowing things up because of me."

"Not people."

"*Vampires* are blowing things up because of me. Maybe this proves that vampires and druids don't mix."

"No, it proves that Miles would do anything to get you."

"I'm just so glad that no one was hurt. No one was in the car, right?"

"No, no one was hurt."

"It's Halloween. What if people had been out on the street? Innocent bystanders just taking a walk could have been injured—or worse, killed by that explosion. I don't think I can do this," she said raggedly.

"Do what?"

"Any of this."

"There is a way to end it."

"Tell me what it is."

"Have sex with me."

Nick welcomed the fact that a loud pounding on the door prevented Daniella from replying to his comment. He could easily read the shock on her face, however. And perhaps a bit of interest as well? Or was that wishful thinking on his part?

The pounding continued.

"It's Pat," Nick said.

"How can you tell?" Daniella asked.

"His scent." Nick went to open the door.

"You're needed elsewhere," Pat curtly told Nick.

"I can't leave Daniella."

"You can't bring her with you," Pat said. "I'll watch over her until you return."

"Where are you going?" she asked Nick.

"It's better you don't know," Pat said. "We're at Code Red," he told Nick.

Nick nodded, but kept his eyes focused on Daniella as she answered a phone call from her father, no doubt wanting to make sure that she was okay. He watched the play of emotions race across her face: concern for her family, relief that they were fine, worry about the explosion.

Worry wasn't an emotion that Nick had experienced very often since he'd been turned. It took a great deal to worry him. He'd displayed no emotion upon seeing his Jaguar in flames, other than relief that he had Daniella safe in his arms.

Normally an explosion of that magnitude would have blown out the windows on the block, but they'd had special windows put in during the last flare-up of hostilities with the Gold Coast clan. Unbeknownst to Daniella, they'd had the same specialty glass installed in her windows as well.

She completed her call with her father and turned to Nick. "What about my shop? I need to go downstairs and check it out."

"No way." Nick firmly took her by the shoulders and looked her right in the eye. "Your shop is fine." Nick held up his smartphone and showed her a feed from the surveillance camera of the front of her shop. "You need to stay here with Pat."

"You can't compel me," she reminded him.

"I'm trying to appeal to your common sense."

"If I'm such a damn good soothsayer, then why didn't I see that explosion coming?"

"Your skills aren't as strong when it comes to vampires."

"Great. That's just great. What's the point in having visions of the future if you can't do anything about it? That sucks."

"Soothsaying is not a perfect art." Nick said.

"Clearly it's not." She tried to make sense of it all. "Could every one of my visions come true? What if a dream is just a dream or a nightmare just a nightmare and not some indication of an event yet to come?"

"I'm not certain of the way all this works," he said. "I wish I was."

"Yeah, me too."

"Have you had any visions lately?" he asked.

She shook her head.

"So that's a good thing, right?"

"Says the man whose Jaguar was just blown up."

Nick valued the slight smile she gave him ten times more than he valued his luxury vehicle. And that was a problem.

"We're at Code Red," Pat reminded Nick.

"Understood."

What Nick had yet to understand was exactly how he was going to convince Daniella that having sex with him was a good idea. He hadn't wooed a woman since his Regency days.

Yes, they were definitely at Code Red here. Which meant Nick had better come up with a plan. And it had better be a damn good one for it to get Daniella into bed.

* * *

Daniella sat in her favorite chair and stroked the soft linen, proud to see that her fingers barely trembled at all. Nick had left her alone with Pat, which wasn't a problem. Not really. After all, she'd been alone with Bruce and that had been fine. But that had also been in her shop and not her living room.

Not that Pat was intimidating. Okay, he was a little intimidating. "I assume you know about this legend business?" she said.

Pat nodded.

"Pretty weird, huh?" Now she was strumming her fingers nervously on the arm of the chair.

"My definition of *weird* is no doubt different from yours."

"Probably. But even you have to admit that this druid thing is kind of out there."

"The facts have been confirmed."

"It's a legend."

"It *was* a legend," Pat said. "Now it's a fact."

His certainty was giving her the willies. Time to change the subject. "I'm sick of talking about myself and this mess. Let's talk about you instead. Nick told me a little about his background."

"He did?"

"He's a Regency vampire. What about you?"

"I go back farther than that," Pat said.

"Care to share?"

"No."

"What about when you first came to Chicago," she asked. "Or is that off limits, too?"

"This car explosion tonight reminds me of my arrival in the city," he admitted.

"It does? Why?"

"It was 1865. I was hanging out with the elite of

the city. The Palmers, the Fields, the McCormicks. Those were exciting days. Or nights."

"Were you able to go out in the sunshine as you can now?"

Pat shook his head. "My activities were restrained to the after-dark hours."

She wasn't sure she wanted to hear about those activities. "Is this going to get icky?"

"Icky?"

"You know, bloody?"

"Not if you choose not to learn about those episodes."

"I'd rather not if you don't mind," she said.

He gave her a very direct look. "You do understand that vampires drink blood, correct?"

"Of course I know that. And I know you're getting it from my family's funeral home."

"That's where we are currently getting it," Pat said. "Obviously we didn't get it from there when I first came to Chicago." He paused and once again gave her a look, only this time it was tinged with disapproval. "I fear you have a romantic idea of what our life is like."

"I do not have a romantic bone in my body where vampires are concerned," she said. She did have plenty of lusty hormones where one particular vampire named Nick was concerned, however. Not that she had any intention of telling Pat that.

"Have you seen Nick feed?" Pat said bluntly.

She gulped. "No. Some things should remain private."

"Hmm." Pat stared at her so long she started to squirm. Was he eyeing her as a meal? Okay, she really needed to stop being so paranoid. But that was difficult to do when banker vampires were blowing up cars on her block.

Like that Jennifer Lopez song, Daniella considered herself to just be Dani on the Block. She didn't appreciate all this attention, especially from pissed-off bloodsuckers. She just wanted to bake her cupcakes in peace and quiet.

Clearly that wasn't going to happen anytime soon. Unless she had sex with Nick.

Yeah, right. Like that was going to simplify her life. *Not.*

"Do you know the difference between feelings and emotions?" Pat asked.

She was too confused to come up with an answer for that one, so she just shook her head.

"Vampires feel hunger, lust, anger."

She noted his use of *lust* and not *love.* "Are you saying vampires don't have emotions? That they aren't capable of love?"

"Love weakens us."

"So you don't love Bruce? He sure seems to love you."

"He wears his emotions on his sleeve," Pat said. "The sleeve of his clown costume sometimes."

"And what about your emotions?"

"I have been a vampire centuries longer than Nick. I have come to terms with my . . . emotions."

Daniella frowned. "I don't understand. Are you saying Nick isn't old enough to experience love?"

"He hasn't experienced it so far."

"Maybe he just hasn't met the right . . . um . . . partner," she suggested.

"Perhaps. But such a partner would have to be able to handle his life as a vampire. That would take someone special."

"Well, I've been told I'm special."

"So I hear."

She waved her hands in the air. "Let's talk about something else. Can we get back to your early days in Chicago?"

"I assume you've heard of the Palmer House?"

"Of course. It's one of the city's oldest hotels."

"I remember when they were laying out the plans to build it. Potter Palmer built it for his new wife, Bertha. It opened on September twenty-sixth in 1871. The hotel burned down thirteen days later in the Chicago Fire."

"I didn't know that."

"I'm not telling you this as a simple history lesson. I'm telling you because a vampire's life is not an easy one. Humans fear us, and when they fear something, they seek to destroy it. The fire was not caused by Mrs. O'Leary's cow as is frequently reported."

"I heard that story had recently been proven inaccurate," Daniella said. "It was a way to blame the Irish, who were recent immigrants and therefore at the bottom of the pecking order."

"It was a way to burn out the vampires."

Her eyes widened. "Are you serious?"

"Very much so."

"You're telling me that the Chicago Fire—"

"Was intended to get rid of vampires. But it got out of control and ended up burning down most of the city. Some vampires died, but some survived."

"Why didn't you leave?"

"Did the Palmers or the Fields leave? No. They rebuilt instead, even bigger and better than before. In fact, Potter Palmer built the world's first fireproof hotel. He was a real mover and shaker, that man. His wife was even more successful. After his death, she doubled the fortune she'd been left."

"Was this Miles vampire around in those days?"

"Yes. Miles the Mustache was the catalyst to the trouble leading up to the fire."

"He didn't start the fire, though, right?"

"No. Vampires are not fans of fire."

"Yet Miles blew up Nick's car tonight. He's the one to blame for that explosion, right?"

Pat nodded.

"Maybe if I was a better person, I'd go see Miles and ask him to stop all this."

"If you did that, you would be a very stupid person. And probably a dead person after he had sex with you."

Her legs turned to jelly, and she started to shake. "Wow, you don't pull your punches, do you?" she said unsteadily.

"It is best if I'm blunt about this situation."

"I'm not just a person. I'm a druid hybrid, or so I'm told."

"That would not help you survive Miles if he chose to end your life."

"Okay, that's good to know. Since you're being blunt, I'll do the same. What about Nick? Would I survive if he chose to end my life?"

"Probably not."

She started to hyperventilate.

"The difference is that Nick would never choose to end your life. He's not evil. Miles is. Nick takes no pleasure in killing. Miles does."

"Wow. Okay. Uh, again, good to know." She practically stumbled over the words.

"I'm not trying to frighten you."

"You haven't frightened me. *Frightened* is much

too mild a term. So is *scared*. *Downright terrified* comes a little closer to how I feel right now."

"Actually that could be a good thing," Pat said.

"How do you figure that?"

"It could keep you alive."

Chapter Nineteen

Nick was already in a bad mood when he entered the Vamp Cave. The news delivered from Bruce didn't improve it any.

"We took a vote and we decided that you should have sex with Daniella the cupcake maker druid hybrid ASAP. Like tonight. Like in the next hour."

Nick stared at the members of the Vamptown Council with flinty eyes. "So you decided this, have you?"

Bruce nodded. "We have. It was a unanimous vote. Except for Tanya, who abstained."

"I only abstained from voting," Tanya said. "Not from sex." She came closer and ran her fingers down Nick's T-shirt-covered chest. "When you're done with the druid drone, you can come to me and I'll show you—"

"Nothing," Nick growled. "You'll show me nothing." He never used to growl before Daniella came into his life. Or his afterlife.

Tanya pouted but wisely stepped away.

"We don't want to keep you from your designated

task," Doc Boomer said. "If you are unable to fulfill your duties, you can delegate the job to someone else."

"Just not me," Bruce said. "Because that's not the way I roll."

"And I may not be able to do a good job because I had prostate trouble before I was turned and while it hasn't gotten any worse, it hasn't gotten better and frankly I'm not sure I'm up to the job if you get my meaning," Doc Boomer said.

"You'd think we're all a bunch of has-beens, but we all have plenty of young and fit and powerful vampires working for us here in Vamptown," Lois said. "Not as powerful as you, Nick, but I'm sure they are up for the job."

"There's no time to waste. What's it going to be, Nick? You or someone else?" Doc Boomer asked.

Nick's glare and his bad mood intensified. Hell yes, he wanted to have sex with Daniella, and not just because of the legend. But he did not appreciate being ordered to do so by the council. "This entire discussion is ridiculous."

"It's not a discussion, it's a ruling," Doc Boomer pointed out.

"Are you worried about performing in front of the cameras? We agreed to turn off the surveillance cameras in Daniella's bedroom while you do the deed," Bruce said. "It's not like we want a vamp sex tape showing up on the Internet."

"I'm sure there are already some on YouTube," Neville said. "Not that I've ever checked them out myself."

"The thing is, Miles blew up your car," Bruce said.

"I had noticed that," Nick said curtly. "Hard to

miss the still-glowing charred remains and all the firefighters."

"They want to talk to you, by the way," Bruce said. "And the police also want to ask you a few questions. I don't think we're going to be able to compel our way out of this one."

"I'll go deal with them now," Nick said.

"Don't take too long," Bruce called after him. "Remember, you've got a date with destiny and Daniella."

Nick approached the first cop outside the bar. "I'm Nick St. George, the owner of the Jaguar that went up in flames."

"I'm Officer O'Malley and this is Officer Romalotti. Damn shame about your car," the cop said.

"That'll teach you to buy foreign," his slightly overweight partner said. "Just kidding." He flipped open his notebook in his hand. "Any idea who would want to blow up your vehicle?"

"No," Nick lied. Human law enforcement didn't have a chance against vampires, so they were never involved in clashes and disputes between the clans. The less contact between the two worlds, the better—and the less chance their existence would be discovered.

"Any enemies you can think of?"

Nick shook his head.

"Any unhappy customers at the bar lately?"

Another shake of his head.

"Any pissed-off ex-girlfriends?"

"No."

"Thank God the explosion didn't damage the cupcake place," the skinnier cop said. "My wife loves those cupcakes. Especially the red velvet and the cookies 'n' cream. I'm more partial to the Killer Chocolate myself."

"The maple and bacon ones are great, too," his partner said. "I never would have thought of putting them together in a cupcake. Have you tried them?" he asked Nick.

"No."

"Not the chatty sort, are you?" chubby cop noted.

"No. I think this car explosion was just some sort of Halloween high jinks," Nick said, on the verge of compelling them both to agree with him. He didn't have time to stand around here making small talk with Chicago's finest.

"Seems like more than a prank to me," skinny cop said. "Lucky thing no one was hurt. Where were you when the explosion occurred?"

"I was upstairs visiting a friend." Nick pointed to Daniella's apartment above the cupcake shop.

"Hey, the cupcake maker lives there," chubby and chatty cop said. "So you two are friends?"

"You could say that," Nick replied.

"Tell her we think her cupcakes are the best."

"I'll do that."

They stood around a little longer, gathering more information from him, like his driver's license number and his car insurance card. Then they got another call and had to leave. "We'll let you know if we find something," skinny cop said. Nick thought he was O'Malley but he wasn't sure. He didn't really pay that much attention to humans normally.

"Halloween." Chubby cop shook his head. "Every doped-up dickhead, every gang banger, every moronic asshole is out looking for trouble." He grinned. "Best day of the year to be a cop."

His partner laughed. "Yeah, right." He paused to

talk into his shoulder radio before speaking to one of the firefighters. Nick kept his distance from his still-smoldering vehicle. He vaguely heard them discussing preserving the chain of evidence for the investigation. Nick was more concerned with preserving his patience at the length of time this was all taking. He could only hope that Daniella was coping okay with Pat.

Daniella laughed at Pat's latest tale. "Mary Todd Lincoln really said that to you?"

"She did."

"I can't believe you went to Abraham Lincoln's inauguration ball."

"You know there were some who, off the record, tried to say that the man who assassinated Lincoln, John Wilkes Booth, was a vampire. But it's not true."

"Were you at the theater that night?"

"No, I was back here in Chicago. I did have some interaction with Lincoln when he was still in the state legislature down in Springfield. Spoke to him in a tavern one night. He was a strange-looking fellow. People said he was a rube, but he was one of the smartest men I ever met. And believe me, I've met plenty over the centuries."

"How many centuries?"

"Three or four, I lose count."

"That's impressive."

"Not everyone would think so. Getting back to Mr. Lincoln, you may have heard about the novel claiming he was a vampire hunter and that vampires were to blame for slavery. Neither is true, of course. There were a few vampire plantation owners, but most were human. Sometimes it seems that every bad thing in the world is blamed on vamps. Although it is true that Miles the Mustache did play a big role in the most recent global economic crash. He did the same in the stock market crash of 1929. But most of the time, humans don't need any help in doing evil deeds. They are more than capable of accomplishing them without any outside influence."

"I guess druids don't have as bad a reputation as vampires."

"They like to stay under the radar. *Far* under the radar, as in off it entirely."

"I'm still having a hard time processing all this," Daniella admitted. "I mean, it's only been a week since I discovered that vampires exist—and now I hear that I'm some sort of weird hybrid. It's all too much."

"It explains a lot. Why you couldn't be compelled. Your strength of spirit and determination."

"Do you ever just wish you weren't a vampire and that you could live a normal life?" she asked.

"For me a vampire's life *is* normal," Pat said.

"I suppose after a few centuries, I can see how that would happen. You've heard that rumor has it I may have a smidge of vampire blood?"

"We need to have Doc Boomer draw some of your blood to substantiate that."

She instantly grabbed her arms and hugged them close to her body. She wasn't real eager to have a vampire draw her blood. How would that even work? Did he use his fangs to do it instead of a needle?

"We would have a human draw your blood and turn the sample over to Doc Boomer," Pat explained. "He runs the Happy Times Emergency Dental Clinic."

"So he's a dentist and a vampire. Those are his qualifications? This Doc Boomer wouldn't just drink my blood from the test tube, would he?"

"No."

"I meant if there was some left over after the test."

"The answer is still no. You have a lot of druid blood, I suspect, and that would have a negative effect on a vampire."

"So no vampire should suck my blood. That's a good thing. That means Miles couldn't kill me by draining me."

"But there are plenty of other ways he could kill you."

"I was afraid you were going to say that," she muttered. "How come my regular doctor never found anything weird in my blood?"

"He didn't know what to look for."

"And you do?"

"Doc Boomer does. If you agree, we can have a phlebotomist here in ten minutes." At her blank look, he added, "That's a medical technician who specializes in collecting blood samples."

"Do you have someone on call or something? Do they bring you blood the way the pizza guy would deliver takeout?"

"If you don't like that option then maybe your brother could do it. He draws blood from people."

"From dead people. Trust me, that makes a difference. A *big* difference."

"Then the phlebotomist it is."

"Hold on. What's the purpose of getting my blood?"

"To verify the amount of vampire blood in your system. *A smidge* isn't exactly a scientific term."

"I'm going to have to give that some thought, so don't go calling anyone just yet." Daniella jerked nervously as her cell phone played Suz's ringtone, the opening to Coldplay's "Viva La Vida."

"Hey you," Suz said cheerfully. "Happy Halloween."

"Are you home now?"

"No. I'm still in Rome. I've decided to stay another week or so."

"Why?"

"I met a man. An incredibly sexy Italian man. He's from Milan, the fashion capital of the world. So I'm going with him to check out some clothes and food. Have I mentioned the food is awesome?"

"You haven't said much at all because our phone connections have been so bad."

"Right. I just didn't want you worrying about me."

"I am worried about you. How long have you known this guy?"

"Long enough."

"You haven't been there more than a week."

"Eight days."

"And you've already hooked up with some complete stranger?"

"He's incredible in bed," Suz said.

Daniella didn't have enough to worry about with vampires and druids and her dad getting engaged out of the blue. Now her best friend was taking off with . . . wait, she didn't even know. "Email me this guy's name and contact info in case he's a criminal or something."

Suz laughed. "You are so cautious."

"You wouldn't think so if you knew what was going on around here." The words slipped out before Daniella could stop them.

Suz, being Suz, latched onto them immediately. "What do you mean? Is something wrong?"

"Nothing I can't handle." Car-exploding vampires?

No problemo. A piece of cake . . . cupcake. A Black Magic Banana cupcake. Too bad druids couldn't do spells. Or could they?

"You're fading out," Suz said. "Talk to you later."

"Don't forget to email me the info on that guy of yours," Daniella ordered.

"You were wise not to give your friend any details," Pat congratulated her.

"It was hard not to. We tell each other everything. Have you ever had a friend like that?"

Pat nodded.

"Is Nick someone like that for you?" she asked.

"Are you kidding? Nick doesn't tell anyone everything. In fact, he tells as few people as little as possible. I'm surprised he told you as much as he did about his past."

"I probably hounded it out of him."

"Nick is immune to hounding."

"Not when I do it."

"Apparently not. What's your secret?"

"I have no idea. It's not like I can tempt him with my cupcakes or anything," she said.

"I think Nick does find you tempting."

"How do you know that? What has he said about me?"

"Don't you want to hear more about Abraham Lincoln?" Pat said. "Or Potter and Bertha Palmer?"

"No, I want to hear about Nick."

"Then you'll have to ask him. Have you thought about the phlebotomist issue?"

"No. I got distracted by Suz telling me she's not coming home now but is instead hopping off to Milan with some sexy Italian guy whose name I don't even know. And did you hear that my father is engaged to some woman he's only known a few weeks? Sure, they knew each other in college, but that was a long time ago."

Pat checked his watch. "Nick should be back soon."

"Right. Like he's going to want to talk about human relationship issues."

"It's not my favorite topic, either. About that blood sample . . ."

"Is that all you vampires think of?" Seeing the look on his face, she said, "Forget I asked that. How much blood are we talking about here? Can't we use something like those diabetes testers?"

"Unfortunately we don't have a druid tester."

"Too bad. How much of my blood would you need?" she asked.

"Hold it right there," Nick growled as he stormed into her apartment. "What the hell is going on here? What's with all the talk about taking blood?"

"Calm down," Pat told Nick.

"He wants a phlebotomist to take a blood sample of mine and have Doc Boomer check it," Daniella said.

"Check it for what?" Nick demanded.

"Its druid and vampire factors, I guess. Did you know you're not supposed to drink my blood because I'm a druid and it could be bad for you?"

"I never had any intention of drinking your blood." Nick turned to confront Pat. "What have you been telling her?"

"Not as much as I could have," Pat said cryptically.

Daniella didn't like the sound of that. Neither did Nick, judging by the look on his face. His eyes were so expressive. They could go from stormy to flinty to smoky.

Right. So the sexy vampire has great eyes. Stay focused here.

"What aren't you telling me?" Daniella demanded. Her question was aimed at both Nick and Pat and she was rather proud of how forceful she sounded, especially considering the fact that she'd just been distracted by Nick's awesome eyes.

Pat's gesture toward Nick clearly indicated that he was leaving this one for Nick to answer. "Nothing you really need to know."

"Why don't you let me be the judge of that?" she said.

"You two work it out," Pat said, heading for the door and his escape.

Nick faced Daniella. "You want the latest news?" he said. "Well, here it is. The Chicago Police Department has impounded my charred Jag and the council has unanimously voted that I should have sex with you immediately."

Chapter Twenty

Daniella couldn't believe what she was hearing. "The Chicago City Council thinks we should have sex? Isn't that illegal?"

"Sex?"

"No, ordering people to have sex. Or ordering a vampire and a druid to have sex. I know we've got a new mayor for the first time in two decades, but come on!"

"You don't like the idea?"

"Of Chicago aldermen ordering me to have sex with you? No, I don't like it at all and I don't believe it. Unless you compelled the entire city council?"

"I wasn't referring to the city council but to our own clan council."

"You mean a vampire council?"

"Yes."

"I've got to tell you, I'm not real happy with them ordering us to have sex, either. I realize I'm repeating myself, but again I say 'Come on.'" She rolled her eyes.

"Come on what?"

"You think it's a good idea? Did you suggest it? Of course you did. Earlier, right before Pat got here, you said I should have sex with you." Her aggravation grew. She was tired of being bossed around. "I'm curious. Did that line work for you in the Regency period? Because I've got to tell you, it's not going over well here in the twenty-first century."

"You're saying the idea is unappealing?"

"It's certainly not romantic."

"It wasn't intended to be."

"So you just want to have sex with me to beef up your powers. Why should I want to have sex with you?"

"Because I'm damn good at it," he said.

"And modest, too," she retorted.

"You already know I'm damn good at it."

"Because you kissed me?"

He nodded. "And it was damn good."

"Yes, it was. But you're not the first man I've ever kissed who is damn good at it."

"But I am the first vampire."

He had her there.

She could tell she was fighting a losing battle here. Because the truth was that the sexual attraction between them was undeniable and nearly irresistible. That didn't mean she was going to blindly fall into bed with him. He was always telling her she needed to be more logical, so maybe she'd try that. "I think we should talk first so I can get to know you better."

"You already know me. I've been living with you for a week."

"True. But you don't talk much. About yourself, I mean. Not that you talk much about other things, either."

"You talk enough for the both of us."

She waved his words away. "I suspect you meant that as an insult, but I will instead take it as a compliment. Either way, you're not getting off the hook. So start talking."

"I'm a Leo."

"Very funny. I'm not referring to bar pickup lines here. Although I'll bet the pickup lines in your bar are rather unique—'Your casket or mine?'"

He glared at her. "Are you *trying* to aggravate me?"

"No, I'm trying to get you to open up about your past."

"It's a very long past."

"I realize that. Let's start with that look between you and Pat when he said he hadn't told me as much as he could have. What was that about?"

"Old history."

"I already figured that much. I want details." She paused a moment. "Wait, first I need some Pellegrino and some Skittles. That's my go-to combo when I am beyond totally stressed. I restrained from having them when I was preparing for my grand opening. I even restrained from having them when I discovered you're a vampire. But now that sex and explosions are in the mix, I can't resist any longer." She went to the kitchen and grabbed a bottle of the imported water from the fridge and dug around in a cabinet to find a bag of Skittles, which she poured into a small bowl. "In the summer, I should come up with Skittles cupcakes." She wrote that idea on a kitchen notepad before returning to the living room and sinking onto the couch. "Okay, now I'm ready for whatever you have to say."

"If you don't have sex with me, you're going to die."

She choked on a Skittle, gasped for breath, and then glared at him. His sardonic smile told her he was mocking her. "It's far more likely I'll die of asphyxiation from having my throat blocked by a Skittle."

Instead of answering her, he answered his smartphone. After a series of curt yeses, he ended the call. "It seems there's a better way to test you than taking your blood."

Feeling snarky, she said, "Is this going to be multiple choice or essay test?"

"Neither. It's a heat sensor test. The surveillance camera takes your image, and our computer can decipher the percentages—druid, human, and vampire."

"That's much better. Taking blood is so old school," she said. "How long until we get the results?"

Nick glanced at his smartphone's screen. "Right about now. Yes, here it is. Preliminary results show that you are one-half druid, one-quarter human, and one-quarter vampire."

"That's just wrong. I am *way* more human than I am vampire!"

"You're right. Updated final results. Forty percent human, fifty percent druid, ten percent vampire."

"So what does all that mean?"

"That you should have sex with me."

"How accurate is this test? I mean, what if it turns out I don't have any druid in me after all and this is just some big mix-up? If that's the case, then I'd be having sex with you for nothing." She paused before abruptly asking, "Can vampires have kids?"

"No."

"Then how did I get vampire blood? Did my mother have any?"

"She was cremated, so there's no way of knowing at this point," he said.

"So my birth father could have had been a vampire?"

"He had to be a hybrid himself or you would have a higher percentage of vampire blood in your body."

She shook her head. "This isn't computing very easily for me."

"I realize that."

"Do you like being a vampire?" she asked abruptly.

"It's not a question of liking or not liking. It just is."

She kept her gaze fixed on him, willing him to tell her more.

The silence dragged on before he spoke again. "I already told you about the woman on the battlefield asking me if I wanted to live. Magdalene taught me how to survive as a vampire. When you're turned, the first blood you get is from the vamp that turned you. She used her fangs to open the vein on her wrist and then held it to my mouth, urging me to drink. I did and that created an irrevocable bond between us."

Daniella wondered if it was weird that she continued to feel jealous of this woman. "Where is she now?"

"Dead." Only one word, but it held a world of fury.

Daniella shivered. "What happened?"

"She was burned to death."

"By the Gold Coast clan?"

"No."

"Who did that to her? Humans?"

"No, vampires." His voice was harsh, and the look

on his face . . . indescribable. "We were in Venice. There was a power struggle between two rival clans. The Master Vampire who had sired her wanted her to turn humans into vampires when they didn't want to be turned. She refused. He retaliated by having us both staked. It didn't kill us but it paralyzed us. He made me watch as he dragged her to a bonfire and threw her in."

Daniella didn't know what to say.

"Then he walked away, leaving me staked, thinking I would die when the sun came up and burned me. But someone from the rival clan saved me and enlisted me to fight for their cause. They didn't need to convince me. I vowed to make them pay and they did. We wiped out the clan that killed Magdalene. I didn't leave any survivors. Including the Master."

Again, she didn't know what to say.

"He wasn't easy to decapitate. I can give you details if you want."

"No, that's not necessary." Her voice sounded strangled. She swallowed the lump in her throat. "You must have loved her very much."

"All I know for sure is that she's the reason I am what I am."

Daniella remembered what Pat had told her about the difference between feelings and emotions where vampires were concerned. Nick might not be able to admit it, but he must have cared for Magdalene deeply. She could see how strongly he was affected by talking about it.

"Everything changed on that battlefield at Waterloo. *Everything*." Nick paused, his eyes stormy. "I said yes when others around me said no. They didn't want to stay in a place filled with so much bloodshed and destruction. They wanted to move on to a better place. But not me."

"You wanted to live."

"By drinking other people's blood."

"I will admit that takes some getting used to," she said. "You never answered the question I asked you before the explosion. If your powers increase, it means what? That you eat more people?"

"How many times do I have to tell you that vampires don't eat people?"

"You just suck the blood from them until they die."

"Some do. Our clan doesn't." Nick paused to look her straight in the eyes. "Are you happy now that you made me talk? Do you feel better about the idea of having sex with me now?"

Daniella recognized that he was mocking her again. Granted, decapitation and bloodsucking didn't exactly make for erotic pillow talk, but the fact that he'd opened up to her meant something to her. She had no idea if it meant something to him—or if having sex with her would mean anything to him other than the obvious.

"How do we even know this would work?" she said. "I mean, has it ever been done before?"

"Has what been done before?"

"Sex between a vampire and a hybrid? Or even sex between a vampire and a human?"

"The latter has been done," he said.

"And how did it turn out?"

"Not well," he admitted.

"Great. So what makes you think that sex with me would turn out better? Wait, what *exactly* do you mean by 'not well'? Not well as in the human didn't have the so called mini death of an orgasm or not well as in the human died?"

"Both of the above."

"Great."

"But not all the time. Sometimes the human experienced an incredible orgasm . . . and then died."

"They all died?"

"It's not like we keep records or anything in the vampire community about such matters."

"Maybe you should," she retorted. "How many humans have you had sex with since you've become a vampire?"

He paused.

"Counting them in your mind, are you?" she said sarcastically.

"None."

She blinked. "None?"

He nodded before glaring at her. "How many humans have you had sex with?"

"That's none of your business."

"So you get to pry into my sex life but yours is off limits, is that it?"

"Hey, nobody dies after having sex with me."

"Same here," he growled.

"Because you've abstained from having sex with humans."

"Female vampires are much less complicated."

"So you're rather have sex with Tanya than with me."

"I didn't say that."

"Because having sex with Tanya won't increase your powers, right?"

Nick yanked her into his arms. "This isn't about increasing my powers."

"Then what is it about?"

"This." His mouth covered hers. She expected him to consume her, but instead he erotically nibbled his way around her lips. She didn't realize he was capable of such tenderness and gentleness. Her passionate response had to let him know that his approach was incredibly successful.

But as was often the case with them, things quickly flared out of control. She parted her lips, he parted his, and the ensuing open-mouth conflagration was wild and exciting. He lifted her. Moaning her approval, she wrapped her body around his. He backed her against the living room wall. His hands gripped her bottom as she tightened her legs around his thighs.

Daniella held on for dear life. Common sense evaporated as she was overcome by desire crashing over her, throbbing through her, increasing her need for him tenfold.

Her feminine core rubbed against his arousal. The clothing they wore increased the friction and therefore the pleasure. Even so, she wanted him naked. She felt herself getting moist, ready for him to enter her body right now. Vampire or not, she had to have him. She was addicted to this incredibly heightened state of sexual awareness. She'd read about the potency of Spanish fly, and this was the closest she'd ever felt to it.

"Now," she moaned. "Take me now."

Instead of freeing his arousal from his jeans, he freed her from his embrace.

"Not like this," he growled. "You have to decide. I'm not going to convince you. It has to be your free will that makes you come to me."

She blinked at him, trying to comprehend what he was saying.

"I'm going to go take a very cold shower." He stormed out of the living room toward her bathroom.

Daniella stood there on shaky legs. He wouldn't compel her. He wouldn't even seduce her, although clearly he could without any difficulty at all.

Instead, he made her think and decide on her own. Free will, he'd called it.

That sucked. Sure, it was noble of him. She wondered how many vampires would do the same in his shoes. She suspected not many. Ditto for mortal men. Most would take the sex and run.

But not Nick. Here was yet another example of his chivalrous side. The part of him that might have slayed dragons for a princess.

So far it had been one hell of a Halloween. She discovered she was part druid, Nick's car was blown up, and now they had to have sex to save the world. Perhaps it was more accurate to say to save his *vampire* world. Oh yeah, and there was also the matter of her dad asking some woman Daniella had never even met to marry him.

Her cell phone rang. It was her dad.

"I just wanted to make sure you're okay," he said.

"I already told you I was when you called me after the explosion."

"Yes, but that was several hours ago. I was just checking in again. No law against that, is there? It's been a hell of a Halloween."

"Yeah, I was just thinking that myself," she said.

"Your brother is pretty upset with me about my engagement. I know you are, too. I'm sure you'll both feel better once you meet Franny."

"Have you set a date for the wedding yet?"

"Next week."

She gasped.

"Just kidding," he quickly assured her. "Geez, can't anyone around here take a joke?"

"No, Dad, we can't. Not when cars are exploding on our block."

"Do they know what happened? Was it an accident?"

"The police are looking into it." Daniella tried to be as vague as possible.

"I don't understand. This has always been such a quiet neighborhood," her dad said.

"I know."

"Was there trouble while I was on vacation that you and your brother aren't telling me about?" he asked.

She hated lying to her dad, but she couldn't tell him the truth. "No."

"Has your brother been gambling again?"

"Whoa. Where did that question come from?"

"My parental radar is telling me something is up. Something happened while I was away. I haven't figured it out yet. But I will."

"I sure hope not," she muttered. Because if he figured out that vampires were his neighbors and the funeral home's business partners, then he'd have to be compelled to forget.

"What did you say?"

"Nothing, Dad. Look, I've got to go."

"Okay. You know I love you, right?"

"I know. And I love you, too."

As she disconnected the call, she brooded about the complications love created. Did she love Nick?

That wouldn't be wise at all. Or was it only lust? Could she give him her body and not her heart?

She was preparing to turn her laptop off for the night when the screen suddenly went blood red. Then a face appeared, followed by an eerie and scary Satan-sounding voice. "Allow me to introduce myself. I'm Miles Payne. I hope you'll forgive this intrusion, but I need to speak with you."

Shrieking at the top of her lungs, Daniella slammed the laptop shut.

Nick was instantly at her side, still wet from the shower, water dripping from his muscular body. "What's wrong?"

"Miles." She hated the fact that she gasped, but hell, seeing that face suddenly appear on her computer screen totally freaked her out. "He was here."

"Where?" Nick looked around. "I don't sense him here."

"There." She pointed to her laptop and leaned away. "He suddenly showed up on the screen and . . ."

"And what?"

"Introduced himself."

"Tell me exactly what he said," Nick ordered.

Nick's naked body was so incredibly distracting, Daniella had to close her eyes. Otherwise she might just leap into his arms.

She cleared her throat. "Like I said, Miles introduced himself. Apologized for the intrusion, he called it. Then he said he needed to speak with me."

"What did you tell him?"

"Nothing. I shrieked and slammed the laptop shut so hard I probably broke it. But there's something I need to tell you."

"Go ahead."

Daniella opened her eyes and stared directly at Nick. At his eyes and not the rest of his very male and very impressive anatomy. "I've made my decision. Let's do it," she said. "Let's have sex."

Chapter Twenty-one

Nick responded with unexpected calmness, actually reaching for a throw from the edge of the couch to wrap around his waist, restricting her view of his naked body. "I thought you said you wanted some romance."

"That was before Miles creeped me out. No, let's just do it and get it over with." She squeezed her eyes shut. "I know this is a wimpy question but I have to ask. Will it hurt?"

"Are you a virgin?"

"No."

"Then it shouldn't hurt. It's not like I have fangs on my privates."

Her eyes flew open. "You don't have to get all crabby about it."

"Let's keep this simple," he said.

She nodded vehemently, trying to dislodge the vision of Nick's previously naked body from her mind. "By all means."

"You lust after me. I lust after you. We have sex."

"Does the lusting part include foreplay?" she

asked. "Because frankly I'm going to need some foreplay."

"That's doable," he said.

"So how exactly *are* we going to do this?" she asked.

"The usual way."

"You're a vampire and I am a hybrid. There is no usual way."

"We'll do it any way you want."

"Okay, now you make it sound like I want you to do something exotic out of the Kama Sutra or something."

"I could do that if you want me to."

She nervously stood up, banging her elbow into the bowl of Skittles as she did so and sending the candies flying into the air. One landed down her shirtfront. She wasn't about the dig it out now. She had more important things on her mind.

Instead she quickly tidied up the mess and dumped the rest of the Skittles in the trash.

She tilted her head toward her bedroom, indicating Nick should follow her there. "Miles might be able to see us in the living room," she whispered. "What if he has the place bugged?" The possibility made her sink onto her perfectly made bed. Her legs were too shaky to hold her up at the moment.

"He'll leave you alone once we've had sex. It's only the first vampire to have sex with a hybrid who gains additional power."

"You're sure about that?"

Nick sat beside her on the bed. "As sure as anyone can be in this situation."

"Just lie and tell me you're sure," she ordered.

"How about you? Are you sure about this?"

"As sure as anyone can be in this situation," she retorted.

He smiled at her.

"You should do that more often," she said.

"Do what?"

"Smile." She lifted her hand to his mouth and traced his lips. "It looks good on you." She traced her way down his jaw, his throat, to his chest and his abs. "Naked looks good on you, too."

"I'm sure it will look great on you as well once we remove more of your clothes."

"I am a little overdressed," she agreed. "Comparatively speaking."

"I can take care of that." He slowly slid one of her shirt buttons out of its buttonhole.

She quickly undid the remainder.

He lifted a dark eyebrow. "In a hurry, are we?"

"Well, yeah. Miles may be planning something else."

"Forget about Miles."

"Easier said than done."

"I can help with that." He turned her to face him.

"Are you going to do some kind of vampire thing?"

"I was actually going to unfasten your bra. If that's okay with you?"

"Sure." She cleared her throat and tried to sound more confident. "That's fine with me."

"Good." His fingers brushed against her breasts as he worked on the front fastener of her lingerie. The white bra was not one of her sexier pieces.

"I should have put on something more appropriate," she said nervously. "I have a lacy black bra."

"I'd just be taking it off."

"Right."

He finally undid her bra. He held her breasts together and bent his head before lifting it again to smile at her. "You store your extra Skittles in your cleavage?"

She snatched the candy away from him. "Of course not." Her eyes slid away from his and focused on his left shoulder. "Wait, you've got a Skittles on you, too." Instead of tossing it away, she leaned forward and licked the candy from his skin. He tasted unlike anything she'd ever experienced before. It was the best Skittles she'd ever had.

"Mmm," she murmured, licking her way over his collarbone.

Her moans of pleasure increased as he made good use of his hands, caressing her breasts. He brushed his thumbs over her nipples, creating shards of pleasure deep within her core.

Tightening her hands on his body, she shifted her tongue-teasing to his male nipples.

Growling deep in his throat, he lowered her to the bed and yanked the throw from around his waist. She stared up at his bare body. Wow. He was even more impressive close-up.

And he was big. Would he even fit? Would their merging be physically possible?

She hated being suppressed by her fears. She wanted to let go. She needed to let go.

She studied him closely. Okay, he was big but not humongous. This should work. This was going to be good. Really good.

When he undid her jeans, she lifted her hips so he could yank them off and throw them onto the floor. Her underwear followed.

Now she was as naked as he was. She wished

she'd thought to turn off the light first. Yes, she was afraid of the dark, but the night-light would go on automatically and somehow make her look skinnier? Sexier?

Those thoughts flew out of her mind when Nick gripped her hips with both hands, brushing the ball of his thumb against her. He was so close to the part of her that cried out for his touch. He took his time until she was wild with anticipation. Then she was wild with pleasure as he caressed her clitoris. She threw her head back and raised her knees on either side of his body.

He watched her as she came. Then he lowered his head and did incredible things to her down there with his wicked mouth. Hot suction and tantalizing tongue touches. She curled her fingers into his hair as she was overcome by another set of even stronger sexual surges ripped through her again and again.

Eventually Nick kissed his way back up her body. She could taste her essence on his mouth, "Now," she whispered, shifting hungrily against him.

"Was that enough foreplay for you?"

"Yes!" she practically screamed as his hands worked on her again.

"Are you sure?"

"Yes!" She curled her hand around his penis and guided him in. She took all of him. His powerful thrusts created rapture. Pure rapture. Insanely wild rapture.

The walls of her vagina clenched with the force of their joining as her orgasm began to take over. They were meant to be together. This was meant to happen. And it was about to happen big-time. Her spasms grew from a sensual ebb and flow to a mind-blowing force that propelled her from this world to some other plane of infinitely raw and reckless ecstasy.

She gripped the metal uprights of her headboard in her fists and held on for dear life as her pleasure kept growing and erotically exploding and then growing yet again. Her vision was getting blurred but she still saw the expression on Nick's face of dark desire before she was nearly overcome. The bliss was almost more than she could bear.

He arched his back and came, lodged deep within her.

Daniella had no idea how much time had passed before she was able to form words. But she couldn't decide what to say because there was no way to accurately describe what had just happened to her. To them both.

"Bloody hell, that was exceptional," Nick said, his English accent suddenly apparent.

Daniella grinned as she felt what else was apparent—him hardening inside her once more where they were still joined together. "Vampire rejuvenation?"

Nick grinned back. "Allow me to demonstrate."

And he did.

Daniella got little sleep that night, but she wasn't complaining. She opened her eyes the next morning before the alarm went off. Nick was still asleep. He had his back to her. For the first time she saw his tattoo, at the base of his neck. His dark hair normally would cover it. She recognized the fleur-de-lis design, but the dagger at a forty-five-degree angle through the center was unique.

Reaching out, she barely brushed her fingers over

it. A millisecond later he had her pinned to the bed. His eyes had a strange glow she'd never seen before.

Gulping, she said, "It's me. You don't like anyone touching your tattoo. Sorry. I won't do it again."

His eyes returned to a more familiar smoky gray as he gently cupped her cheek with his hand. "No, I'm sorry. I'm just not accustomed to waking up with anyone in bed with me."

"Did you sleep in the same bed with Magdalene?"

"No."

"Why not?"

"It was complicated," he said.

"So are you and I."

"True." He tenderly slid a tendril of her hair behind her ear. "Are you okay?"

"I'm better than okay. I feel energized despite the fact that I didn't get much sleep last night. But then I've never needed lots of sleep. A good thing given that I have to get up so early to make the cupcakes."

"Hmmm." He was nuzzling her ear.

"Or maybe it has something to do with the naked vampire in my bed."

"I'd like to think so," he said with false modesty.

She glanced at the bedside clock. "We still have some time before I have to get up."

"I'm already up." He moved against her.

"Yes, you are." She reached for him, running her fingers up and down his tumescent length. "Show me again how well you fit inside me . . . Yes, yes, yes!" she chanted over and over again as he thrust into her. The feeling of him filling her up was just as excruciatingly exciting and sexually hyper-satisfying as it had been the first time. And the second and third times. No, this was even better because now he knew exactly where to touch her to lift her climax to the stratosphere.

Her orgasm was fast and furious and left her saturated with satisfaction yet more energized than ever. Afterward, she hopped out of bed and wrapped a robe around herself. Then she turned to Nick, where he lounged in her bed and watched her. Her floral sheet pooled low on his hips in a way that was ridiculously sexy. "I have to ask you something," she said.

"Go ahead." He whipped the sheet completely off. "I'm an open book."

She tried not to drool as she also tried to remember what the hell her question was. Oh yeah. It was about her best friend. "Did you send a vampire to compel Suz to stay in Italy?"

"No."

"Did you or one of your vampire clan compel her via Skype or something on YouTube?"

"No. Why are you asking me these dumb questions?"

"They aren't dumb and I'm asking them because it's not like Suz to change her plans because of a guy she just met," she said. "First my dad gets engaged to someone he hasn't known very long and now Suz is staying longer in Rome to be with Enrico. What's next?"

"You falling for me?"

"That would be a really dumb thing for me to do," she muttered, turning away.

He was in front of her in the blink of an eye. "Why is that?"

"Because you wouldn't have looked at me twice if you'd been able to compel me not to open my shop that first day we met. And you certainly wouldn't have wanted to have sex with me if I wasn't a hybrid."

"I wanted you right away when you wore that prim sweater the first time I met you. I wanted you even when your stubbornness was driving me crazy." Seeing her face, he added, "Why do you find that so hard to believe?"

"Because I'm not the kind of woman that men like you notice. You may have been curious about the fact that you couldn't compel me but that's all it was."

"Why do you belittle yourself so?" He sounded like he'd just stepped out of the pages of one of her historical romances.

"I'm just being realistic."

"Our reality is different from anyone else's," he said.

"I realize that."

"Do you?"

"Yes." She waved a hand at the badly rumpled bed. "I've never experienced anything like that before."

"Neither have I."

She didn't want to dissect their relationship. It was too early. And she had to take a shower and get dressed. By the time she did that Nick was waiting for her, wearing his customary black.

"Do you feel any different this morning?" she asked him. "I mean, your powers were supposed to increase after we . . . uh . . . did the deed."

"I don't think it's an immediate thing."

"Oh." It had been for her. He only had to look at her the way he was doing now and she wanted to jump back into bed with him. "Um, was something supposed to change with me once I had sex with you?"

"Why? Do you feel different this morning?"

"Hell yes."

He grinned at her. "Yeah, me too."

"Do you think this merging between us somehow made us addicted to having sex with each other?"

"I sure hope so."

"Me too." She grinned back at him. "That doesn't mean I'm going to fall for you."

"You really should."

"Maybe you should fall for me."

"Maybe I already have," he said.

Her heart actually skipped a beat or two. "Do not give me that look."

"What look?"

"That *let's have sex* look," she said. "We are *not* going back to bed."

Nick leaned close to whisper in her ear. "We could do it against the wall."

"Or we could go downstairs and bake cupcakes. I have to open the shop."

"I'm going with you," he said.

"Why? Shouldn't I be safe from Miles now?"

"I hope so," he said. "But I'm not taking any chances."

Daniella had been taking plenty of chances lately. Boatloads of them, in fact. First by opening her shop. Then by opening herself to Nick.

That realization was scary, so she focused on the rituals of her baking routine the minute she stepped into the shop. Xandra joined them a short while later. The sun had yet to rise but it was time to make the cupcakes.

Baking was therapeutic for Daniella. She didn't remember exactly when she'd had that aha moment. Maybe she'd always known it.

Her mother, of course, had considered the baked goods she'd made as comfort for those in need of it. So while mixing the butter and sugar and flour was work, it was also a labor of love. Loving cupcakes was one thing. Loving Nick was something else entirely.

He was a vampire who lived forever. She was a hybrid who didn't know what she was doing or who she was. It hadn't even been twenty-four hours since her father had handed over her mother's letter and yet so much had changed.

Nick remained focused on his smartphone as he had most mornings this past week when he was with her in the shop. She did sense a new tension emanating from him, however. Xandra headed to the front to ready the display case of cupcakes for the shop's opening.

"What are you doing?' Daniella asked Nick as he abandoned his phone in favor of getting close to her.

He paused, leaning even closer. She thought he was going to kiss her. Instead he devoured the red velvet cupcake she'd just started to ice. And he did so with super speed. He closed his eyes in apparent ecstasy . . . or maybe pain?

"Should you be doing that?" she whispered.

"I can eat," he said in disbelief. "I can eat food." He licked his lips. "Neville said it might be possible. Oh my God, I can eat. Steak. I want steak. And a pizza. Fish-and-chips. Ale and whiskey. Mexican food. I've never had Mexican food. Or a hot dog. Or a hamburger."

Daniella stared at him. "The first food you could eat in two hundred years and you picked one of my cupcakes." She blinked away tears. "That's so sweet of you." She paused as she realized he'd just devoured another five cupcakes in a second flat. "Hey, take it easy! All things in moderation."

"That's not what you said last night."

She kissed the cream cheese icing from his mouth. She just had to. She couldn't help herself.

"Be patient," she told him before whispering, "You've got forever."

Daniella was able to hold out until noon. Then she couldn't take it anymore. Nick was eyeing her and the cupcakes with increasing hunger. She was afraid that he might devour both her and the food if she didn't do something to satisfy his newfound appetite.

"Xandra, do you think that you and Lois can manage the shop today? She'll be in shortly."

"Sure," Xandra said. "No problemo."

Nick pulled Daniella outside.

"Where are we going?" she asked.

"Someplace where we can eat," he said. "Which rules out my bar."

"I think it might be safer to order in and stay in my apartment until we have this food thing figured out."

He was on his smartphone an instant later. By the time they were upstairs he'd phoned in four delivery orders. One from the nearest sandwich shop, one from a Chinese place, one from a Mexican place, and one for a Chicago-style deep-dish pizza.

He headed straight for her kitchen as soon as they entered her apartment. "Peanut butter." He opened the lid and swiped his finger in it before sticking it in his mouth.

"It's better if you drizzle chocolate syrup over it." She held up the container.

He grabbed it and her and headed for the bedroom.

"What are you doing?" she said.

"It'll be another twenty minutes until the food arrives, so I'm going to test your claim that it's better with chocolate syrup over it." He whipped off her Heavenly Cupcakes T-shirt and her bra and drizzled chocolate syrup on her bare breasts. Bending his head, he licked the chocolate from her skin. "Mmm, you're right. What a clever cupcake maker you are, Ms. Smarty Knickers."

He had that English-accent thing going on again, which she found to be incredibly sexy. A darkly erotic Mr. Darcy. Oh yeah.

She was so distracted that she didn't even notice he'd peeled off her shoes and jeans and was now removing her knickers. But then he was doing all that with vamp hyper speed. He slowed down greatly when he administered the chocolate syrup to the rest of her body, layering the most on her breasts with creative swirls. He lowered her onto the bed.

"These are the most perfect cupcakes in the world," he murmured huskily, before taking her into his mouth and sucking the sweetness from her. She was burning with pleasure when he moved on to her navel and below. A lick, a nibble, and she was a goner. She came with rolling waves of ecstasy.

He came into her, sliding his way home before almost withdrawing, only to thrust back in. The ensuing friction was deliciously arousing. Daniella didn't think it was humanly possible to have as many orgasms as she'd had in the past twelve hours—but then she wasn't all human. She was part druid. Maybe they had super sex lives. She knew she sure was right now.

By the time the banquet started arriving, they were dressed and back in the living room. Daniella had to smile at the way Nick admired every little thing set out for him to sample—from the pot stickers to the cheese on the deep-dish pizza. He paced himself, trying some of everything rather than gorging on any one item. He sampled the burritos and tacos last.

"Today and tomorrow are the Days of the Dead in Mexico," he noted. "Días de los Muertos. A time when family and friends remember their loved ones who have died. I was down there one year for the event."

"Did you fly?" she asked.

"Yes. I prefer first class to coach."

"I meant without a plane. Can you fly without a plane?"

He lifted an eyebrow in one of his classic moves. "You must have mistaken me for Superman."

"After your performance last night and today, I'd say that *super* is an accurate description."

They spent the rest of the day and most of the night exploring new foods and new moves with equal amounts of supreme gastronomical and sexual satisfaction.

Nick walked into the Vamp Cave early the next morning to find Pat and Bruce grinning at him. He'd left Daniella at her cupcake shop, guarded by Lois.

"We were starting to think that we'd never see you again," Pat said. "Oh, wait, we did see you. Devouring cupcakes yesterday morning. So I guess Neville was right about the food thing, huh?"

"There's only one thing I want to know," Bruce said. "Was it good?" He deliberately waited a beat before adding, "I mean the food, not the sex."

"I can tell by the look on Nick's face that both were good," Pat said, slapping him on the back.

Nick turned his attention the Neville, who wiped the grin off his face the instant he realized Nick was glaring at him. "I need to know how Miles hacked into Daniella's laptop the other night," Nick said. "She saw and heard him."

Neville nodded. "He got into her Skype account. It's been corrected."

"It never should have happened in the first place." Nick's voice reflected his anger as he gripped the back of a steel chair, bending it without even realizing what he was doing.

"Agreed," Pat said, taking the chair away. "It appears your powers have been increased as predicted. At least your strength has increased. What about other abilities?"

Nick didn't know if his sexual abilities had been improved or if it was just Daniella that did it to him. And she did it to him big-time over and over again. He couldn't wait to get back to her. "We'll just have to wait and see what develops."

Daniella was preparing to decorate a special order of cupcakes for a baby shower when Lois ran into the back room. "You're in danger. We must leave right now." She yanked Daniella to the back door, using vampire strength for the first time.

"What about Xandra?"

"They're not after her. They're after you, and there's no time to explain."

They ran past the back entrances to Nick's bar and grill as well as Pat's Tats and the Happy Times Dental Clinic along the alley to Tanya's Tanning Salon.

"This way," Lois said. She tugged on the corner of a storage rack, opening a secret doorway that led down a small spiral staircase.

"What's going on?" Tanya demanded as she joined them.

"Miles is after Daniella."

"So you didn't have sex with Nick?" Tanya asked Daniella.

"No time," Lois gasped. "Miles is coming!"

"Then I'm coming with you two," Tanya said, following quickly behind them before slamming shut the door to her salon. "I'm not staying behind with a pissed-off Miles the Mustache."

The lighting on the stairway was dim, barely enough to keep Daniella's fear of the dark at bay. "Where are we going?"

"To the tunnels," Lois said.

Daniella didn't like the sound of that.

"Don't be afraid." Lois used her maternal voice. "The tunnels were built during the Prohibition by bootleggers wanting to move their product."

"Illegal booze," Tanya inserted.

"Congress was foolish to pass a bill prohibiting the consumption of alcohol," Lois said.

"And Congress continues to be foolish at times," Daniella said. Were vampires political? She didn't want to get them riled up or anything. She already had enough vamps mad at her.

They reached the bottom of the staircase and

quickly started moving. The place was like a maze. The tunnel had a lightbulb every ten feet or so, but there were too many shadows for Daniella to feel comfortable.

She took a deep breath, which ended in a gasp as even that pitiful amount of illumination abruptly disappeared, plunging them into utter darkness and Daniella into total panic.

Chapter Twenty-two

"Where's Daniella?" Nick growled, staring at the screen displaying the back of the cupcake shop. Pat had asked him to review some damn security report for a second and the next thing he knew Daniella was gone and Miles had invaded Vamptown.

"Daniella is safe," Neville said. "She's with Lois."

"And Tanya," Bruce added.

"Lois will look after Daniella," Neville said.

"Where are they now?" Nick said.

"In the tunnels." Neville switched screens.

"Why is it pitch dark down there?" Nick demanded.

An instant later the lights in the Vamp Cave blinked out along with all the high-tech equipment.

"The backup generator will kick on," Neville said.

"When?"

"It should already be on," Neville admitted. "I don't know what's wrong."

"Where's Miles right now? He's nearby." Nick's voice was grim.

"I don't know." Neville was frantically pounding on various keyboards and touch screens to no avail.

Nick closed his eyes and sniffed, concentrating all his increased abilities on locating Miles. He was close but not in the building. Not yet.

Vampires had excellent night vision, so it wasn't the darkness of the Vamp Cave that disturbed Nick. It was the fact that with their security system and its multiple backups disabled, they had to fall back on their inherent skills.

"Time to go old school," he said curtly.

Nick couldn't afford to think about the fact that Daniella, who was terrified of the dark, was down in the tunnels. At least she wasn't alone. She had Lois with her. Tanya might not be any comfort, but Lois would.

"Bootleggers were simply supplying a need," Lois said. "The Eighteenth Amendment to the US Constitution banned the production and sale of alcohol. Prohibition. And with that law came the birth of the speakeasy. Now anyone could get a drink, including women. We weren't allowed in the saloons but we were welcome in the speakeasies. They were magical places, full of life and music. The Jazz Age. I heard Duke Ellington play when I had my first drink."

"Who cares?" Tanya said.

"Daniella cares. She likes history. I'm distracting her because she's afraid of the dark," Lois said.

"*Terrified* comes closer to the truth," Daniella said.

"Boo!" Tanya said from behind her, making Daniella jump.

"Don't be mean," Lois said.

"Keep talking, Lois," Daniella said, reaching out to hold her friend's cold hand. "Were you a flapper?"

Lois laughed. "I was. It was such an exhilarating time. So much newfound freedom. We wore our dresses and our hair shorter. We smoked. Those were the best of times. They ended with the big crash on Wall Street in '29." Lois's voice turned somber.

Daniella's eyes had adjusted enough to the dark that she could see the outlines of Lois and Tanya. But she hadn't adjusted as far as her fear was concerned. "When will the lights go back on?" Daniella asked.

"When they need to."

"I need them to go on right now. Does Nick know they're out? Does he know I'm down here in the dark?"

"Of course he knows," Lois said.

"Then he'll fix this," Daniella said.

"You sound like you have a lot of faith in him," Lois noted.

"I do," Daniella agreed.

"That's a shame."

Lois's words shocked her. "What do you mean?"

"Nick used you to ramp up his vamp skills. It was all very premeditated. Nick told you he was adopted, right?"

"Yes."

"It's not true," Lois said. "He just said that to make you confide in him."

Daniella would expect Tanya to say something like that, but not Lois. "Why are you saying this?"

"The truth hurts," Lois said.

Tanya laughed. "I've got to say I'm enjoying this conversation more than the boring talk about Prohibition."

"Am I really in danger from Miles right now or was that a lie?" Daniella demanded.

"No, Miles is really here," Lois said with certainty.

As if on cue, a dim light went on above their heads. The rest of the tunnel in both directions remained pitch dark. Lois's eyes had a strange glow as she reached into the pocket of her pants and pulled out a vial filled with something red. Daniella didn't think it was red food coloring in there.

"You must drink this now." Lois's voice was grim.

Daniella eyed her and the vial suspiciously. "What is it?"

"Blood," Lois said bluntly.

"No way! I am not drinking that." Daniella vehemently shook her head. The rest of her body was already shaking, and her fear had just notched up several thousand degrees.

Lois hissed and shoved the now open vial at Daniella's mouth. "Drink!"

"Look, I dislike the cupcake maker as much as the next vamp," Tanya said. "But if she doesn't want to chugalug blood, that's her loss. Don't go all full vamp on her."

"Stay out of this," Lois growled.

"Whoa, chill out," Tanya said. "What's with the fangs?"

"I told you to stay out of this." Lois leapt toward Tanya, knocking her down.

Tanya shoved her aside. Her eyes had that strange glow now, too, and both of them showed their fangs. Lois rolled off the tunnel wall and attacked Tanya again.

Girl-on-girl fighting, or in this case female-vamp-on-female-vamp, might intrigue some people but Daniella sure as hell wasn't one of them. How had she gotten into this mess?

She had no idea what she should be doing. Running away? In the pitch dark? When either vampire had supreme speed and could outrace her in the blink of an eye? And what about Miles? What if he was there in the darkness?

Daniella stood there frozen. Why had Lois turned on her? What had gotten into her?

"Lois, why are you doing this?" Daniella said.

"Miles wants you to drink his blood so he's inside you."

"Yuck!" Daniella almost hurled.

While Lois was momentarily distracted by Daniella, Tanya grabbed the opportunity to take off. Lois looked like she was about to chase her when the single dim bulb above Daniella went out.

"Leave her," a male voice said from the darkness. It wasn't just any male voice; it was the Satan voice of Miles Payne. She'd recognize it anywhere. "I have what I want."

Okay, her panic now increased a billionfold. "I don't suppose you could turn the light back on? No? Anyone have a flashlight handy?"

Miraculously one was turned on and aimed at Miles's face. "Get that out of my eyes," he hissed.

"Sorry, sire," a male vampire said, redirecting the light so it was beneath Miles's chin. Now he really looked like something out of a horror film.

Daniella dropped the vial onto the floor where it shattered and left a pool of blood.

* * *

Tanya burst into the Vamp Cave. Nick had her by the throat an instant later. "It was *you*. You led Daniella down into the tunnels and to Miles."

Tanya gurgled, unable to speak.

Pat intervened. "Release her, Nick."

He did but he wasn't happy about it.

"I was the one who tried to save her," Tanya said. "And I'm the one who's come to get help for her. Lois is the bad one here. Miles did something to her. I don't know if he compelled her or if she's been a secret cell all by herself for him all these years—but she turned on us. She turned on Daniella. She even tried to get her to drink Miles's blood so he'd be 'within her.' I'm telling you the truth. See for yourself." She pointed to one big screen, which had just come back to life.

"If I can't have you, then I'll have the blood supply from your family's funeral home," Miles was telling Daniella as he held her in his grip.

"I already told you that I don't have anything to do with the family business," she said.

"I realize that. But Nick does have something to do with it. Isn't that right, St. George?" Miles called out. "I've cleared the security system so you may see us now. Briefly."

A vacant-looking Lois stood to one side of Miles while a subservient Andy stood on the other. Seeing Miles with his hands on Daniella made Nick wild with rage. But he couldn't afford to lose it right now. He couldn't let human emotions get in the way of his vamp powers.

"Let Daniella go." Nick prayed the sound of his voice would stop Daniella from going into full-blown hysteria. Her face was pale, and he sensed she was in danger of losing it.

Miles's smile was filled with icy contempt. "I will. As soon as you give me the rights to the blood. In writing."

"This is between you and me," Nick told Miles. "Let the cupcake maker go now."

"Let her go now?" Miles laughed. "Ain't gonna happen. You're in no position to be making demands. Don't bother trying to find us down here in the tunnels. Through the miracle of modern technology this is a delayed feed to your surveillance cameras. Your pretty little friend and I have already moved on."

Nick could sense that they were still nearby, perhaps closer than ever. Concentrating, he pinpointed their location. "You're in my bar," he said.

Power was restored, lighting all the screens and showing Miles still holding Daniella in his grip, only now he had a large knife at her throat as they stood inside the All Nighter Bar and Grill. Nick could see the Blackhawks hockey jersey in the background along with the singing fish on the wall.

Nick's growl was feral as he went full vamp, fangs fully emerged and ready to rip into Miles.

"Don't do anything stupid," Pat warned him

"That's right, St. George," Miles mocked him. "Don't do anything stupid because as everyone knows, I never lose."

One second Daniella was alone with Miles in the deserted bar and grill—and the next Nick was there.

"You've heard that joke, right?" Miles mocked Nick. "A vampire and a druid walk into a bar." His laugh was as Satanic as his voice.

Nick barred his fangs and hissed.

"Take a good look at him," Miles told her. "Lois

told me you'd never seen St. George go full vamp. What do you think of your lover now? Not so sexy, is he?"

Like she was going to think about sex when a crazed deadly vampire held a knife to her throat. Her eyes remained on Nick. She refused to look away or be freaked by his vampire side. He'd saved her life before. She sure hoped he could do it again.

"One last chance. Let the cupcake maker go," Nick said as he had earlier.

Wait a second, Daniella thought. Is that all she was to Nick? The cupcake maker? Nothing more? Not *soul mate*? Not *love of my life and afterlife*? Miles had just called Nick her lover yet Nick called her the cupcake maker. Not even *my* cupcake maker.

Not that she should be worried about stuff like that when she had a knife held to her throat. Nick had said yesterday and today were the Days of the Dead. She sure hoped she didn't end up that way. Dead.

"Cat got your tongue, sweetheart?" Miles mocked her, toying with her as he shifted the knife, nearly cutting her but not drawing blood.

"Why are you doing this?" she gasped. "You're rich. You don't need more blood."

"How astute of you," Miles said. "Now, now, keep your distance, gentlemen," he warned Pat and Bruce as they joined Nick.

"Is this another example of your love of making trouble?" Pat demanded. "Like the time you instigated the Chicago Fire? Or the crash on Wall Street? You can't increase your powers—"

"I know the hybrid druid has already mated with St. George," Miles said.

"Then you know my powers have increased," Nick said.

"Doesn't matter," Miles said. "You're no match for me."

"We outnumber you," Pat said. "Where are Lois and Andy?"

"They're in the tunnels. I ordered Andy to decapitate Lois. I had no further use for her. Don't go fainting on me," Miles warned Daniella. "I might slit your throat by accident." Ruthlessly tightening his hold on her, he continued. "Discovering I could compel Lois was a lucky fluke. Mind control usually doesn't work on vampires. But it worked on her. I could sense that when I saw her working at the bakery on your surveillance cameras, which I hacked into. Maybe it was the fact that she knew me when she was still human. We met in a speakeasy and shared a drink or two. It doesn't matter. She served her purpose."

Daniella felt tears coming to her eyes. Lois deserved better.

"Mating with the cupcake-making hybrid may have increased your powers, St. George. But it's only temporary," Miles said. "Because you're no longer immortal. Oh, you'll live longer than most humans, but from now on you will grow old at the same pace she does. I'll bet you didn't know that when you agreed to shag her, did you?"

Daniella remembered Lois's accusation that Nick had only had sex with her in order to ramp up his vamp skills.

"It doesn't matter," Nick growled.

"It doesn't matter because you've fallen for this hybrid, haven't you, St. George? You're wrong when you said this isn't about blood," Miles told Daniella. "And don't even think about it," he warned Nick. "Yes, you're superfast, but so am I and I can kill her before you get to me. Now, where was I . . . oh yes. This *is* about blood. About family."

"We've done nothing to hurt your clan," Pat said.

"I'm not talking about my vamp clan. I mean my *human* family. In Venice. When I was Milo Panetti."

Daniella saw recognition hit Nick's glowing eyes.

"That's right, St. George. I was a human cousin of the clan you destroyed in Venice over a hundred years ago. I wasn't a vampire at the time; I became one just to get you. But the thing was, I had to wait until the right time for my vamp vengeance." Miles paused a second before adding, "You like this cupcake maker, don't you, St. George? You like her a lot. You fell for her big-time."

She shuddered as Miles licked her cheek.

"If you try to suck my blood, it will kill you," she said.

"I have no intention of sucking your blood. Instead I'm going to slit your throat and make Nick watch. Just like he had to watch his last love Magdalene being tossed onto the bonfire she deserved after disobeying orders."

"Take me instead," Nick said, his voice tortured and harsh. "Let her go and take me."

"That wouldn't make you suffer. And I really want to make you suffer." As Nick moved toward him, Miles warned, "Stay back!" He took a few steps, pulling Daniella with him, until his back was against the wall. "I don't appreciate you pushing me against the wall of your pitiful establishment. I mean, a talking fish?" He tilted his head toward the decoration on its wooden base. "Come on. Very bad taste."

As if on cue, the fish started singing "Don't Worry, Be Happy" before falling to the floor and shattering. A large shard of wood from its base bounced up into Daniella's hand. Without even thinking, she immediately lifted it over her shoulder and jammed it into Miles's chest with all her might.

Chapter Twenty-three

An instant later Miles disintegrated, his clothing falling to the floor in a pile. The clatter of the knife hitting the floor echoed in the deathly silent bar.

Nick rushed forward and tugged her into his arms. "Are you okay?"

"Wha . . . at happened?" Daniella stuttered. "I was just trying to stake him, not to . . ."

"Make him go up in dust?"

Pat surveyed the destroyed plaque. "The base is oak."

Daniella didn't get the connection. But then she wasn't exactly thinking clearly at the moment. "So?"

"So remember how druids once locked up vampires in the hollows of ancient oak trees? The combination of angry druid and oak is apparently still deadly for a vampire," Pat said.

"It's like in *The Wizard of Oz,* when they throw water on the witch. They changed that in the play *Wicked,*" she said. "I'm in shock and I'm babbling." She looked at the pile of dust and clothing on the floor. It freaked her out to think a few moments ago that had been a person. Well, not a *person* per se. A vampire. An evil vampire. "You don't think he somehow got away, do you?"

"No, you're safe now," Nick said.

"Am I? What about the rest of his clan? The Gold Coast vamps? Won't they come after me now that I've disintegrated their leader?"

"Normally they might," Pat inserted. "But Miles was no longer their leader. Neville just texted me that Miles had been recalled through a vote of their council. It's a very rare occurrence, but they didn't approve of his actions or his instigating this war with us. They didn't need blood; they have their own blood bank franchise they've just started."

"Now that the dust has settled . . ." As everyone groaned, Bruce said, "What? Too soon? So I'm guessing it's also too soon to say that the last laugh about a vampire and a druid walking into a bar would be on Miles?" He eyed the designer men's clothing on the floor. "Do you think that suit of his can be saved? It's an Armani." He paused. "No, you're right. It probably has bad karma and should be burned."

Pat held up his hands in the universal sign of surrender. "I didn't say a word."

"You didn't have to," Bruce said. "I saw the expression on your face."

"What about me?" Tanya demanded as she sauntered into the room. "I could use some thanks here. I'm the one who fought off Lois to go get help. But does anyone express their appreciation for my efforts? Noooo." Putting her hands on her hips, she stared at them all. "Well?"

"I appreciate your help," Daniella said.

"I should hope so. I'll bet I surprised you, huh, sticking up for you the way I did?"

Daniella nodded.

"Lois sure surprised me," Tanya said. "Have you figured out what was going on with her? I mean, I know she was obeying Miles the Mustache's orders. I just don't know why."

"He said he compelled her," Pat said.

Tanya frowned. "But she's a vamp. We can't be compelled."

"She *was* a vamp," Pat said.

"Poor Lois." Daniella, still held in Nick's arms, shivered. She'd considered Lois to be a friend as well as an employee. She remembered bonding with her the very first time they'd met, when Lois had mocked Nick.

"To misquote Mark Twain, the report of Lois's death was an exaggeration," Doc Boomer announced as he walked into the bar with Lois and Andy.

Daniella couldn't help it. She cringed back. Sure, she'd just annihilated a very powerful vampire all by herself with nothing but a hunk of oak—but that didn't mean she thought of herself as Buffy the Vampire Slayer. After all, she was in love with a vampire.

Whoa, where had that thought come from? Was it the fact that being in Nick's arms made her feel she had found her place in the world? Or that him whispering *"You're safe"* in her ear made her feel so secure?

"I'm so sorry, Daniella," Lois said. "I didn't want to do what I did but I couldn't seem to stop myself. Miles looked into my eyes and ordered me to obey. Perhaps he was able to compel me because I was infatuated with him when I was still human. I was turned into a vampire within an hour after my last encounter with him. Not that Miles was my sire. I was turned by the bartender at the speakeasy."

"I've heard that if a human has unrequited love for a vamp shortly before she is turned by another vamp, she will remain vulnerable to the object of her feelings even after the transformation," Doc Boomer said. "It sounds complicated, I know, but then we are dealing with vampire lore here."

"The Mustache said he ordered Andy to behead you." Nick's voice was hard and edged with suspicion as he stared at Lois.

Lois nodded. "That's true. But Andy disobeyed."

"Why?" Nick barked the question. Daniella could feel the tension in his body. He was ready to face trouble at a nanosecond's notice.

"Because we had a vamp vow," Lois said. "I saved his life when Doc Boomer wanted to behead him that time Andy came to Vamptown the night before Halloween. That's when Andy vowed that he would save my life."

"Only if I was present and only if it was within the next twenty years," Andy qualified nervously. "Is it true? Did the druid whack my sire? Did he really bite the dust?"

"He *is* the dust." Pat pointed to the pile of fine particles on the floor.

Andy looked at Daniella with respect before telling Nick, "She's got some powerful mojo going on, dude."

Nick gave him a steely glare that made Andy duck behind Lois before realizing what he was doing and returning to his original stance.

"We're glad you're not dead, Lois," Bruce told her. "I'm glad Andy didn't behead you. I thought maybe he was influenced by the *Happy Days* marathon on cable TV last night and the fact that you look like Mrs. C's twin sister," Bruce said. "I thought perhaps that's why he didn't decapitate you."

"A vampire would never allow himself to be influenced in such a stupidly emotional way," Andy stated. "Besides, I like the Fonz better."

"Really? I had no idea you rolled that way," Bruce said.

"I don't roll that way," Andy said.

Lois stepped forward. "I don't know how to express my regret. I realize that my actions will require you to banish me from Vamptown . . . or even worse."

Staring at the other vampires in the bar, Daniella had to speak up. "You are not going to kill her! Not after Andy saved her."

"We can't trust her," Pat said regretfully. "If one vampire could compel her, another might be able to as well."

"But Doc explained that," Daniella said.

Pat shook his head. "It doesn't matter."

"Can't you do a mind meld with her or something to make her immune to compelling?" Daniella said.

"You're getting us confused with Spock on *Star Trek*," Bruce said. "We don't do mind melds."

Daniella refused to give up that easily. "There must be something you can do."

"Do not get her upset," Bruce said, eyeing Daniella warily. "Remember what she did to Miles with that chunk of wood. There are still pieces of the plaque on the floor along with little iddy biddy pieces of Miles."

"Why are you trying to save me?" Lois asked Daniella.

"Yeah," Tanya said. "Why are you trying to save

her? Because she said she's sorry and that's supposed to make it all okay?"

"She was forced against her will to do the things she did," Daniella said.

Nick turned Daniella to face him. "That doesn't make a difference."

"Well, it should," she said.

"There is one thing we could try," Pat said slowly. "It hasn't been done in centuries."

"What is it?"

"Have the druid forgive her," Pat said.

"How would that prevent some other power-hungry vamp from compelling Lois?" Nick said. "I know what Doc said, but he also said it's only vamp lore that that was how Miles got to her."

"Forgiving would make Lois a distant part of the druid clan and therefore immune to any vampire compelling. That's vamp law, not lore."

"What about Andy?" Lois said. "And even if you do forgive me, Daniella, looking at me would still bring back terrible memories."

"You tried to make me feel better by talking about the Prohibition when I was so terrified of the dark," Daniella said.

"And then I tried to make you drink blood from Miles. So even if I am forgiven, I think it's best if I leave Vamptown. I have vamp friends in Seattle. Andy and I could go there. He's not as immune to the sun, so Seattle would be a good location," Lois said.

"Are we all in agreement then?" Daniella said. "I forgive Lois, and she's immune to any future vamp compelling her—and she can move on to Seattle."

Nick nodded.

"Okay then, how exactly do I do this?" Daniella asked.

"Lois has to kneel before you," Pat said.

She did.

"Daniella, you must put your hand on top of her head and tell her you forgive her," Pat continued.

"That's all I say?" Daniella asked. "No special words or spell or anything?"

"You're part druid, not part witch. Let's keep it simple, okay?"

"I like simple," Daniella said. "As long as it works. Which hand?"

"Right hand."

Daniella did so. "I forgive you, Lois."

Lois shuddered and collapsed to the floor.

Daniella stared at her in horror. "Oh my God! I've killed another vampire!"

Pat knelt beside Lois. "She's fine. Her reaction is an indication it worked."

"You could have warned us about that," Daniella said.

"And risk the chance that Lois might fake her reaction? No, it had to be done this way." He helped Lois to her feet.

It was now official, Daniella decided. Her nerves were totally shot. That fact was reinforced by how startled she was at the arrival of someone new.

"It's okay," Nick told her. "It's just Neville. He's one of us."

He looked more like a computer nerd than a vampire, but Daniella was learning you couldn't tell who was a vampire by their appearance.

"Nick, you showed up on infrared and none of the other vamps did. You know what that means, don't you?" Neville said.

"What does it mean?" Daniella demanded, afraid that by forgiving Lois she'd somehow injured Nick.

"I believe Daniella and I need some time alone to discuss matters," Nick said with that touch of British formality she found so sexy. "We'll be in my office and don't want to be disturbed."

"Or watched on camera," Daniella warned them.

Nick held the door open for her as he ushered her into the small room at the back of the bar. The only thing on the wall was a large framed watercolor of an English manor house and the surrounding countryside.

Noticing her interest, Nick said, "That's Marchmore, my family's estate in Gloucestershire. It's a tourist hotel now."

"Lois told me you lied about being adopted."

"I did," he acknowledged. "I was trying to get you to confide in me about your adoption. I thought if it was something we had in common, then you'd be more likely to talk to me about it. I wasn't adopted, but I was born on my father's estate of Marchmore. That much is true."

"Did he ever know you became a vampire?"

Nick shook his head. "I was officially listed as dead. My father had a heart attack when he heard the news and my older brother took over the estate. There was no going back. It wouldn't have done any good." He paused. "Do you forgive me for lying to you?"

She didn't have to take a moment to think about it. After all, the guy had just saved her. Okay, technically, she'd sort of saved herself by jamming that wood into Miles. But hearing Nick's voice down in the tunnel had given her the strength to do that and not turn into a mass of quivering jelly early on in the ordeal. In the grand scheme of things, his lie about being adopted wasn't that bad. "Yes, I forgive you.

Just don't lie to me again and don't ask me to put my hands on your head and make the pronouncement. I don't want you falling over on the floor the way Lois did."

"That was generous of you to forgive her and let her go."

"Would you all really have killed her?"

He shrugged. "It's the vampire way."

"There's a lot I still don't understand about the vampire way. For example, what did that guy with the geeky glasses mean when he said he could see you on infrared?"

"It means I'm no longer one hundred percent vampire. I still have my powers but I have other traits. I can eat food."

"So Miles was right about you no longer being immortal?"

"Miles's reasons for coming after you were to get to me," Nick said. "Getting involved with me put your life at risk."

"Getting involved with me put your *afterlife* at risk." Her breath caught, and it took her a moment to shake off the threat of tears. "You won't live forever anymore. You'll grow old. Not at the normal human rate, granted. At a slower pace."

"At the same slower pace you'll grow old."

"Is that okay with you?" she asked unsteadily.

"I don't want to live without you," he said huskily. "I love you."

"I love you, too."

He tenderly wiped away her tears. "Why are you crying?"

"You could have lived forever but I ruined that."

He cupped her chin in his hand and lifted her face to his. "Listen to me: You didn't ruin anything. You brought me back to life. I can experience things I haven't in two hundred years."

"Like eating roast beef."

"Like love."

"So you love me because I made you able to eat?"

He shook his head in exasperation. "I love you because you're *you*. Stubbornly cheerful, ridiculously chatty . . ."

"Gee, thanks."

"Unbelievably sexy, incredibly compassionate, intensely loyal."

She grinned. "Right back at ya. Except for the chatty part. But we can work on that."

"I'd rather work on this." He lowered his head and kissed her.

Mouth to mouth, tongue to tongue, heart to heart. Their passion was even more powerful than before. Reaching around her, Nick swept everything from his huge mahogany desk and perched her on the edge of it.

As he whipped off her Heavenly Cupcakes T-shirt, Daniella remembered her Regency vampire fantasy of him seducing her on the desk in the library of his manor home. Not that Nick had to seduce her. She was already all his.

Pushing her knees apart, he pulled her flush against his arousal. She leaned back, allowing him unlimited access to her breasts, which he quickly freed from the confines of her bra. She shivered with pleasure at the feel of his fingers caressing her nipples. Anticipation built within her. She knew what was coming and she couldn't wait. Yet she did because she knew that every move he made, every caress increased her sensual bliss.

He bathed both her breasts with kisses. She

clutched his head, her fingers winnowing in his dark hair to hold him closer. He rewarded her by taking her into his mouth, his tongue swirling over the rosy peak. The suction was enough to set up sexual surges deep in her womb.

He handled her as if she were the only reason for his existence, erasing her lingering fear from being held captive in the dark and replacing those memories with new blissfully erotic ones. He had the ability to heal her pain in ways she couldn't even begin to fathom. Not only that, he made her feel joyfully alive.

When he dipped his tongue into her navel, she lifted her hips to let him tug her pants and underwear out of his way. The tilt of her body increased the intimacy of their embrace. He dropped to his knees and opened her further to his exploration. She felt his warm breath on her before his tongue delved into her moist inner recesses. His kisses brought a powerful orgasm that would have had her screaming had she not been aware of those outside the office.

He leaned back long enough to tell her, "My office is soundproof."

Then he returned to taste her again, this time focusing on her clitoris. She came again even more forcefully than before.

"Yes!" she screamed. "More!"

She felt him smile against her.

He slanted a roguish look up at her. "You're insatiable for a cupcake maker."

"You're chatty for a vampire."

"I thought you wanted chatty."

She tugged him to his feet and undid his black jeans. "I want you. All of you. In me. Right now!"

Freed from the confines of his pants, she could

see how much he wanted her. Taking her at her word, he wasted no time. He drove into her with wondrous power until he was buried deep within her. Then he moved with a wildly satisfying rhythm, binding her to him with masterful finesse. She dug her fingers into his shoulders as wave after wave of pulsating ecstasy oscillated through her. Her eyes locked on his as he shouted her name before coming.

Eventually they both came back down to earth.

"What's wrong?" Nick tucked an errant strand of her hair behind her ear. "I recognize that look on your face. What are you worrying about now?"

"There's still so much left unfinished."

Nick frowned. "I felt you come. Several times."

"I didn't mean *that*. The sex was the best ever."

He grinned. "I certainly thought so."

She cupped his face with her hand, "Everything makes sense when I'm with you. But there's a complicated world out there. My dad and his fiancée. My brother and his gambling. Suz and her Italian lover. Not to mention your vampire ways and my druid stuff."

"Don't overthink it. That's life," he said.

"Not the life *you're* accustomed to," Daniella said. "You used to have forever."

"I don't need forever. I only need you."

Nick's words were powerful enough, but it was the way he said them and the look in his smoky gray eyes that convinced Daniella that this was meant to be. This was why she'd gotten the letter on Halloween. Her birth mother had known that Daniella wouldn't need to know she was a druid until the moment she'd merge with Nick and her life would be forever changed.

Lifting her eyes upward, Daniella whispered, "Thank you."

"Who are you thanking?"

"Both my mothers."

"For what?" Nick asked.

"For you." Daniella placed her finger over his lips. "No more questions. It's time for less talking and more doing. Agreed?"

Nick nodded and kissed her.

Legend had it that druids and vampires didn't get along. But Daniella was determined to create a new legend with this vampire who was her soul mate. She had a feeling it might be a bit of a bumpy ride, but in the end it would be the most awesome experience of her life.

Turn this page for a special excerpt of Cat Devon's next novel

THE ENTITY WITHIN

Coming in July 2013 from St. Martin's Paperbacks

Chapter One

"I don't want any trouble," Zoe Adams said as she eyed the two vampires staring at her from across the table at the All Nighter Bar and Grill.

One of the vampires, Damon Thornheart, had an extremely threatening aura. Everything about him was dark, from his inky black hair to his deep blue eyes. He was glaring at her as if he wanted to consume her for lunch.

Zoe tugged her red cashmere shrug more tightly around her as if it could protect her. This was her first interaction with vampires, and it wasn't going very well at the moment.

"*We* don't want any trouble," Zoe amended her earlier statement with a tilt of her head toward her grandmother, Irma Adams in a knock-off vintage Chanel suit, sitting beside her. With her white hair and twinkling blue eyes, Irma was the epitome of elegant and classy grannies everywhere.

"We don't want any trouble either," the non-glaring vampire said. His name was Nick St. George, and he was the one who'd invited Zoe and her grandmother to this meeting today. Zoe had been nervous about the get-together, unsure of its purpose and uneasy about its possible outcome.

Looking at Damon now only increased Zoe's misgivings. He did not want her there and he made no attempt to hide that fact. The sardonic gleam in his deep blue eyes conveyed the message that he planned on making her life very difficult if he let her live at all.

"That problem back in Boston was not my fault," her grandmother piped up to say.

"We don't want any problems here," Damon growled. "No trouble. No problems. We like to stay under the radar."

"I understand," Zoe's grandmother said with a nod of her head. "But all I did back in Boston was attend a motivational seminar given by Dr. Martin Powers."

"And what did *you* do?" Damon directed his question to Zoe.

"Nothing," she said.

"I find that hard to believe, witch," he growled.

Zoe held her head high. She'd been called worse. And the fact was that he was speaking the truth. She was indeed a witch. In fact, she came from a very long line of witches. The Adams women had more than a few blessings and more than one curse.

"Yes, I'm a witch," Zoe said, even though she wasn't real proud of that fact at the moment. There had been a time when she'd gloried in her powers and felt empowered by her magical abilities.

Her mother's death two years ago had changed all that. Now she just wanted to lead a quiet life.

But enjoying a peaceful existence was difficult to do with her grandmother around because Irma was also a witch and not a very quiet one. Not that Zoe intended to share that bit of information at the moment. Oh, the two vampires knew Gram was a witch. They just weren't completely aware of *all* her escapades, and Zoe planned on keeping it that way.

"I'm a witch and you're a vampire," Zoe told Damon. "That's old news. Very *old* in your case."

Damon's glare intensified. He looked scary even to a witch.

Reminding herself that she'd said she didn't want trouble, Zoe dialed it back a notch. "As my grandmother said, what happened in Boston wasn't her fault." Gram had already told Zoe that she'd seen the motivational speaker in an interview on the local Boston affiliate TV station. He'd talked about his seminar but what had caught her grandmother's attention was the fact that there was something strange and devious about his aura. Gram felt she had to attend to learn more. Once in the audience, she'd tried to keep an open mind, but when Dr. Powers started talking about how he had the secret to happiness and would only share it if people paid a large sum of money, Gram hadn't been able to keep quiet. She hadn't cast any spells. Instead she'd spoken out, which was her constitutional right as an American, albeit an American witch.

"That's right. It wasn't my fault," Gram said in that uber-cheerful voice of hers. "All I did was ask how anyone could be stupid enough to think that simply giving Dr. Powers money would give you absolute happiness? How was I to know my comment would cause a stampede?"

"As Vamptown's new head of security it's my job to make sure there aren't any stampedes here," Damon said.

"And I'm sure you're very good at your job." Gram patted his hand.

Looking like he wanted to rip her head off, Damon snatched his hand away.

Zoe downgraded this face-to-face meeting from bad to train wreck. Nothing in her experience had prepared her for this. She'd heard about vampires, of course. It was hard not to given all the movies and press they got. She could understand their need to keep things quiet. Most humans didn't believe vampires really existed and that's the way they liked it.

The same was true for witches. That witch-burning disaster in Salem might have occurred over four hundred years ago, but the memory remained. Sure, there were plenty of websites and books about covens of Wiccas who practiced white magic instead of the darker magical elements, but no human was eager to have a witch move in next door.

Apparently few vampires were eager to have a witch move in nearby, either. Zoe had seen enough episodes of *The Vampire Diaries* to know that witches and vampires had issues. But then, vampires didn't seem to get along with anyone other than vampires.

Damon appeared to be proof of that fact although Nick had been extremely welcoming in Gram's time of need. And Gram's time of need was also Zoe's time of need. Her grandmother had always been there for her, so Zoe couldn't let Irma come to Chicago by herself.

Besides, Zoe had her own reasons for leaving Boston that had nothing to do with stampedes or motivational speakers. Her reasons were very personal and had to do with matters of the heart.

They'd had to leave their hometown of Boston in

somewhat of a hurry. Zoe didn't know where they'd go, but Gram said she had a friend named Nick St. George whom she'd met at a local occult bookstore years ago and formed a bond with because of their similar interests. Nick had moved to Chicago, but he and Gram had kept in touch. He'd told her that if she ever needed help, he'd be there for her.

Gram hadn't told Zoe much about Nick—just that she trusted him. The bottom line was that their options had been limited so they'd had to accept Nick's invitation to stay rent-free in a house he was managing.

Zoe had only found out about the vampire element to the story that afternoon when they'd arrived in Chicago and were on their way to Vamptown. Not that the neighborhood's name was known outside of the vampire community. Zoe doubted it was known within the witch community, either.

Yet here she was, a witch in the middle of a vampire enclave. So much for living a quiet life.

They'd barely had time to drop their belongings at the brick house a few blocks away that was to be their new home when they'd been summoned to this meeting.

"If we can get back to the matter at hand," she said.

"I've informed Nick that I do not approve of witches moving into our community," Damon said. "It's too much of a security risk."

"What are you afraid we'll do?" Zoe said.

"Make trouble," Damon replied.

"I've already said—"

"I don't believe you," he said.

Nick spoke before Zoe could make a stinging

response. "As I told you, Damon, I met Irma back in Boston when I resided there before coming to Chicago. We became friends. And as her friend, I invited her here when she needed assistance. End of story."

Zoe decided that Nick was nice . . . for a vampire, that is. Not that Zoe knew much about him. All Gram had said was that Nick was a friend. No mention of the fact that the guy had fangs and drank blood. No mention of the fact that the rental sat in the middle of a place called Vamptown. The only thing that looked welcoming was the cupcake shop down the block from the bar.

Damon, on the other hand, didn't appear to have a welcoming bone in his entirely too-sexy body. Instead everything about him radiated danger and power with a hefty dose of arrogance. This was not a man . . . or a vampire who followed the rules.

Thankfully, Nick appeared to be the one with the final say about whether Zoe and Irma stayed or left. And Zoe could tell that Damon hated that fact.

Even so, she detected no personal animosity between the two male vampires. But maybe she was wrong. While it was true that she'd always been good at reading people, reading vamps was entirely new territory for her.

Looking directly at her, Damon said, "If we could have a word alone?" He made it sound more like an order than a request.

No way did Zoe want to be alone with a clearly bad-tempered albeit attractive vampire. "I'm fine right here where I am," she said. She glanced over at Nick looking for reassurance.

Instead he said, "Damon, why don't you show her the sports memorabilia by the bar?"

Nick's lack of support reminded her that she would do well not to count on a vampire, even one she'd incorrectly thought was nice. "That's okay. I can see the Blackhawks' jersey from here," Zoe quickly said. "Not that we were fans back in Boston."

"But we're in Chicago now," Zoe's grandmother said, giving her a nudge. "And we don't want to seem rude to Nick. So let Damon show you the sporty stuff."

That better be all he showed her. She didn't want him flashing his fangs at her, trying to intimidate her. And what was with her grandmother throwing her into the lion's den . . . or in this case, the vampire's bar? Zoe thought she could at least count on Gram to have her back.

"Afraid?" Damon's mocking look would have made a lesser witch leap to her feet just to prove she didn't fear him.

But Zoe was made of sterner stuff. She remained in her seat and calmly returned his mockery with some of her own. "Yeah, I'm just shaking in my boots. Can't you tell?"

"I can tell you twirl your hair around your index finger when you're nervous," he replied.

And she could tell he wasn't going to give up until she went with him across the room. Fine. It wasn't worth wasting her energy arguing with him. She got up and strolled over to the bar where he joined her.

Zoe started the interrogation with a question of her own. "Do any humans live here in Vamptown?"

"Some."

"And you don't . . ."

"Don't what? Eat them for lunch? Only on Tuesdays and Thursdays when they are the special on the menu."

She suspected he was mocking her. She sure hoped so.

"What about you, witch?" he said.

"I don't eat humans ever."

"Glad to hear it. That leaves more for us vamps to consume."

"You think this is very funny, don't you?"

"Not particularly. Annoying as hell, yes. Funny, no."

"What do you have against witches?"

"Everything."

"That's no answer," she said.

"It's the only answer you'll get from me."

"What's the matter? Are you afraid I'll cast a spell on you?"

He laughed. "I'd like to see you try."

"It won't happen, I've given up the practice of witchcraft. Instead I run a legitimate business."

"Yeah, I heard that you run some kind of soap business."

"It's not just soaps, it's bath and body lotions."

"Magical potions," he said dismissively.

"That's not true." She could tell by his expression that he didn't believe her. "Look, I didn't even know there were vampires in this neighborhood until we got here."

"Then you should have turned right around the moment you found out."

"You don't know anything about me."

"Not true. I had you thoroughly researched. You and your grandmother."

Her heart dropped. No, he couldn't possibly know everything. Only the other witches in their coven back in Boston knew everything, and they were bound by their own laws not to reveal a thing.

Keep Calm and Carry On. Zoe had the T-shirt packed in her belongings back at the house. She should have worn it today, but how could she have known she'd be dealing with vampires? As if moving halfway across the country wasn't bad enough, now she had Damon Thornheart to contend with.

So he had them researched. So what? All she had to do was stay calm. Stay calm and carry on. Oh yeah . . . and also lie. Big-time. Because the truth could get them into a cauldron full of trouble.